The Final Mission

Grant and Lee

by

George P. Miga

PublishAmerica
Baltimore

First printing

ISBN: 1-4241-7987-4
PUBLISHED BY PUBLISHAMERICA, LLLP
www.publishamerica.com
Baltimore

Printed in the United States of America

For my family members and their inspiration and support:

Kristin, Jennifer, Tom, and Doree

THE FINAL MISSION

Grant and Lee

Chapter 1

7 a.m.
September 4, 1870
868 10th Street
Washington City

There was a voice pushing at the edge of Spencer's consciousness.

"Colonel," the voice said. "Sir, it's almost seven o'clock."

Spencer's body shuddered when he opened his eyes. Sergeant Major Gideon Barlow stood near the bed. Spencer groaned, wiped the perspiration from his face with his hands, then lightly massaged his forehead. He long ago had become resigned to the dull ache that doctors predicted would be with him always. He lay still for a long moment.

Barlow held a tarnished silver tray on which sat a glass of water and a small porcelain dish containing a white powder.

"I presume you're playing nurse because I was yelling in my sleep again," Spencer said.

Barlow smiled. "Colonel, when we're old and gray and drooling in our porridge, maybe we'll finally be able to put it all behind us."

Spencer nodded slowly, as if testing the ratio of movement to pain. After five years the dream—it really was a memory—didn't occur as frequently. Still, it left him drained and shaken.

Barlow cleared his throat. "Sir, the general asked if you could have coffee with him at eight-fifteen."

Spencer rose to one elbow to take the glass of water, ignoring the pain medication. Dry-mouthed, he drank eagerly.

"Thank you, sergeant major. Tell the general's secretary I'll be there."

"Very well, sir." Barlow went to the window to adjust the drapes to allow a bit more daylight into the room, and then quietly closed the door behind him as he left the room.

Spencer drained the glass. It was always a mystery to him how the memory could leave the acrid taste of gunpowder in his throat.

He touched the small indentation at the hairline where the Confederate ball had struck a glancing blow that day during the Wilderness fighting. The hair near the scar had turned white. John Spencer felt the streak of white made him look older than his thirty-one years.

Colonel John Spencer gingerly swung his feet to the floor, then stood, steadying himself with one hand on the headboard. He considered what the general might want. In Washington, where general officers were as numerous as congressmen, Spencer knew there was really only one "general"—Ulysses Simpson Grant, who by 1870 had served two years as the nation's eighteenth President.

Spencer walked to the window and pulled the drapes wide. His second floor apartment overlooked Tenth Street, deeply rutted after three days of persistent rain and crowded even at this hour with hacks.

Another group of ranking British officers was due any day. Maybe that was what the general wanted to see him about. They probably will visit the White House, Spencer speculated, then want the President to accompany them to West Point.

As Grant's intelligence chief, Spencer's responsibilities included guarding the President. Not that he would have to protect him from the British. They were ostentatiously courting the President and Congress, trying to make amends for having backed the Confederacy during the war.

That wasn't the reason Spencer disliked the British. He wasn't sure he could explain why he felt as he did about them. Maybe it was because they supported the South during the war. Maybe it was because they seemed to talk too much about the glory of war. Maybe it was the way they treated their men.

Spencer opened the window slightly, willing to trade some street noise for fresh September air. He decided he would take Sergeant Major Barlow along, mainly because the British didn't know what to make of him. Barlow didn't trust high-ranking officers, except for Grant, and there were times when Spencer wasn't sure what the sergeant really thought of the general. For that matter, Spencer mused, he didn't really know what Barlow thought of him.

Spencer recalled the night a couple of years before when he and Barlow had shared a bottle of sour mash whiskey. When there were only a couple of fingers left in the bottle, Barlow blurted: "One of the most dangerous creatures God ever created on this earth is an army general. Most of them ain't too smart, and when they make mistakes, a lot of good men don't ever come home."

For the normally taciturn Barlow, the statement was an hysterical outburst. Spencer chuckled as he recalled how embarrassed the burly sergeant was by it.

Certainly, the British officers were impressed with Barlow's size, but they were intrigued by his skill with the .44 caliber LeMat appropriated from a Confederate officer early in the war. The LeMat, weighing nearly four pounds loaded, was the favored sidearm of General J.E.B. Stuart, the Confederate cavalry genius. The double-barreled firepower was awesome. The top barrel fired nine .44 caliber balls. The bottom barrel was an eighteen-gauge shotgun.

Spencer recalled the British colonel who asked to fire the LeMat on the back lawn of the White House. With Grant's almost imperceptible nod of approval, Barlow propped a two-by-eight-inch plank about a foot long at the base of a tree. The colonel, who considered himself a crack shot, fired seven rounds, hitting the board four times.

"Sergeant Major," the Englishman said, "I would not permit one of my men to carry a weapon so obviously incapable of accurate fire."

With another slight nod from Grant, Barlow walked to the board and turned it on its two-inch edge. Back on the firing line, Barlow quickly reloaded the heavy revolver, leveled it, and fired nine shots. Seven slugs tore chunks from the board; two rounds were near misses. Then Barlow fired the shotgun barrel, the grapeshot shredding the board, kicking it high into the air. Spencer knew that Barlow was not satisfied with his shooting.

The portly English colonel, usurping the privilege of rank to have the final word, turned to Spencer: "Colonel, with a proper weapon, I believe your sergeant major could be a rather fine shot."

Spencer smiled as he recalled the incident. Yes, it would be good to have Barlow along to help tweak the British.

CHAPTER 2

8:14 a.m.
September 4, 1870
The White House

Spencer paused at the open door. He caught the aroma of cigar smoke, but it was a moment before he saw the President standing at the rain-splattered window. The President, his hands clasped behind his back and a wreath of smoke wavering over his head, appeared to be deep in thought.

"Come in, John," Grant said without turning. "The coffee will be here in a moment."

"Good morning, general." Spencer moved to the center of the room, waiting to see if Grant would sit at his desk or at the low table flanked by two stuffed chairs in the front of the fireplace. The decision could be significant. Grant handled routine matters, including security, at his desk. But on several occasions the President had asked Spencer to handle sensitive matters not directly related to intelligence or security. Such business had always been handled at the low table.

"If the British are coming, sir, I suspect this weather will make them feel at home."

Grant turned with a quizzical look. Then he smiled. "Oh, yes, the British are indeed coming—the Sandhurst group again." He removed his cigar, pointing it at the low table.

When Grant moved from the window to the chair, Spencer sensed that the President was preoccupied, his mood pensive. As the President paused to snuff out his cigar, Spencer recalled the observation by one of General Meade's staff officers, who said Grant was a man of exquisite judgment, extreme determination, and great calmness.

The man who leaned back in the chair opposite Spencer's did not appear to be all that calm and determined.

"Colonel, before I begin, I want it understood that what we are about to discuss must be held in the strictest confidence. Without an explicit order from me, you are not to discuss any aspect of the matter with anyone."

Each of the President's special assignments began this way, so Spencer nodded quickly. "Yes, sir."

The President paused as an orderly brought in the coffee, placing the tray with silver decanter and china cups on the table, and left the room.

Grant leaned forward to fill the cups.

"Colonel, many of the problems we face today as a nation can be traced directly to the assassination of President Lincoln, and the fact that he was succeeded by Andrew Johnson—a man wrong for the job and wrong for the time. He was heavily supported by the Democratic Party, which proclaimed itself the party for white men, north and south."

Spencer knew that Grant was organizing a premise for his thinking, rather than lecturing to him. "President Lincoln," Grant continued, "had a fine sensitivity for what was required to unite the country after the war, and I agreed, essentially, with what he advocated."

Grant leaned forward, his blue-gray eyes alive as he warmed to his subject.

"Mr. Johnson, however, was initially more interested in proving that he was capable of punishing the insurrectionists. Are you aware that if Johnson would have had his way, Jeff Davis would have hanged?" Grant slowly shook his head. "That would have left an open grave to haunt this nation for years."

Grant picked up his cup, then returned it to the saucer without drinking. He got to his feet and walked to the window. Spencer heard the wind pick up, whipping sheets of rain against the glass.

"The hard fact, colonel, is that the South, and to some extent the West, do not have faith in my leadership." Grant paused, then said so softly that Spencer could barely hear, "Perhaps not with insufficient cause."

The President turned to face Spencer. "If I may inquire, what are your personal plans for the future?"

The question surprised Spencer. "Well, sir, I guess I'm not certain." Spencer considered whether to say what had been on his mind in recent months. "When I graduated from the academy in sixty two, I planned to make the army my life." Spencer paused. "Now...now I guess I'm not as certain. The West intrigues me—as a civilian, rather than a soldier."

Grant nodded understanding. "Yes, our future is in the far West."

The President returned to his chair, again leaning toward Spencer.

"I hope you will remain in the army, colonel, but the assignment I am about to give you can jeopardize your military career, whether or not your mission is successful. You must understand that if your involvement is discovered, the reaction in certain influential quarters may be so negative that I might be powerless to defend you."

Grant looked at Spencer for a long moment. "In fact, colonel, it is conceivable—even probable—that both your life and mine may be jeopardized.

Spencer was alarmed by Grant's words—not so much regarding any risks to his own life. He had long before made the decision that his life would be secondary to the President's.

"Sir," Spencer said carefully, "if this assignment poses a risk for you, perhaps we should reconsider—"

Grant waved away Spencer's concern with his cigar.

"With respect, sir," Spencer persisted, "and to put a point on it, as chief of security I should be aware of any threats to the President."

Grant smiled. "I sincerely appreciate your concern, colonel." Grant reached across and patted Spencer's forearm. "I plan to let General Sherman determine whether the risks outweigh the benefits."

Grant, clearly indicating that the subject of risk was closed, reached over his cup into the humidor for another cigar. The briarwood case had been a gift from a private who had carved it with a penknife after the victory at Chattanooga. Grant clipped the cigar carefully. Holding a match just under the tip, he locked eyes with Spencer while he drew on the cigar, slowly rotating it over the flame.

Grant, his words distorted somewhat by the cigar, said, "The rebellion is now five years into history, and too much hatred still lingers and too many factions seek to subvert our efforts to move ahead as a single people."

Spencer watched as Grant exhaled the rich, blue smoke. Deep in thought, Grant gently rolled the Havana between his thumb and forefinger, examining the glowing tip. On several occasions Spencer had seen Grant on the battlefield and was impressed by his energy and confidence. Now, Spencer noticed Grant's chestnut brown hair and short beard were going gray, making him look older than his forty-eight years. Grant had always been self conscious of his left eye, which was a little lower than the other. His current mood made him appear even more dejected.

As if sensing Spencer's thoughts, Grant clenched down on his cigar and continued.

"What I need, colonel, is a man at my side who both the North and the South respect, one who can help me pull this nation together so that we can get on with the work at hand."

Grant reached into an inside pocket and retrieved two envelopes and held them out to Spencer. Taking the envelopes, Spencer noted that one of them was addressed to General W.T. Sherman. Nothing was written on the other.

"I want you to personally deliver those letters to General Sherman. He is attending a meeting at the Metropolitan Hotel in Baltimore. He is expecting you. He will telegraph his response to Sergeant Major Barlow who will deliver it to me. The letter specifies the language General Sherman should use to maintain security."

"I understand, sir." Spencer held up the unaddressed envelope. "Will General Sherman tell me who receives this one?"

"Yes. He will direct you to deliver that letter or he will order you to return to Washington. In the latter event, he will destroy it."

Spencer knew that Sherman was the one man whose judgment the President most respected. Spencer wondered who would receive the blank envelope, who the general felt would help him achieve national unity. He felt a momentary chill. *It can't possibly be that man. Not again.*

"Colonel, I suggest you make your travel plans immediately."

Spencer slipped the letters into his jacket pocket and started for the door. He paused when he remembered the scheduled visitors.

"General, what about the British? Will you be taking them to West Point?"

"The British? Oh, yes. I suppose I can't avoid that, but I won't leave until I hear from you."

"I'll assign someone in my absence to provide security."

"If you think it necessary." Grant smiled. "I presume you have Barlow in mind."

"Why, general, I can't think of anyone the British would enjoy more than Sergeant Major Barlow."

Grant, who many considered to be a humorless man, chuckled, then laughed openly. Spencer suspected the reaction was in part a release of the tension generated by whatever was in those letters.

The President was then silent for a long moment, tapping his fingers lightly on the arm of his chair, his eyes on the rain-whipped windows. Then he rose quickly and motioned Spencer to walk with him to the door.

"One thing, John, see if you can convince the sergeant major to get rid of that old LeMat. The requests by the British to fire the damn thing on the back lawn are causing some complaints from the staff—they apparently don't have much faith in British marksmanship."

At the doorway, Grant paused, the smile gone. "Your mission is very important to me, John." Grant again paused, as if searching for the right words. "There is one thing more: General Sherman may discuss with you a concern that he has—and that perhaps I have, as well—about what may be the real reason for the visit by the British."

"Do you mean, sir, something other than the visit to the academy?

Grant dismissed Spencer with a pat on the shoulder. "Good luck, John."

A moment after Spencer departed, the President's secretary, Abner Babcock, walked into the room. "Senator Logan has been waiting to see you, general."

"In a moment, Abner; in a moment."

Grant closed the door and went to his desk. He sat quietly for a moment, then opened the center drawer and withdrew a yellowed newspaper editorial from the New York *Herald.* Even though he had nearly memorized the article, he carefully unfolded the clipping dated August 15, 1868:

> *If the Democratic Committee must nominate a soldier—if it must have a name identified with the glories of war—we will recommend a candidate for its favors. Let it nominate General R.E. Lee. Let it boldly take over the best of all its soldiers, making no palaver or apology. He is a better soldier than any of those they have thought upon and a greater man.*
>
> *He is one in whom the military genius of this nation finds its fullest development. Here the inequality will be in favor of the Democrats for this soldier, with a handful of men who he had molded into an army, baffled our greater armies for four years; and when opposed by Grant was only worn down by that solid strategy of stupidity that accomplishes its objective by mere weight.*

Grant slowly and carefully refolded the clipping and returned it to the drawer.

"Mr. Babcock," the President called, "please show in Senator Logan."

Chapter 3

7:30 p.m.
September 5, 1870
Georgetown

Rachel Brockton was pleased with her image in the full-length mirror. The black velvet dress had been delivered that afternoon. The low cut neckline was complemented by the emerald and diamond necklace. The dress and her hair, black as washed coal, contrasted dramatically with her fair skin. There were few who would disagree that she was one of Washington's most beautiful women. Certainly she was becoming one of the most wealthy and influential.

Rachel noticed Mattie Monroe's reflection in the mirror, surveying her. Rachel saw her shaking her head disapprovingly.

"I know, I know," Rachel said, "you think it's cut too low."

"Rachel, child, you lean too far forward in that dress and one of them Yankees will bite a chunk out of his champagne glass."

"Mattie, dear," Rachel said as she turned her head slightly from side to side to examine her hair, "most of those people can make fools of themselves without the prompting of a little cleavage."

Mattie moved closer to smooth the folds of the dress. Despite her more than fifty years, Mattie herself was a beauty. Her rich brown skin, high cheek bones, short-cropped silver hair, and still trim figure drew stares of appreciation from men of both races.

Mattie had cared for Rachel when she was a child. When Rachel was old enough to realize Mattie was exceptionally intelligent, she insisted that her tutors also educate Mattie. Her father, Alfred Chase, president of Chase Foundries, objected. He believed it was dangerous to educate Negroes. He relented when he realized that Mattie was Rachel's closest friend and, since her mother's death, her only confidant. Besides, Alfred Chase rarely said no to his daughter. Alfred Chase, the once powerful industrialist, was in a room down the hall. He rarely left his bed, his mind shattered as if by the same charges Union sappers used to destroy his factory.

While she adjusted her hair combs, Rachel recalled the first time she and Mattie had ridden into the country to purchase vegetables, shortly after the Georgetown mansion had been completed. The weather was cool enough to require coats. When they stopped at a farm they had been directed to, Mattie said she would make the purchase. When she stepped down from the buggy and removed her coat, Rachel was shocked to see Mattie wearing a tattered cotton dress. Mattie took a faded red bandanna and tied it around her head, then picked up the wicker basket.

"Why on earth are you wearing that costume?"

Mattie just smiled and waited until the farmer approached them.

"Suh," Mattie said, her head bowed, one foot pawing the earth like a nervous colt, "mah mizzy sho'nuf wants sum fresh greens, if'n y'all gots 'em. If'n y'all don't gots 'em, she gonna wup mah ass raw."

"My lord," Rachel groaned, covering her face with gloved hands. "I don't believe this."

The farmer, perhaps the abolitionist Mattie had hoped for, glared at Rachel, and took the basket to fill it. Later, they figured that he had charged double, but the price was worth the joke.

Mattie put the black velvet cape over Rachel's shoulders, helping her with the clasp on the short gold chain that held the cape closed at her throat.

After one final look in the mirror, Rachel gracefully turned a full circle, the cape's red satin lining flashing as she turned. She had a child's delight in beautiful clothes and parties, and Rachel saw Mattie smile knowingly.

"I will be home late," Rachel said as she pulled on her gloves, "so please don't wait up for me."

The two walked downstairs, where they found John asleep on a rug in front of the fireplace. The boy clutched an elegantly engraved oval picture frame. The picture was typical of those made of Civil War officers on both sides. The young soldier's stance was rigid, angled slightly away from the camera, his expression stern, his left hand gripping the hilt of his sword. A small brass plate at the bottom of the frame read: "Capt. Charles Brockton—CSA."

Rachel felt a surge of emotion when she saw her seven-year-old son clutching the captain's photograph. "The older he gets the more he looks like his father," she said softly. Rachel knew that Mattie was concerned about the boy. He could not, or would not, understand why his father had not returned from the war. Mattie had said her concern was that the boy was developing his mother's hate for the North.

"I'll get Nelson to carry him up," Mattie said. Rachel kneeled to kiss him, gently smoothing his hair. A moment later they heard the crunch of carriage wheels on the crushed stone driveway.

"Your escort has arrived," Mattie said from the foyer.

Chapter 4

8:40 a.m.
September 5, 1870
Metropolitan Hotel
Baltimore

Spencer was immediately engulfed by the energy level of the hotel suite. William Tecumseh Sherman was standing in a circle of field grade officers, giving them instructions in a voice so low that Spencer caught only an occasional word.

The U.S. Army's top general was a sharp, almost painful, contrast to the rumpled Grant. Sherman stood nearly a head taller than the officers around him. The man's eyes, Spencer thought, were fierce. They were a weapon.

Sherman was outspoken, a man who talked freely of the exultation he felt in battle. Grant was prudent and guarded, a man whom Spencer saw turn in his saddle to stare sadly at a bloated corpse whose uniform was so blood-drenched and shredded by shrapnel that it couldn't be identified as blue or gray.

Sherman concluded his meeting and the officers gathered their papers. When they were gone, the general invited Spencer to be seated.

"I've been told to expect you, Spencer," his rich, articulate speech filled the room. "I understand you have something for me from the President."

"Yes, sir." Spencer handed the two letters to Sherman. "I have been advised that I will receive any further orders from you, sir."

Sherman briefly examined the envelopes before leaning back in his chair. He gently tapped the unopened letters against his finely tailored trouser leg, surveying Spencer. For several seconds neither man would avert the other's gaze.

"You know, Spencer, I can't help but be suspicious when an intelligent and highly decorated officer survives in that viper pit called Washington City. It must be difficult for you, considering all the temptations available to a young, bachelor officer who has the President's ear."

Spencer was startled by Sherman's words. "Sir, you may not recall, but the order assigning me to the President was signed by you."

"I am damn well aware I signed the order, colonel, because your services were requested by the President." Sherman, his eyes hard, rose from the chair, dropping the envelopes onto the cushion.

"What concerns me," Sherman said, as he paced the large sitting room adjoining his bedroom, "is that you frequently are seen at those damnable social events that politicians seem unable to resist."

The general stepped to within a few feet from Spencer's chair, looking down at him. "You have also been seen in the company of some of those Radical Republicans who still cry for southern scalps."

Spencer was mystified by the direction of Sherman's conversation. "General Sherman, I can explain what—"

"Colonel Spencer, based on my discussions with the President, I have an idea of what those letters contain."

Sherman took his seat, his demeanor now cool and detached. He stretched his long legs onto the low table. "You should know that you were not my first choice as the President's chief of intelligence and security. I, in fact, offered the names of two other more senior officers who I thought were better qualified."

"I was not aware of that, sir. I presumed you approved the order because you believed I was qualified."

Sherman, his eyes hard, leaned toward Spencer. "Are you being impertinent, Colonel?"

"Sir, that was not my intent." Spencer was alarmed at how badly this meeting had begun.

Sherman leaned back in his chair. "Before you leave this room, colonel, you must convince me that you are not only worthy of whatever may follow the opening of this letter, but that you are worthy of continuing in your present assignment."

Stunned, the last thing Spencer expected was that his competence and loyalty to the President would be questioned. He forced himself to collect his thoughts, the room now so quiet that the sounds of the Baltimore traffic filtered into the third floor suite.

"General, it is my understanding that providing security for the President involves much more than protection from a lunatic assassin. I believe it is also my responsibility—and the President agrees—to provide intelligence about those individuals who want to subvert efforts to put the war behind us."

"Proceed with caution, colonel," Sherman said, his voice measured. "You are on the verge of lecturing me on policies with which I am intimately acquainted."

"Sir, I am talking about intelligence in the broadest sense," Spencer said, forging ahead, "ranging from protection for the President to the effectiveness of his policies."

"Do you mean to say, colonel," Sherman, his face twisted in disbelief, said, "that you dabble in *politics?*" Sherman enunciated 'politics' as would an evangelist forced to utter a profanity.

"No, sir; not at all. But to accomplish my mission, I must meet socially with those people. They are potential sources of important information, precisely because of my link to the President. In effect, sir, I consider myself to be another set of eyes and ears for President Grant."

Spencer paused to assess what he had said and to consider what more he should say. For a moment, he lightly massaged the scar at his hairline. He was confused and angry. He knew what to say next, and he knew he must say it without losing his temper.

"Sir, my assignment is to protect the President and to support him with intelligence services. I wish to continue in that assignment. However, if you have cause to question my loyalty and ability to serve the President, then I respectfully request that I be reassigned as soon as practical."

If he does reassign me, Spencer thought, *I will resign my commission.*

Sherman nodded slowly. "We will see, colonel; we will see. Why don't we first find out what specifically the President has in mind for us?"

Sherman used a miniature cavalry saber to slit the flap of the envelope.

September 6, 1870
W.T. Sherman
General-in-Chief

You and I have discussed on several occasions our mutual concern that Reconstruction has been a failure because of political and economic greed, especially as evidenced by the Radical Republicans.

As a Republican President, who was supported by the Radicals, I hoped to exercise some control over this reactionary wing of the party, but I have discovered I had far greater effect on the destiny of this nation as general than I do now as President.

When I assumed this office, I viewed my responsibilities as those of an administrative nature. I agreed with your brother when he said the President should obey and enforce the laws, leaving the will of the people to be expressed in the Congress. I have endeavored to follow Senator Sherman's advice.

But I am presiding over a vindictive Reconstruction, a course I feel powerless to alter.

As you are aware, the Radicals managed to divide the South into five units, each governed by a military administration. They succeeded in doing what we fought the war to prevent—making two nations out of one—one nation the conqueror, the other the vanquished. All southern states have been readmitted to the Union, the final, Georgia, just a few months ago. To secure the perpetual hegemony for their party in the South, the Radical Republicans have enfranchised the black population, but the votes of these former slaves are being shamefully manipulated by carpetbaggers and scalawags.

I am at a crossroads, my friend, one that requires your good advice. I have found it increasingly difficult to judge the character of the men upon whom I must depend. In some cases I have erred in my judgment of them. Nor do I have faith that Congress will disengage its preoccupation with politics long enough to act in the best interests of our future generations.

Therefore, I have decided I must exercise whatever authority I can muster as chief executive. My first objective must be to dilute the influence of the radicals with southern blacks, northerners who sympathize with the South, and those in the South and West who still cannot find it in their hearts to support a national government led by a former Union general.

However, there is one man who, if I can gain his support, can carry us to the threshold of our objective. He is perhaps the one man who is respected by the constituencies above. He is the one man who can tell the nation that the gauntlet must be buried.

That man is Robert E. Lee.

One month from the date of this letter, there will be a small, quiet reunion in Atlanta of many of the senior officers of Lee's Army of Northern Virginia. I understand that Lee, for reasons that include his failing health, has not yet decided to attend. It has been Lee's inclination not to participate in any demonstration commemorating the war. Certainly he avoids any public comment regarding political issues.

Considering all of the above, I believe the timing is appropriate to approach Lee and urge him to attend the reunion.

Further, Lee must be persuaded to consider my appearing with him before his corps of officers. I would not expect him to support my administration, but if he will openly support the theme of unification, then all else that is good will flow from that.

My friend, it is still the old issue of whether the United States "is" or the United States "are".

I value your judgment highly in this matter, as I have so many times in the past. If your consideration is that I should abandon the effort, then destroy both letters.

If the effort is worth the obvious risks, then use the army telegraph to send the word: Reunion. *The second letter is to be carried by Spencer to Lee. The letter asks Lee to respond, either in writing or orally.*

For your information, what I have learned about the reunion came from reports prepared by Spencer. I first met the young man when he was disguised as a Confederate colonel so he could escort me behind the lines one night. You may wish to have him tell the story. He is a good man and an excellent soldier, facts that I hope you will remember when he is considered for promotion. He does have one fault, however; he is somewhat overly protective of me. Either he or his hulking sergeant major seem to appear nearly everywhere I go.

Finally, although I have not discussed with Spencer your specific concerns regarding the British and Gen. Nathan Bedford Forrest, I did mention that you have some concern regarding British intentions. I made no mention of General Forrest. I leave it to you whether to brief Spencer on the matter, as well as to determine whether he should be involved in any investigation you may decide to initiate. Keep me advised of your decision.

I look forward to your recommendations.
U.S. Grant

Sherman neatly folded the letter. He held it in his hand for a moment, his eyes turned toward the lace-curtained windows.

Then the general's thick-fingered hand began to crush the letter into a wad. His fist trembled slightly, then slammed into the arm of the chair.

"*Lee!*" Sherman's voice was rasp. "I did not think you would ask *him*; I did not think you would seek *his* help."

Chapter 5

9:05 a.m.
September 5, 1870
Metropolitan Hotel
Baltimore

A legend had grown around Sherman's unpredictable volatility. Some said its lightening-bolt force could crack boulders; some swore they saw Rebel bullets that should have killed him diverted by the sheer energy of his anger. Nothing could be accomplished during such fits of anger, Spencer overheard Grant say, until the passion cooled.

Sherman appeared to suddenly become aware of Spencer. He looked down at the crumpled letter and slowly shook his head.

"You know, I refused to vote for Grant in sixty-eight." Sherman's voice was subdued, controlled. "I didn't vote for that damned Horatio Seymour, but I did not vote for Grant. I told him that a general could not function as a politician. They are different animals. When placed in the same cage, the politician is a python who stalks, interested only in filling his belly. What chance has the hunting hound, trained to obey and serve? He will be swallowed head first."

Sherman abruptly shook his head, as if to fling away the image he had created.

"I thought he would be angry. But he just smiled and said he understood. It reminded me of the time we discussed which of us was better educated, although we both were at West Point. I attended reputable prep schools, excelled in French, and am somewhat of an expert on Shakespeare. Grant had difficulty with French and appears bored with Shakespeare."

Sherman chuckled at the recollection. "His response to such impressive credentials was to blink that sorrowful eye at me and reach for another cigar."

Spencer became aware that more than mutual respect was at the root of the relationship between Grant and Sherman. They obviously were close friends who turned to each other in times of stress. Sherman, in fact, was among the few men who called Grant "Sam," the nickname given him by fellow academy cadets.

Sherman, his voice flat, said, "Colonel, I do not believe this letter should be delivered. "Nor do I believe Lee would agree to the request."

Spencer was relieved that the President's most trusted friend clearly believed that Grant's vision to unify the country in one spectacular gesture would fail. Spencer not only agreed that Lee would reject Grant's request—again, but was disappointed that Grant would even want to try to persuade Lee.

"Then I presume, sir, that I will return immediately to Washington to inform the President?"

Sherman again turned to the curtained windows. Then he sighed and Spencer saw sadness in the general's eyes.

"No, colonel," Sherman said softly. "The first thing I will do is to telegraph the single word 'reunion' to the President. Then you will proceed from Baltimore to Washington College in Lexington. You will deliver Lee's letter."

"Excuse me, sir," Spencer said, confused, "but a moment ago you said that General Lee probably will not agree to the President's request."

"I am aware of what I said." Sherman's voice was firm now. "And you will not repeat any of those words to the President."

"Yes, sir, I understand." Spencer hesitated, choosing his words. "But I have personally seen Lee reject the general twice before, and I expect he will do it again."

"Although I do not recall inviting any discussion regarding my decision, colonel," Sherman said, "what is your point?"

"My point, general, is that..." Spencer paused for a moment, breathing deeply to calm his nerves. Spencer came to believe long ago that he could not trust his gut instincts. Barlow was the only man he knew who seemed instinctively to know the right course of action. Spencer always needed plans meticulously built on logic and calculated risk. Spencer wished that Barlow could be at his side now. He wondered if what he was about say was based on fact or gut instinct.

"My point, sir, is that I respectfully request to be released from this assignment."

"You, *what?*"

"Sir, when the President briefed me, he clearly was counting heavily on this effort. You obviously have doubts that the mission is either appropriate or possible, and I agree, and you seem to have doubts in my ability. If we proceed, it is logical to presume that Lee will once again reject the President's request for help."

"Are you saying, colonel," Sherman's words were measured as he leaned forward, resting his elbows on his knees, looking intently into Spencer's eyes, "that you are *refusing* this assignment?"

"No, sir." Spencer quickly shook his head. "Of course not, sir. It's just that Lee—"

"*General* Lee!"

"It's just that I believe General Lee is more consumed by having lost the war than he is with helping to deal with the problems caused by the war. He's not going to help—."

"Did you tell the President that?"

"No, sir," Spencer said softly. "I didn't have the heart to do that."

"Well, young man, on occasion your brain does work."

Sherman rose from his chair and slowly began to pace the room. "Tell me, colonel, do your views of General Lee reflect your views of the South generally?"

"I'd prefer not to discuss my view on that subject, general. Besides, I don't see how it matters."

"I will be the judge of that." Sherman walked a few paces, then turned to face Spencer. "It's because of your sister, isn't it?"

Spencer was surprised that Sherman knew about Eleanor. "How did—"

"The President mentioned it some time ago. She was at Bull Run—the first battle—when a confederate artillery round landed near her carriage."

Spencer nodded. "It was stupid of my father to take her there. They were in Washington City, and they were going to have a damned picnic while they watched the battle." Spencer was quiet for a long moment. "She was beautiful, full of life, and only 19."

"Yes," Sherman said softly, "there were a lot of civilian spectators there expecting to see an easy Union victory, and they stampeded back to Washington when the Rebs sent our boys packing."

Sherman returned to his seat. "Colonel, let me be clear about this—you *will* carry out this mission."

"I understand, sir."

"But you will fail unless you set aside your feelings—your hatred—of the South."

"General Sherman. I have the highest regard and respect of President Grant—which is why I suggested that someone else may be better qualified for this assignment. Rest assured that I will be totally committed to do whatever is required to achieve success in this mission."

Sherman nodded slowly and for the first time Spencer saw a trace of a smile. "Yes, colonel, I believe you will try your best." Sherman smoothed Grant's crumpled letter on the chair's arm. "Did the President share with you the contents of his letter?"

"No, sir, but he discussed what apparently is the premise of that letter."

Sherman tore off the bottom of the letter, the portion referring to Spencer and the British, and handed him the rest. "Read that quickly, because we have a lot of work to do. You have just been demoted from courier to diplomat."

Sherman walked to the door, opened it, and called to his aide. "Mason, cancel my schedule for the day. Make arrangements for Colonel Spencer to travel by train to Lynchburg tomorrow morning. He will travel on horseback from there to Lexington, so draw thirty dollars from my personal travel allowance."

Sherman paused to look back at Spencer. "By chance, colonel, do you have civilian clothes with you?"

"Yes, sir, I always carry them."

"By damn." Sherman's expression was of mock surprise. "A rarity—a cavalry colonel with brains." Then Sherman smiled. "On the other hand, you just missed an opportunity for the army to add to your civilian wardrobe."

Still standing in the open door, he turned back to his aide. "Arrange for quarters in this hotel tonight for the colonel. And get my telegraph officer in here."

Spencer heard the scurry of bodies before Sherman closed the door.

"Now, colonel. You are still working for the President—in the manner that you and he apparently prefer." He paused to point his long arm like a rifle at Spencer. "But you now belong to me. From this moment, you will communicate to me, as well as to the President, all developments involving this matter. I will so advise the President."

Spencer found the general's growing enthusiasm infectious. He quickly nodded.

Sherman pointed to the letter in Spencer's hands. "No matter how well written and cogent the argument, that alone will not move Lee. You must support the President with solidly persuasive oral argument. To do that effectively, you must know Robert E. Lee; you must know the man."

Sherman began to pace the room, his words punctuated by his characteristically impulsive gestures.

"Lee lives by codes that have served him well. He is, first and always, a gentleman. He is socially correct even with dunderheads, although his demeanor with such people can be cold to the point where ice would not melt. He has been described as quiet, grand and cold."

Sherman walked to the window and pulled the curtains aside to look down into the street. "His allegiance is to Virginia and the South—but in that order." Sherman continued to stare down at the traffic and said more softly, "We all know how well he fought for that allegiance."

Sherman turned to Spencer, saying more firmly, "Appeal to that concern for his people, especially for his former soldiers; convince him of the opportunity—perhaps the last for either him or Grant—to furl the battle flags once and for all and to link the corners of this nation."

The room was quiet for a long moment. "General Lee is old, weary and sick," Sherman continued. "But he has always been a fighter. Convince him, Spencer," Sherman's voice now filled the room. "Convince him to stand before the elite of what was the Army of Northern Virginia—with Grant at his side—and say for all the world to hear that it is finally over, that the damnable thing is behind us."

Sherman struck his palm with a fist. "If you can do that, then by God you have paired the men who can rip the gut from the lesion that drains our national spirit."

Sherman stood for a long moment, looking at Spencer, then he walked slowly to a sideboard, splashed whiskey into two glasses, and handed one to Spencer. He resumed his seat, examining his cut crystal glass. He spoke more softly, less passionately.

"Among your attributes for this assignment is your youth. Lee always had a soft spot for young, bright officers in his command. He said they are the nation's future." Sherman locked eyes with Spencer. "Talk to him of the future—your own and for others like you."

Sherman was reflective for a moment, then sipped from the glass. "One other thing: Lee is a deeply religious man. His faith is the hand that guides his life. He measures other men by those values. Be certain that in his presence you do not damn God and—equally important—when you arrive, the only odor on your breath is that of fresh spring water."

There was only a moment's silence before both men chuckled.

The discussion continued until mid afternoon. Spencer felt drained. They both stretched and walked about the room to loosen cramped muscles. Both men paused in the center of the room.

"One thing more, Spencer—what do you know about General Nathan Bedford Forrest?

Spencer was surprised by the question. "I am aware, sir, that he was a Confederate general who was considered one of the finest cavalry officers on either side."

Sherman smiled. "Yes, that in fact was a rumor I initiated. Early in the war, his admirers called him 'Wizard of the Saddle', and I personally described him as 'That Devil Forrest'. Are you aware, Spencer, that he did not attend the academy?"

"I heard, general, that he didn't have much of any kind of formal education."

Sherman nodded. "Which makes his military accomplishments all the more impressive. I personally observed that he adopted the three battlefield principles used by Napoleon and Alexander—anticipate, adapt, and react—which I am confident helps explain the fact that he never lost a battle."

Sherman sat in one of the easy chairs and motioned Spencer to sit in the other.

"What do you know of the Ku Klux Klan?" Sherman asked.

"Not much, sir. I am aware of reports that they are former Confederates who have committed some serious acts against blacks, and that General Forrest is their leader."

"*Was* their leader, colonel. Last year he ordered the KKK to disband, and he supposedly disassociated himself from the organization. According to reports, he said he *deplored* the violence against blacks. Despite his order, many independent Klan organizations remain throughout the South.

"And they have been opposed to Reconstruction," Sherman continued, "especially regarding provisions to give blacks voting and other rights. But Forrest's stance on Negro rights has been inconsistent. He is quoted as saying when he learned of the Klan's objections to equality for blacks, '*That's a good thing; that's a damn good thing. We can use that to keep the niggers in their place.*'"

Spencer nodded. "I'd heard that he made his fortune as a slave trader, which he lost when slavery was abolished. But, sir, may I ask what relationship you see between General Forrest, the KKK and my visit to General Lee? The President also mentioned that you have some concern regarding the British."

"Did he mention my specific concern?"

"No, sir."

"That is a discussion you and I may or may not have at a later date. My immediate concern is that the KKK, and perhaps Forrest, may take some action to prevent a meeting between Grant and Lee, which is the last thing the Klan wants to see."

"How might they do that?"

Sherman shook his slowly, thoughtfully. "I have no idea at this point," he said softly. But Forrest said when he was the KKK leader that he had a half-million members nationwide and that he could in five days mobilize more than 40,000 in Tennessee alone."

Sherman rose from his chair and stepped to the window. For a long moment he stared down at the traffic. "Depending on the outcome of your meeting with General Lee, I may have a discussion with Forrest." Sherman turned from the window and looked at Spencer for a long moment.

"Spencer, do you carry a sidearm?"

"Only when in uniform, sir."

"One moment, before you leave." Sherman walked into his bedroom. When he returned he carried an ornately carved walnut case, from which he retrieved a revolver. Spencer recognized it as a Colt Patterson. It was the belt model in thirty-one caliber, the barrel less than five inches. The gun was heavily engraved, the barrel marked: "General W.T. Sherman."

Sherman handed the revolver to Spencer, who ran his fingers over the grips, puzzled by the wood.

"They wanted to use ivory," Sherman said with disdain, "but I've always preferred the grain of the Circassia."

"I've never heard of that wood, sir."

"The intricate grain is characteristic of the English walnut. The Colt people delivered the weapon a few days ago. Save it for your first-born son, Spencer. It may be worth a lot of money one day—even if it does have my name on it."

Both men smiled.

Considering how the day began, Spencer was at a loss for words. The two men stood awkwardly silent for a moment, then Sherman held out his hand, firmly gripping Spencer's.

"My aide, Captain Mason, should have your arrangements. Good luck, colonel."

With Spencer gone, Sherman poured from the decanter until the crystal glass flashed hues of rich amber. He leaned back in the chair.

Sherman replayed the meeting. He did manage to rattle Spencer, but the young man's head worked well under pressure, and he even wants to do all he can to ensure the success of his mission, despite his negative feelings for the South and the realization that Lee will do nothing. Sherman believed that Spencer only wanted to abandon the mission because he sincerely believed that there might be someone else who could be successful.

Well, Sam Grant, Sherman thought, *you always could measure the worth of soldiers. It is the rest of the world that confounds you.*

Sherman drained his glass and refilled it. He closed his eyes as Grant's letter churned through his mind.

"Sam," he said aloud, "you have stepped into the cage with the politicians to do battle in a noble cause, and they have locked the door behind you. They are clever and slippery and their values and tactics confuse you.

"Now, in desperation, you turn to the *aristocrat* who never considered you his equal. Will he enter the cage and fight at your side? Or is he just a sick, old man who will kneel and pray only for the honor and virtue of his Virginia? Remember, my friend, he is their Arthur. If we soil him as he approaches the grave, they will haunt our souls through eternity."

Sherman's concern for his friend triggered a churning ache deep in his belly.

"You are staggering in darkness, Sam Grant. They are stalking you, and your honesty and naiveté leave an easy mark. They will devour you."

Later that evening, Jeptha Daniels decided to check the sitting room before he finished work for the day. Daniels had delivered lunch to General Sherman and the colonel. He had returned twice to pick up the dishes, but had been told to return later. Even though Daniels was an assistant food service manager, he wanted to pick up the dishes himself.

But Daniels's interests went beyond those of a dedicated employee of the Metropolitan Hotel. Bits of conversation he'd caught earlier were intriguing. He'd heard General Lee's name mentioned several times. He was standing outside the sitting room talking to Captain Mason when Sherman asked that travel arrangements be made for that colonel—Spencer was his name—to Lynchburg. Daniels was a member of a group that certainly would be interested in such information, perhaps interested enough to pay for it.

Daniels opened the door to the sitting room. He saw Sherman asleep in a stuffed chair, a glass lying on the floor nearby. Something else caught his eye. Near the glass were several sheets of crumpled paper. Pausing for a moment to make sure no one else was in the room, Daniels entered. He gathered up the dirty dishes from the sideboard and on his way out quickly picked up the pieces of paper. He paused in the hall outside the door, which he left partially open, and hurriedly read the letter.

Daniels carefully pushed the door again and put the letter back where he'd found it. He knew he would have to hurry and telegraph the information to friends who felt as he did—that the war hadn't stopped when the fighting stopped. Reconstruction had strangled the South and only the Klan could do something about it.

But for Jeptha Daniels to hurry was always a painful ordeal. A Bluebelly's bullet had blown away his right kneecap. The doctors had managed to save the leg, but he would go to his grave with a leg that would never bend at the knee.

8:40 p.m.
September 6, 1870
The White House

President Grant and his wife, Julia, lingered over breakfast. They talked about how much they like New York City. Some day they hoped to live there. For now, they discussed the possibility of spending a week or so there visiting friends and shopping.

Julia wanted to get her husband away from the White House for a while because she was concerned about him. He seemed to be confused by the growing talk of scandals and swindles.

A gentle, considerate woman, Julia was never heard to complain about her husband's long absences during the war years. She reached across the table to put her delicate hand on his. For some reason, people were surprised to discover how dedicated Grant was to Julia. They loved each other deeply.

There was a polite tap at the dining room door.

"Come in."

The door opened and Abner Babcock took a step into the room. The secretary clearly was flustered.

"Excuse the interruption, general. Sergeant Major Barlow says he has an urgent message from General Sherman that only he can deliver."

"Well, send him in, man; send him in."

Barlow stepped around Babcock and handed the message to the President.

"I received this less than ten minutes ago, sir."

Grant tore open the envelope, unfolded the sheet of paper and read the one word he both hoped and feared would be sent.

"Thank you, Sergeant Major. There will be no response."

Julia, sensing a mood change in her husband, asked, "Is it something important?"

"Perhaps," Grant says as he shredded the message. "Perhaps."

Chapter 6

9:15 p.m.
September 6, 1870
Mayflower Hotel Ballroom
Washington City

"Do you see the beauty in black?" The way James Fisk asked the question made it clear that he was impressed. Jay Gould turned to see the object of his associate's comment and caught occasional glimpses of her through the ballroom crowd.

"Ah, my dear James," Gould said. "Not just a beauty in black; she is a black widow. Because of our work, she now walks in powerful company, and she earned a reputation for cutting a man's gizzard in a business deal."

"If that is Rachel Brockton, I would gladly risk my gizzard."

"She is indeed our Rachel—wife of a dead Confederate war hero, daughter of the famous Chase dynasty of Richmond, and currently the darling of the moneyed interests driving this city."

Fisk, only partially distracted by Gould's words, watched as Rachel removed her cape and handed it to her escort. In a hoarse whisper, Fisk said, "She is magnificent."

"Curb your desire," Gould said. "Her only passion is gold. Notice that she is on Brewster's arm—his reward for helping her acquire those New York properties his bank foreclosed on."

Both men watched as Rachel moved from group to group, greeting acquaintances, acknowledging introductions.

"All right," Gould said, "I think it is time we met the dazzling Mrs. Brockton."

Fisk stepped away from the group and approached Rachel and Brewster. Ignoring Brewster he spoke directly to Rachel.

"Good evening, Mrs. Brockton. My name is Jim Fisk. My business partner, Mr. Jay Gould, has asked that I invite you and your escort to meet our group." Obviously accustomed to having such requests accepted without delay or question, he turned to lead the way.

As Rachel approached the group, she didn't offer her hand to Gould. He nodded his head slightly in her direction, apparently as much of a bow as he would permit.

She had heard about his eyes, and thought that if ever she met him she would be prepared. From three feet away, his eyes seemed devoid of human emotion. They were steel lances poised to slash, even though a hint of a smile appeared through his beard. Although his physical appearance was less than imposing, the others seemed to anticipate his needs and wants. He was smallish, hardly more than thirty years old, the hair above his forehead thinning noticeably. An outsized beard dominated his face, some said to mask a weak jaw line.

Rachel saw Gould run the fingers of one hand through his beard. It was a habit, she had heard, a gesture revealing that his quick mind was evaluating an opportunity. His ability to seize financial opportunities was the basis for his reputation as the "Shark." Many victims of his ruthless dealings described him as "the meanest man born since the beginning of the Christian era." He inspired respect and no small measure of terror among his adversaries, as might be expected of a man who had earned his first million by the age of twenty-one.

As for Fisk, the man whom the press called "Jubilee Jim," Rachel found him repugnant. He had an equally insatiable appetite for money, a zest for high living, and an eye for the kind of women only his money could acquire. It was said of Fisk that he was "first in war, first in peace, and first in the pockets of his countrymen."

Even his expensively tailored suit failed to flatter his short, lumpy frame. As she was introduced to the others in the party, she could feel Fisk's eyes on her. When she turned to confront him, Fisk smiled, his tongue moving languidly over his pink lips, leaving the gleam of saliva.

Gould leaned toward Rachel, so that he could be heard over the string ensemble playing on a dais nearby. "You are to be congratulated, Mrs. Brockton, on your successful negotiations involving the New York properties."

Despite the fact that Gould intimidated her, Rachel felt more comfortable with him than with his partner. "Thank you, but I am surprised that you know about it. In any event, the credit should go to Mr. Brewster here, who advised me in the matter."

"Yes, we are aware of Mr. Brewster's role. His bank is one of the institutions that handles similar negotiations for us," Gould said.

For some reason Rachel couldn't identify, Gould's comment made her feel uneasy. Brewster's firm also handled her gold transactions several months earlier. Brewster had, in fact, urged her to speculate on the price of gold, which she had been reluctant to do. She wondered how much Gould knew about that.

"Mrs. Brockton," Gould continued, gesturing toward the other two men standing behind him. "Permit me to introduce our associates, Mr. Hollis Connor and Mr. Charles Wells, both of Washington City." The men nodded their greeting. Rachel thought Wells appeared to be benign. Connor's demeanor was sinister.

"Mr. Fisk and I solicited invitations to this event, and we traveled from New Jersey with the sole purpose of meeting you. We would like you to consider a business proposition that I am confident you will find very interesting."

Rachel glanced at Brewster, who at that moment sipped too much champagne, dribbling some. His eyes darted to Gould as he wiped his chin.

"We were so confident of your interest, Mrs. Brockton, that I have reserved a small meeting room down the hall to discuss the matter."

"Are you saying that you want to have the meeting now?" Rachel asked.

"It will take only a few minutes, after which Mr. Fisk and I and our associates will leave and you can rejoin Mr. Brewster in time for the dancing."

Gould extended his arm in the direction of the side exit. "Shall we?"

Rachel was hesitant, yet she was intrigued, perhaps even flattered. Certainly she was curious.

Gould led the way. Fisk fell in behind her and the other two men behind him. Gould walked the length of a short corridor that led off the main hall. He opened the door to a small room and turned up the gas jets.

A meeting table dominated the room. On a sideboard along one wall was a tray of liquor, a pitcher of water, and glasses. Fisk went immediately to the liquor and poured brandy into a snifter for himself. "Mrs. Brockton, may I pour some refreshment for you?"

"Nothing, thank you," she replied without looking at Fisk. He held the bottle questioningly to the other men, none of whom expressed interest.

Gould pulled the chair at the head of the table and offered it to Rachel. He sat at her left. The two associates sat at the far end. Fisk remained standing.

Gould shifted his chair so that he was more nearly facing Rachel. Then he began.

"Early last year, Mrs. Brockton, you made inquiries with several financial institutions about making an investment." Gould's voice was very soft, even in the confines of the small room. The only other sounds were the barely discernible refrains of the string ensemble, and Fisk's heavy breathing. Apparently, she thought, the short walk was an exertion for him.

"When you contacted Roger Brewster, he was intrigued—by your beauty, and by the fact that you are the daughter of Alfred Chase, who had dealings with Mr. Brewster's father before the war."

Rachel felt the room was too warm. She had difficulty not looking at Fisk to see if he were staring at her.

"Mr. Gould, the mysterious nature of this meeting is making me very uncomfortable. Please get to the point."

Gould leaned close, his eyes narrowing. "My purpose is not to make you uncomfortable, Mrs. Brockton. My purpose is to make clear to you that the good fortune you are enjoying in your financial transactions was a carefully orchestrated strategy that I approved."

"Are you saying that I did not earn that money?"

"You most certainly did earn it," Gould said, smiling. "Let me take a few more moments to explain. As you know, the country went off the gold standard early in the war, which meant that speculators could trade in gold as in any other commodity—buying and selling for future delivery or gambling on the difference between inflation and deflation."

Gould pressed on. "Now, if the price of gold ever gets too high, then the Secretary of the Treasury can release government gold supplies into the market to stabilize the price, even force it down. It became evident to Mr. Fisk and me that knowing in advance when the government was going to release gold would provide us with a significant advantage. Better yet, if we could stop the Treasury Secretary from acting for a period of time, then we could drive the price of gold up to fantastic heights."

Rachel noticed that Gould's eyes were hard as flint in the wavering light of the gas jets.

"When the price got high enough," Gould continued, his murmuring voice almost hypnotic, "we squeezed the living devil out of speculators who gambled that the price would fall. To do all of that, however, we had to—shall we say—hoodwink President Grant; we had to influence the right people in the right offices for our plan to work."

Fisk, drinking from the brandy snifter as if it contained water, stepped closer to the table and sat next to Rachel.

"What we counted on, Mr. Brockton," Fisk began, "was Grant's ignorance of the market and that he was naive enough to think the people around him could not be influenced by hard cash." Fisk burst into a sudden laughter that triggered a coughing fit.

Rachel, who had been resting her arms on the table, pulled them quickly away when Fisk's laughing released a spray of spittle.

"I have a beautiful yacht, Mrs. Brockton," Fisk continued when he recovered, "which I hope some day soon you will give me the honor of visiting."

"Let me assure you," Rachel said sternly, wondering about the abrupt shift in conversation "that I have absolutely no intention of visiting your boat."

"*Yacht*, my dear Mrs. Brocton. It is a *yacht* described as a floating palace." Fisk chuckled. "Even President Grant and his wife agreed to accompany Mr. Gould and me on a night cruise. Each of the staterooms has a canary," Fisk said, "and each canary is named for the dignitaries who occupied the room. There are canaries named John D. Rockefeller, J.P. Morgan, Leland Sanford, and, now, one named General Grant."

Gould interrupted, indicating that he was becoming impatient with Fisk. "We found, however, that Grant—despite the luxury of Mr. Fisk's floating palace—would not divulge his policy on gold."

Rachel noticed that when Gould smiled, his eyes became even more sinister.

"It proved to be a relatively simple matter," Gould said, "to manipulate a few people, including Grant's own brother-in-law, to prevent the government from selling gold to control its price. On September twenty-third of last year, when Grant's brother-in-law told us the President would be traveling and distant from a telegraph, we struck. The price of gold soared from one hundred thirty-five dollars to one hundred sixty-one before noon. And all the time we knew the government would not act."

Rachel, as the story unfolded, became uneasy as she began to understand how she benefited from what these men had done. "I am becoming impatient with these stories of *yachts* and your exploits in the gold market. Please get the point or I will leave."

Gould, nodded, saying, "Please, bear with me a moment more." He paused, placing his hands on the table, spreading his long, slender fingers as he collected his thoughts. "Grant eventually discovered our plan and ordered the Treasury Secretary to immediately sell government gold—but we knew when that message was received and were prepared for it."

Gould turned to smile at Fisk, obviously proud of how well his plan had worked. "Although we do not know precisely how much money we made, it was certainly in the tens of millions. One side benefit was that many small brokerage houses closed down, shaky banks defaulted, export commodities could not be sold, imports could not be unloaded, and credit ceased. It is probable that September 24 will be known as Wall Street's Black Friday. But the chaos provided the opportunity to purchase a number of attractive properties at a greatly reduced price. A significant side benefit, wouldn't you agree?"

Now Gould pushed his chair back, walked to the sideboard, and poured himself a small brandy.

"At this point, Mrs. Brockton, you enter the picture. You will recall that only a few days before Black Friday, Mr. Brewster advised you to invest in gold. During the discussion you had with him that day, you were rather candid about your feelings regarding the North. You revealed the tragic circumstances of your husband's death and the current state of your father's health.

"You see, Mrs. Brockton, one of Brewster's contributions to my organization is that he has the kind of personality that people tend to find comforting. Brewster contacted me. Since he knew of our pending manipulation of the gold market, he suggested I permit you to take advantage of the opportunity."

"And what were Mr. Brewster's motives for offering such an…an opportunity?" Rachel asked.

Gould ignored the question. "If you will recall, Mrs. Brockton, you sent Brewster a message to sell your gold when the price hit one-hundred-forty. You also will recall that he not only urged you to stay in the market—that the price would climb still higher—but he also urged you to invest all you could. Although you were understandably hesitant to do so, I am pleased—as you no doubt are—that you took Mr. Brewster's advice."

Gould held up his hands, indicating that the narrative was complete. "Consequently, Mrs. Brockton, you earned the tidy sum of three-hundred-fifty-thousand dollars. Since then, you have continued to invest successfully with Mr. Brewster's guidance. In fact, you have made some very interesting investments on your own, demonstrating excellent business judgment."

Rachel was aware that Gould and Fisk went through a great deal of trouble to make sure she understood their role in her successful investments. What she wanted to hear now, was what the outcome would be of this conversation.

"Mr. Gould, it should be obvious that I am curious about several things," Rachel said, worried that she would show her alarm. "I am especially curious as to why you included me in the manipulations you have described."

"Ah, Mrs. Brockton, I'm afraid I can not tell you that."

"Why not?" Rachel asked indignantly.

"It isn't that I won't; it's just that I can't."

Rachel shook her head in confusion and anger.

"You are a beautiful woman, Mrs. Brockton. You now are wealthy, you are popular in Washington social circles, and your father was highly respected by businessmen and politicians in the North and South."

Gould now stood and rested his elbows on the back of his chair. "All of those qualities are—or will be soon—of value to my associates and me."

"How?" Rachel now was frightened and angry. "What do you want from me? I demand to know"

Fisk laughed. "We will make that clear to you soon enough."

"I can assure you now that I refuse to have anything further to do with you people?"

Gould smiled. "You are well beyond that choice. Just so there is no misunderstanding, let me make this clear." Gould leaned very close now, his eyes cold and menacing. "I can destroy you in less than twenty four hours. Money is a trap, dear lady, because once in its grasp you never are free. The signs are clear that you are entwined as if in the arms of your lover. If you lose everything, consider carefully what will happen to your son, your father—even the black woman who manages your new and beautiful Georgetown estate."

Gould pushed his chair back to its place at the table. "When the time is right, Mrs. Brockton, you will receive an assignment from us. It will come from me and will be delivered by Mr. Connor and Mr. Wells. Until then, feel free to continue seeking investment advice from Mr. Brewster."

Gould smiled. "You see, Mrs. Brockton, if you cooperate with us I can assure that you will become one of the most wealthy women in the nation."

Gould bowed slightly and walked from the room. Connor and Wells, neither of whom had uttered a word, left with him.

Fisk now moved very close to Rachel, leaning his elbows on the table, his face only inches away.

"I thought you would be pleased to know," he said, his expression filling Rachel with disgust and fear. "I have purchased a new canary for my yacht. It is a rare beauty—light blue and yellow. I've named it Rachel."

Fisk moved his right hand very close to Rachel's arm. He lightly ran his small finger over her arm from the wrist to the elbow.

"That lovely creature, my dear, will reside in my stateroom. Very soon, I expect to introduce my beautiful canary to its namesake."

Then Fisk reached for his brandy snifter, held it in a toast to Rachel, then drained the glass. He wiped his wet mouth with the back of his hand, then erupted into laughter at the look of disgust on Rachel's face. Shaking his head, he left the room. Rachel could hear his high-pitched laughter as it faded down the corridor.

Chapter 7

9:15 a.m.
September 7, 1870
Lynchburg, Virginia

Spencer liked the roan mare the stableman brought out for him to examine. She was young and stood about fourteen hands. Her mane and tail were black. She had one white sock and a star on her forehead. She was muscular and Spencer liked her spirit.

"Put a saddle on her. What's the charge?"

"You say you're ridin' up to Lexington for a few days?" The stable owner seemed reluctant to rent the horse.

Spencer nodded.

"Then that'll be three dollars a day, two day's charge in advance. And make sure you bring her back to my place," the stable owner said brusquely. "Lately, folks've been leavin' my animals at stables all over Lynchburg, then I gotta go huntin' for 'em."

Spencer paid the stableman.

"I'm gonna need your name."

"Spencer—John Spencer."

After the saddle had been cinched under her belly, Spencer walked the horse in a circle, watching her feet. He examined the fit of the bridle, then mounted and pulled on one rein. She turned a full circle in her own length.

"You know," the stableman said, "there's another way to Lexington, if you've a mind. You can take a boat up the Kanawha Canal. Takes about twelve hours. If the boat's not loaded too heavy, they'll even carry the animal."

Spencer shook his head, suspecting the stableman was worried that the horse would be ridden too hard.

"Thanks, but I prefer to ride. I'll take good care of your horse."

"All right. Just remember to bring that animal back to my stable."

Spencer walked the roan to the northwest edge of town. When he touched her flanks lightly with his spurs, she quivered and broke into an easy run. He decided to hold the run for a few minutes. It had been long time since he'd been on horseback in open country. The air was cool and refreshing after more than a day on a rail car. He'd caught the morning train from Washington to Richmond, then made the connection to Lynchburg.

Spencer reined the horse back to a walk after a mile or so. It was perhaps thirty miles to Lexington, and he didn't want to tire the animal. In a couple of hours he would find a place to eat lunch. He checked his map. If he followed the north bank of the James River for a few miles, then headed northwest, he'd be at the small town of Pedlar Mills. Surely there would be a tavern or boarding house where he could buy a meal. Even with a stop for lunch, Spencer estimated he'd be in Lexington by dark.

There was a Federal garrison in Lexington, but Sherman's orders were to avoid contact with the commander. In fact, Sherman made it clear that, aside from the meeting with Lee, Spencer was to avoid any situation that might force him to reveal his identity or his mission.

The traffic had thinned considerably. Spencer encountered only an occasional buggy or horseman. The James River was out of sight on his left, masked by heavy woods. Ahead, Spencer could see the rolling countryside rise to the Blue Ridge Mountains. The country was as beautiful as he'd remembered it, and as disturbing as his memories made it.

A few miles to the east—perhaps only twenty or thirty miles—was the village of Appomattox Court House. This was the road over which Lee had desperately fought so his tattered and starving army could escape to the mountains Spencer could see in the haze. Lee wanted to escape Grant's encirclement so he could fight a few more days. Lee knew the cause was lost, but he felt that each day he prolonged the war might improve the chances for concessions from the North.

The road was deserted now. Spencer urged the roan into a trot again, its hooves kicking up spires of dust. Feeling a chill, Spencer pulled the collar of his coat closer around his neck.

Spencer was a scout with General Phil Sheridan's cavalry in those final days. He had, in fact, spotted the rear guard of Lee's army as it attempted to escape down the Lynchburg Road. When he reported to Sheridan, the general wanted Spencer to immediately get the information to Grant, who was more than a dozen miles east.

Because it was nearly dark and the battle lines so fluid, Sheridan wanted Spencer to wear the uniform of a captured Confederate colonel. The message Sheridan wrote urged Grant to move up immediately because Lee might be trapped by first light. Written on tissue paper, Spencer wrapped the message in tin foil and concealed it in a wad of chewing tobacco.

More than two hours later when he found Grant, the general was amused by the young captain's uniform. "If General Sheridan wants me with him that urgently, we'd better get up there now. Lead the way, *colonel.*"

Grant, his headquarters staff, and a small cavalry security guard followed Spencer into the woods toward Sheridan's camp. Spencer stayed well ahead of the group in case they encountered a Confederate patrol. He was aware of the risk if he ran into a Union patrol.

The night was unusually black and Grant moved up alongside Spencer.

"Captain Spencer," the general said softly, "I can't imagine how you know where we're going, but I'm sure you can appreciate the consequences for us all if we are captured."

"I'm confident of our position, general," Spencer replied, "but I suggest that the security guard drop a little farther back. Cavalry units just can't move very quietly in woods."

Grant gave the order.

It was nearly midnight when Spencer located Sheridan's camp, and that's when the young scout made the one mistake that nearly cost him his life. Spencer's approach to the camp had been too quiet. Two sentries, tense and jumpy because of the blackness, were completely unnerved by the ghost-like appearance of a Confederate colonel with the unbelievable message that he was escorting General Grant to see General Sheridan."

Both sentries had cocked their Springfields and were prepared to fire when Grant moved up alongside Spencer.

"I am Ulysses Grant. Escort me to General Sheridan's tent."

The rifle muzzles wavered between Spencer and Grant. Fearful that one of the sentries would fire at any moment, Grant slowly urged his horse forward until he was only a few feet from the guards.

"Soldiers, I want you to take me to General Sheridan, and I want you to do it now!"

One of the sentries asked the other: "You know what Grant sounds like?"

"Nope. Never heard him. I can't see him clear, but he sounds like a general."

"And he don't talk like no Reb," the other said, "so I suppose we'd better do like he says."

Later, when he received word of Lee's intention to surrender, Grant asked Spencer to accompany him to Appomattox. Spencer was among the Union troops waiting outside the red brick private residence where the surrender document was signed. He saw Lee walk out onto the porch where he paused for a moment, slamming one gauntleted fist into the other. Then Lee mounted Traveler and rode slowly between two columns of Union troops, each man saluting as the general passed.

Spencer clearly remembered that Lee was resplendent in a new uniform, his tops of his boots embroidered in red silk, the hilt of his jeweled sword capped by a lion's head, the blade sheathed in a gilded scabbard. Virginia had presented it to him.

Grant wore a mud-splattered private's coat with the stars of a general on his shoulders. He rarely wore a sword and didn't that day. He felt wearing a sword on horseback was awkward. One of the few times he did wear a sword, a Rebel bullet took off the hilt.

The morning after the surrender, accompanied by an aide and bugler, Grant arranged to see Lee once more. This time the meeting would be between the lines. As he rode toward the meeting, Grant paused when he saw Spencer sitting on a rock at a campfire drinking coffee. When Spencer saw Grant he started to stand, but the general motioned for him to remain seated. Grant hunkered down next to him.

"I'm still curious about something, captain. I don't see how any man could have found his way through those woods on such a black night. Tell me, did you really know where you were going?"

Spencer smiled. "Well, sir, I had been through those woods several times over two days. But I guess the most important thing is that we did make it."

Grant chuckled. "We did, indeed. Get your horse, captain. Let's see how well you can lead the way in daylight. We're going to see General Lee again."

Spencer rode ahead of Grant, carrying a white flag as a precaution, even though all of the Confederate and Union troops had stacked their arms.

For more than thirty minutes Grant and Lee talked in plain view of thousands of men, most of who still found it hard to believe that after four terrible years it was finally over. Many of those who watched also recognized that they were witnessing a unique moment in history.

Lee, despite the fact that he had removed his hat and put it on the pommel of his saddle, still sat astride Traveler with the same erect dignity he always maintained. The soldiers from both sides would remember years later how Lee's silver hair and beard shimmered in the early morning sun.

Grant, who also removed his hat, looked stooped and small in the saddle. His horse, Cincinnati, aside from an occasional quiver, seemed rooted to the ground.

The two men talked casually about the old army in which they had served.

Only a few feet away, Spencer heard Grant tell Lee that several of his officers wanted permission to enter the Confederate camp to visit old friends they hadn't seen since before the war. Lee said he would make the arrangements.

Finally, Grant posed the question that prompted him to seek the meeting. He asked Lee to use his influence to urge all Confederate armies to surrender and, and most importantly, to advise the civilian population to accept the peace.

Lee considered the request for a moment, then said that he couldn't comply without the permission of Jefferson Davis. Lee didn't, however, volunteer to seek such permission. Grant nodded his understanding, and the meeting ended.

During the ride back to their lines, Grant rode quietly. He obviously was disappointed. He hoped Lee would agree to immediately stop the fighting throughout the South.

The wind coming down off the Blue Ridge Mountains had turned much cooler, especially for so early in September. Spencer could see clouds thickening ahead. He hoped it wasn't going to rain.

Spencer estimated that Pedlar Mills was less than an hour up the road. He was making good time, mainly because the roan wasn't a hard trotter.

Lee and Grant met one other time, just last year. Lee had been in Baltimore, part of a delegation urging the laying of a railroad through the Shenandoah Valley. The line would serve Lexington, as well as aid the growth of Washington College.

Grant quietly sent an invitation to Lee in Baltimore, inviting him to visit the White House. The President said he hoped the visit would dramatize the ending of the war's bitterness.

Spencer assigned Sergeant Barlow to serve as Lee's escort. The meeting didn't go well. Anything of importance either man could say to the other apparently had been said in that open field outside of Appomattox. At one point Grant attempted a bit of humor to relieve the tension. Referring to Lee's effort to promote the building of a railroad, he said, "You and I, general, had more to do with destroying railroads than building them."

Lee wasn't amused. He didn't even smile. Apparently, Lee found it impossible to exchange humor with the man who had beaten him.

The meeting lasted less than fifteen minutes, and then the old soldiers parted.

Spencer recalled a feeling of great personal sadness as he and Sergeant Major Barlow escorted Lee to the train station.

He couldn't shake the memory of Grant's disappointment after his two meetings with Lee. How ironic, he thought, that five years after the war, Grant, the victor, was still appealing for Lee to use his influence to help solve the problems that continued to divide the nation.

A cold drizzle began as Spencer topped a small hill. Pedlar Mills was less than a half-mile ahead. Spencer spurred the roan into a gallop. In a few minutes he pulled up to the stable at the edge of the little village and walked the horse into the building. A young boy, perhaps no more than twelve or thirteen, was in one of the stalls rubbing down a dapple.

Spencer dismounted and reached under the roan's belly to loosen the cinch. "How about rubbing this one down, son, and give her some feed and water. Where can I get something to eat?"

The boy nodded, his fresh chaw so big that he leaked tobacco juice at the corners of his mouth when he smiled. "I'll take good care of your horse, mister. You can eat across the street. The widow McLaws serves food in her dinin' room for travelers. Her man, Henry McLaws, got hisself kilt in the war. I run the stable for the widow. It'll be a dollar for your horse."

Spencer flipped the boy a silver dollar in advance. He pulled his saddlebags and threw them over his shoulder.

Pedlar Mills was a cluster of no more than a dozen buildings. The street was deserted. Spencer felt chilled to the bone. The wind picked up, whipping the misting rain as he walked to the small white frame house across from the stable. He climbed the three steps and tapped lightly on the door.

A woman opened the door, the swirling wind fluttering her apron and wisps of hair that she pushed back from her tired eyes.

"Ma'am, the stable boy said I could buy a meal here."

The woman nodded and opened the door wide.

"You can hang your things there," she said, pointing to a row of pegs in the narrow hallway. She waited while Spencer got out of his coat, then led him into the dining room.

The room was just large enough for the table and six chairs. The furniture was plain but sturdy, typical of what he had seen in many homes in the South, except for the sideboard along the north wall of the room, which seemed out of place. It was delicate, ornately carved, obviously an old country heirloom. On the opposite wall a small fireplace spread its warmth.

The woman motioned Spencer to a chair, then left for the kitchen. He sat with his back to the fire, but near enough to the window that he could see the stable across the street.

Spencer was surprised by how comfortable he felt in the house. It was neat and spotlessly clean. He could hear the kitchen noises as Mrs. McLaws prepared the meal. He could also hear the murmur of voices, then the suppressed giggle of a child. Spencer stretched his legs under the table and leaned back. The room felt comfortably warm, especially when he could hear the cool wind moaning around the little house. Spencer could not remember when he had felt so relaxed. It had been a while since he'd ridden so long on horseback. His eyelids were getting heavy when Mrs. McLaws brought in his lunch.

She put the plate of sliced cold ham and boiled potatoes in front of him. There were sliced onions on a small side dish.

"I've got some coffee made."

"Some coffee will be just fine, ma'am."

In a moment she brought in a mug of coffee and another plate with two slices of a coarse, dark bread.

The ham was deliciously sweet, and Spencer realized how hungry he was. When he'd finished the meal and Mrs. McLaws had refilled his cup, Spencer felt he had enough time to savor the comfort of the room. He noticed that although the misting rain had stopped, the wind seemed to be blowing even harder. It hadn't rained hard enough to soak the ground, and the wind was churning up swirls of dirt that occasionally made the stable hard to see.

A movement in the street caught Spencer's eye. He saw two riders stop at the stable. One of them, a big man with a heavy black beard, his hat low over his eyes, was talking to the stable boy. After a moment the boy pointed to the McLaws house, then the men walked their horses into the stable.

Spencer presumed the travelers were looking for a meal. He thought the little dining room he enjoyed so much in the last hour would be less comfortable with two strangers. He decided it was time to leave. Mrs. McLaws came into the room when she heard Spencer slide his chair back on the polished hard wood floor.

"That was a fine meal, Mrs. McLaws. How much?"

"Fifty cents, if you've already paid the boy to take care of your horse."

Spencer started to say that he had, then decided to leave two dollars beside his plate.

"Thank you. I'll probably stop on my way back in a day or two."

Wiping her hands on her apron, Jessie McLaws nodded her thanks. For the first time, Spencer noticed the little girl, no more than seven or eight, standing shyly behind the woman. He could see only some of the blond hair, much lighter than her mother's, and a blue eye peeking around the coarse gray material of the dress. Then he could hear the giggling when the head disappeared.

Spencer smiled, and for the first time the woman's face softened. She was an attractive woman, Spencer thought, despite the rough clothes and the apparent fatigue of the chores that consumed her day—and despite the fact that she was Southern. He buttoned his coat, not looking forward to the cold wind and the lonely road. But in another three or four hours he should be in Lexington. He picked up his saddlebags and stepped into the street.

Spencer stood in the doorway of the stable, unable to see the boy. He called several times, but the only sounds were the wind, which occasionally kicked up bits of straw near the door, and the nervous stomping and soft knickers of the horses. Since he had paid the stable fee, he didn't have to see the boy, but he wanted to make sure his horse had been fed and watered.

Spencer looked up the street. It still was deserted.

Spencer was impatient now to move on. As he walked to his horse, he saw his saddle on the floor just inside the entrance. He picked it up, then jerked the saddle from the floor to his right shoulder.

At that instant, the muzzle blast of a heavy caliber rifle flashed from the shadowy end of the stable. The saddle deflected the bullet, which would have struck Spencer just above the right ear. The impact knocked him off balance, and he fell into the roan's stall.

Scrambling under the belly of his spooked horse, Spencer dug for the small Colt tucked into his belt. He carefully rose to his feet, peering over the back of the horse, which now was blowing nervously and stomping the dirt floor of the stable.

Spencer saw a big man running toward him from the corner of the stable. Pointing his pistol at arm's length, the man was only a few feet away when Spencer reached over the horse's back with his Colt. But the nervous roan spoiled his aim just as the other man got off two quick shots.

The first bullet struck the stable wall more than two feet above Spencer's head. The second round hit the horse in the neck six inches behind her ears. The roan screamed and reared back, knocking the Colt from Spencer's hand. She backed out of the stall so suddenly that the other man could not avoid the collision. Knocked to the ground, he tried to roll clear of the roan, but one flaying hoof grazed his forehead, tearing away a large strip of skin.

The big man tried to sit up, trying to shake away the blood pouring into his eyes. Spencer ran toward the man, slammed into him, knocking him back to the floor. Both men rolled over several times, each trying to pin the other.

Spencer scrambled to his feet, pulling the man up, pounding him in the face with three short, rapid punches.

Desperately trying to blink away the blood flowing into his eyes, the big man grabbed the front of Spencer's coat, pulled him close with his left hand while he slammed his heavy fist into Spencer's stomach and chest.

Spencer grabbed the man's blood-soaked beard with his left hand and jerked viciously, holding him while he drove his fist again into the side of his face.

The man groaned and staggered back a step, pulling Spencer with him by the coat sleeve. He locked one hand on Spencer's forearm and pulled his wrist into his mouth, biting down until blood bubbled up around his teeth. Spencer writhed in agony, then drove his knee repeatedly into the man's belly and groin.

When the man grunted in pain, Spencer pulled his wrist free and scuttled a few feet away to examine the wound, fearful that his hand wouldn't work.

Wiping the blood from his eyes on a coat sleeve, the man screamed at another man who Spencer had not seen standing in the shadows. He was holding a Henry rifle. "Choka, shoot him, you dumb bastard! What the hell you waiting for? Kill him *now*!"

When the rifleman didn't raise his weapon, the big man's voice quavered with fury. "Choka, you sonafa*bitch*! When I finish with him I'll come take care of you, you goddam hunky!"

Both the big man and Spencer were splattered with blood. Spencer knew the fight couldn't last much longer. The big man reached for a sheath sewn into his boot and pulled a twin-edged knife. He lunged at Spencer, who took a step back as the six-inch blade gashed the front of his wool coat.

Spencer grabbed Morgan's knife hand, bending the wrist inward, the blade pointing at the man's chest.

It became a test of strength, a test that Spencer knew the big man would win. In a few seconds, Spencer knew the blade would be turned toward his chest.

Both man strained, fighting for control of the knife, their hands slippery with each other's blood. They were locked in a hellish dance that moved to animal-like grunts that rasped through clenched teeth, boots churning the dirt and straw of the stable floor.

Spencer thought he had one chance, but he had to move quickly. He took two steps back, suddenly, to pull the man off balance. Then Spencer drove his forehead into the man's face hard enough to hear his nose break. When the man's head snapped back, Spencer pushed as hard and fast as he could.

The man tried to keep his balance by moving backward as fast as he could, but Spencer was gaining momentum. Spencer sensed that strength was leaving the other man's arms.

When the big man was falling, when he was blinded by the blood in his eyes, when the air rasped through his shattered nose, when he must have known he was about to die, he used the final moments of his life to scream Choka's name.

As both men crashed to the floor, Spencer's weight drove the blade to the hilt into the man's chest.

Spencer sat for a moment, breathing so fast he was afraid that he would never catch his breath. He sensed the movement before he saw it—the muzzle of the Winchester only inches from his head, the barrel pointed very near the indentation at his hairline.

Spencer had trouble focusing his eyes when he looked from the muzzle to the man—what had the big man called him? Choka? The roar of his heart hammering in his eardrums made it difficult to understand Choka's words.

"He was crazy man," Choka said, gesturing toward Morgan's corpse. "He like to kill with his hands." Spencer noted the heavy European accent.

"Who was he?" Spencer gasped.

"He was Morgan—Silas Morgan."

Spencer was chilled by how readily Choka gave him the name.

"Why did he try to kill me?"

Choka shrugged his shoulders. "He was crazy man," he repeated.

Spencer sensed that Choka hated Morgan, but that his fear of the man apparently had been greater than his hate.

"Are you going to kill me?" Spencer asked evenly.

"You fight good, but now I kill you because they give me money."

"Who gave you money?"

Choka ignored the question. He backed up several steps, apparently aware of what the .44 Henry cartridge would do to Spencer's head at close range. He slowly started to raise the Winchester to his shoulder.

Spencer couldn't pull his eyes from the muzzle of Choka's rifle. It occurred to him that he knew precisely the sequence of events that would follow the pull of the trigger. His mind flashed back to the Wilderness—the Reb with his elbow poking through his ripped shirtsleeve. The scraggly red beard. Like Choka, the unhurried, workman-like motions.

At the last moment, Spencer willed his eyes to lock with Choka's. He was surprised. The eyes sighting down the barrel were dark, large, almost liquid.

When it came, the roar filled the stable like a thunderclap. As if time had slowed, Spencer saw Choka's hat fly from his head, the liquid eyes and the face dissolve in a red spray, the body stagger back against a support post.

Already dead, Choka's body thumped into a sitting position with the suddenness of a heavy grain sack. It lay propped against the post. The gory head, its neck obviously shattered, was tilted grotesquely back over the left shoulder.

Spencer didn't move for several seconds. Then he forced himself to turn to look at the stable entrance.

It was the widow. He couldn't see her face because of the daylight behind her. But he knew it was Jessie McLaws. When she lowered the shotgun, Spencer could see the stable boy behind her, his face reflecting the shock.

Jessie slowly walked into the stable, pausing at Morgan's body, the knife handle protruding from the center of his chest, his face covered with blood.

"Great God almighty!" she whispered. "What has happened here?"

The stable boy edged toward Choka's body. Working his chaw nervously, his body twisted toward the entrance, ready to run if his courage failed him, the boy tentatively leaned forward to see better in the dim light.

"Who-*e-ee*, Miz McLaws," he said in a soft voice. "You danged near blowed his head clean off with that scattergun." The boy's voice broke as he gagged.

"Shush, boy!" Jessie said, her voice now firm. "Get away from that dead man and come take this shotgun."

Jessie looked at the two bodies, running one hand through her hair.

"Who were these men, mister?"

"I don't know."

"What have you done that they'd want to kill you?"

Spencer shook his head.

"Look, mister. How do I know you aren't the one that deserved killing?" I've shot and killed a man, and I've got to know that the wrong one isn't sitting there dead against that post."

Spencer struggled to his knees, then stood, feeling dizzy and nauseated.

He remembered Sherman's order that he divulge his mission only to Lee. But it appeared this woman might send someone to bring local or county police to the scene. He had no choice. He'd have to trust her.

"Mrs. McLaws, my name is John Spencer. I'm a soldier assigned to Washington City. I have a letter that I'm to deliver to someone very important. I suspect that these men were trying to stop me."

Jessie considered Spencer for a moment. She'd known immediately that he was a Yankee. But he had been kind, and she liked the way he had smiled at her Amanda.

"What in the world could be in that letter that would make someone try to kill you to prevent you from delivering it?"

"I'm sorry, but I can't tell you that."

"Well, then, what are we supposed to do about these dead men?" Jessie's voice reflected her frustration as she swept her arm over the carnage. "Do we just forget about them on your word? Someone needs to get tell the police about all this."

Spencer shook his head. "No, Mrs. McLaws, we can't do that. If you have the stable boy deliver it to the telegraph office in Lynchburg, I'll write a message to my headquarters in Washington. I'll ask that someone come down and investigate what happened here."

Spencer heard a movement at the stable entrance. He turned and saw three men standing there with rifles, all pointed to him.

"What's going on here, Jessie?" one of them asked. "You all right?"

Jessie looked at Spencer. "Have you got papers to prove who you are?"

"Yes, they're in my saddle bags in the stall there."

Jessie turned to the three men. Tilting her head toward the bodies, she said, "Looks like those two tried to rob this Yank. He killed one of them; I had to shoot the other. The Federals will be coming down to investigate."

Jessie motioned the men into the stable. "You'll find some canvas in the back there. Wrap those men in it and bury them shallow in the field behind the stable. I suspect the Federals will probably want to dig them up when they get here."

She took the stable boy gently by the front of his shirt. "You go find this man's saddle bags and bring them to the house."

Spencer remembered his gun. "And look for my Colt pistol, son. It's somewhere on the floor in that same stall."

Spencer saw the roan when he and Jessie walked into the street. The horse was down on her right side, her legs thrashing, a pool of blood around her head. She apparently ran no more than a hundred feet, heading south, toward the safety of her own stable. The animal's eyes rolled as she tried to get to her feet when they approached.

Jessie called to one of the town men to end the animal's misery.

"I'll do it," Spencer said. "She's my horse; it's my responsibility."

Jessie gently took Spencer's arm. "Mister, you've had enough of killing today. Mr. Hayden will take care of your horse. Come to the house so I can see how badly hurt you are."

Spencer reluctantly started for the house, then stopped. He looked down at his blood-splattered hands and clothes. He gingerly touched his swollen and split lips, discovering that one of his lower teeth was missing. He couldn't see well with his left eye because it was swollen nearly shut.

"What's wrong?" Jessie asked.

Spencer shook his head. "I can't go into your house like this—your little girl."

Jessie smiled. "Don't worry, Mr. Spencer. I'll take care of that."

Spencer was about to walk into the little house when the shot rang out. He looked down the road to where the roan lay. The man who had shot her kneeled down and patted the animal's shoulder.

It was a simple gesture, one that a man often does for his horse without thinking about it. Considering the day's events—the fear, the anger, the death—that simple gesture of kindness and concern seemed very important to Spencer. He recalled when he and his squad came across a Confederate soldier cradling the head of his mortally wounded horse. The Reb's unit had moved on, but he wouldn't leave his horse and he apparently couldn't bring himself to shoot it.

When the Reb looked up at the halted Union column, Spencer saw that tears had streaked the man's grimy face. "It ain't right to kill somethin' that don't know why it's being killed," the Reb said, gently stroking the animal's neck. Within thirty feet of the dying horse Spencer counted the bodies of seven men, already turning in the heat. Spencer waved the column ahead. When he looked back, he saw one of his troopers drop his canteen near the Reb.

Spencer slumped into a chair in the dining room he had enjoyed so much. It seemed like hours ago. The room now felt much too warm. Jessie brought in the paper he requested, and she turned up the lamp on the table.

Spencer's hands were so stiff and sore that he had difficulty holding the pencil.

Gideon Barlow
Washington City
Require your immediate presence in Pedlar Mills, Virginia. Suggest detachment of four accompany you to conduct investigation of two deaths. Notify Cump of delay of perhaps two days in my assignment.
John Spencer

Spencer handed the note to Jessie, indicating she should read it. "Colonel, why are you asking your people in Washington City to come here? Shouldn't you send this to your people in Culpepper?"

"Please, call me John. When Virginia rejoined the Union a few months ago, the First Military District headquartered in Culpepper was closed."

Spencer knew Jessie was curious about the name "Cump." Most old army hands knew that Cump was William Tecumseh Sherman. He got the nickname as a West Point cadet by classmates who were intrigued by his middle name.

Jessie folded the message and put it into an envelope. "I can't send the boy," she said, "because it's about seventeen miles. But I'm sure one of the men in the village will deliver it, but he will have to spend the night."

Spencer reached for his money belt, noticing the intense pain in his ribs on the left side.

"Here's five dollars for the expenses and some extra."

It took more than an hour for Spencer to clean up. Jessie had tightly wrapped what she suspected were fractured ribs and applied cool, damp towels to his face to reduce the swelling. The bite wound on his wrist worried her. She drenched it in whiskey, then wrapped his wrist in a mustard poultice.

Now he sat in the dining room trying to eat his evening meal, wondering about Sherman's reaction to the delay. He pushed the plate away, his mouth too sore to chew.

When Jessie had finished with the dishes and Amanda was in bed, she came into the dining room with two mugs of coffee. She took a bottle of brandy and a glass from the sideboard and set them in front of Spencer. "I think a little brandy will help relax you. There's a cot in the back of the house that I make available to travelers. You're welcome to it."

Spencer remembered how Jessie took charge in the stable, how she helped him—how she saved his life. Her gray-green eyes were immense and glistened in the soft lamplight. He remembered the coarse clothes she had worn that afternoon. Tonight she wore a light blue dress. Spencer didn't know much about women's clothing, but he knew that Jessie's dress was expensively tailored.

"Are you all right, Jessie?" he asked.

"Yes," she nodded quickly. "It was just...just all so horrible." She shuddered.

"John, certainly someone else will have to deliver that letter."

"No. Unless my orders are changed, I have to do it."

"But why? Why must you do it? The people who tried to kill you know about the letter and they'll try again. Why can't someone else deliver it?"

"Because it is my responsibility—to General Lee." Spencer could see that Jessie still was badly shaken. "Look, Jessie, the letter I'm carrying could make things better for all of us."

Jessie looked at Spencer for a very long moment. "What difference does it make whether a man dies fighting a war or dies on a lonely road from a killer's bullet. My husband sat at this very table and told me he had to fight for the South." Jessie's voice was faltering. "His exact words were, 'If we win, things will be better.'"

"Your husband fought for the South?"

Jessie nodded. "He was a captain."

Jessie pushed back her chair. She gathered the cups and glass and started to leave the room. She paused at the door and looked back, her eyes welling with tears.

"Men always seem to have passion to squander on causes that require killing. And when the killing stops long enough for men to plan how to start it all over again, it's the woman and children who count the cost.

"General Lee or that damn letter won't make a particle of difference. Your death certainly won't." Jessie started to say more, then shook her head and quickly left the room.

Spencer heard a cup or glass shatter on the kitchen floor. Then Jessie's bedroom door slammed.

Spencer put another log in the fireplace to save the dying flames. Despite the fact that Jessie had saved his life and treated his wounds, he was disappointed that she'd been married to a Confederate officer.

He sat in the rocker by the fireplace and thought back over the day—to the roan, her eyes rolling in terror as she died in the street—to the man who gently patted her shoulder after he put a bullet into her brain. To the gentle, liquid eyes sighting down a gun barrel pointed at his brain.

Spencer tilted the bottle, welcoming the burning liquid that helped dissolve the tension and ease the pain. Who were the two men buried in a shallow grave behind the stable? They were violent men. Killers. The man with the rifle—wasn't his name Choka?—said he'd been paid to kill him. Could it be the letter he carried for Lee? He recalled his meeting with Sherman. Could it be the Klan?

Spencer took a long swallow from the bottle. The brandy didn't burn now. Strange, he hadn't feared the big man—Choka said he was Silas Morgan. The big man was filled with anger and passion. That made him vulnerable.

Spencer grimaced when he recalled the sound of the knife blade plunging through the big man's ribs. He had never killed anyone with a knife. He had killed men before, but never that close. He'd seen men fall when he fired, but even then he often could never be certain whether it had been his bullet or another man's that had done the killing.

Strange, he thought, I am a colonel in the U.S. Army, and I hate violence. Yet, my life has been filled with it.

Spencer had feared the smaller man with the gentle, liquid eyes. Killing had merely been a job of work for him—like that Reb in the Wilderness who fired the bullet at point-blank range, the bullet that caused the pain that would be with him always. Both that Reb and Choka had been unhurried, measured and methodical killers. Spencer touched the indentation on his forehead, where the hair had turned silver.

There were times when Spencer feared sleep more than any enemy. This was a night to fear sleep. He took another swallow of the brandy. He leaned back in the rocker and propped his feet up on a stool. When his eyes closed, he could not control the drift of his mind back to the Wilderness.

The boy couldn't be more than 16. A Rebel ball had taken him low in the belly, knocking him into a sitting position. He clutched his stomach trying to stem the gushing flow, the red glistening in the dappled sunlight filtering through the dogwoods into the tiny clearing. His eyes were locked on the splattered legs of his faded blue trousers.

Spencer lay behind a tree about thirty feet away, his eyes searching for some sign of the Confederates in the tangled underbrush across the clearing.

Spencer's orders were to patrol the south bank of the Rapidan River in a heavily wooded area of north-central Virginia, known as the Wilderness, on this very warm day in May, 1864. He left most of his squad on the road and moved on foot with only a half-dozen troopers. After covering only a couple of hundred yards through the trees and scrubby thickets, Spencer decided the woods were too dense for large enemy formations. He was about to order his men back to the road when the young private was hit.

"Cap'n Spencer! Help me. *Please*!" The boy, his arms wrapped around his middle, was rocking back and forth. "Cap'n Spencer!" Then the boy whimpered, "*Oh, my*...*Oh, my*."

Why had the fool walked into the clearing!

Sound does strange things in deep woods. Where had the shot had come from?

Spencer hadn't even seen the muzzle flash or smoke. All he knew for certain was that the boy—now he remembered that the boy was Heisler,

Peter Heisler from Indiana—was gut-shot, which probably meant the Reb sniper was out in front of them.

Spencer rested his forehead for a moment on the cool loam of the forest floor. The Reb, he was certain, was waiting for someone to try to reach Heisler. Spencer was certain that at least one Reb, probably several more, had the clearing covered. Always a meticulous planner, Spencer learned long ago not to trust his gut, his instincts. Objectively, there was no good reason to risk his life to save the boy. Anyone who was gut-shot rarely survived, and the odds were that Heisler would die even if he could pull him to safety. Always the analyst, Spencer therefore wondered why he even considered trying to save the boy.

The woods were eerily silent, and Spencer didn't know whether he feared the silence or the gunfire. A bird shrilled. Spencer's eyes darted up and off to his left. Had the bird been startled by Rebs moving northwesterly to flank the squad? Spencer had to do something. But what was the right thing to do? Despite what his head told him, he knew in his heart he couldn't just leave the boy, and realization made him angry. He always had been critical of actions driven by emotions.

He looked to his right at Sergeant Barlow. Although he couldn't see the other troopers, he knew they were near.

"Sergeant," Spencer whispered, "pull the men back to the road. I'll try to get Heisler."

Barlow, grimy and with sweat streaming into his gray-flecked beard, shook his head. "Captain, you know they've got the clearing covered. They'll cut you down before you get ten feet. We'll have to come back for the boy."

"Do it now, Sergeant!"

Barlow hesitated, then crawled away to collect his men.

Spencer called softly to the moaning boy.

"Heisler, listen to me. Get down so they don't hit you again. Try to crawl toward me."

The young man, his face contorted with fear and pain, turned momentarily to the sound of Spencer's voice, then resumed his rhythmic rocking.

A heavy volley suddenly erupted. The bullets cut through the trees, triggering a shower of leaves and small branches and striking all around the boy, even plucking at his clothes. Heisler seemed dazed.

"Get down, Heisler!" Spencer shouted. "*Damn* you, boy," Spencer yelled as he began to crawl toward the boy, "get down or they'll kill you!"

When he saw a line of a half-dozen skirmishers move into the clearing, Spencer dropped behind another fallen tree. He cocked the hammer of his single-shot saddle carbine, wiped the sweat from his eyes, and fired when he had a clear shot. He then drew his revolver, resting it on the tree trunk, and carefully placed his shots. Three more men went down. The sporadic Reb fire shifted toward him, several rounds thunking into the fallen tree.

When he fired all six rounds, he watched helplessly as two Rebs walked up to Heisler. One looked at the boy for a moment, as if examining his wound. Then, without apparent hatred or anger, he drove his bayonet into the boy's chest. Heisler pleaded silently, with outstretched arms, as the point of the bayonet passed through his body and pierced the back of his shirt. The boy convulsed as the Reb jerked his blade free.

Spencer slowly, deliberately got to his feet. He drew his saber, the blade rasping as it swept clear of the metal scabbard. Spencer's clenched fist held the saber extended in front of him. For a moment the blade wobbled and danced. Then he raised the weapon over his head and charged the two men.

The tangle of brush and low hanging limbs clawed at his body, slowing his rush. A rising panic gripped Spencer. He realized he wouldn't reach the Rebs in time. Despite his furiously pumping legs, Spencer felt as if he were pulling a tremendous weight that would forever keep the two Rebs just out of reach.

Curiously, despite the panic and anger, Spencer's brain seemed almost eager to register details. When the nearest Reb raised his Enfield, Spencer noted the man's scraggly red beard, an elbow poking through a ripped shirtsleeve, the bayonet stained with Heisler's blood. He heard the series of frosty snaps as the hammer was cocked.

From no more than ten feet, the muzzle blossomed, the deadly white petals soundlessly filling Spencer's vision. He felt the tremendous hammer-blow to his forehead, and he began a long spiral into darkness.

Spencer awakened with a spasm, kicking over the stool. He was lathered in sweat. The fire was out and the room was dark. As terrifying as the memory always was, Spencer dreaded his first waking moments. "Did I do the right thing?" was the question he always struggled to answer. "There was no hope of saving that boy, so why did I charge those skirmishers?" His conclusion always was that he acted without thinking—always dangerous in life threatening situations, especially for a soldier. And especially so now that he was responsible for the safety of the President.

Spencer noticed the lantern in the hallway leading to the bedrooms. Jessie stood there in her robe.

"John, are you all right?"

Spencer quickly righted the stool and whipped his face on his sleeves. "Yes…yes, I guess I must have dozed off."

Jessie set the lamp on a table next to Spencer's chair, then sat on the stool. She gently pushed his damp hair away from his forehead. She smiled softly and took his hand in both of hers. He looked into her beautiful gray-green eyes and saw concern, perhaps even understanding.

"You can't sleep in that chair," she said softly, briefly squeezing his hand before rising. "Why don't you go to the guest room? I'll leave the lamp."

Spencer nodded. "Yes, thank you. I will in a moment."

She stood for a moment in front of Spencer, her arms folded tightly across her chest and her head tilted slightly to the left. "I'll call you when breakfast is ready. Then I'll change those bandages."

She smiled again. "Good night, John."

"Good night."

He lingered a moment before heading to the guest room. Yes, he thought, there is something very special about this woman. She can be as tough as a gun barrel or as gentle as a dove.

CHAPTER 8

11:35 a.m.
September 7, 1870
Chicago

Joseph Medill confessed that what he disliked most about traveling by train were the crowds. As he and Ernst Pohlman stepped down from the train, the LaSalle Street Station was jammed with humanity. "You see what I mean?" Medill said, his hand sweeping toward the crowd.

Almost immediately a filthy old man hobbled up to Medill trying to sell something.

"No thank you," Medill said several times. Pohlman saw that Medill was trying to maintain his temper and his dignity. Finally, the old man gave up, mumbled something under his breath, and moved toward a fashionably dressed young woman.

As they moved with the flow of passengers from the large, ornate terminal, Medill heard someone calling his name.

"Mr. Medill! Mr. Pohlman! This way, please."

A young man dressed in livery was waving at them.

"I knew the paper would send a carriage for us," Medill said. "Thank goodness the driver was able to find us in this madness."

The driver had managed to park the landau at the curb in front of the hack line, which Pohlman suspected infuriated the cabbies. The driver placed their portmanteaus in the boot, and a moment later snapped the reins over the backs of two sleek grays that pulled the landau into traffic.

"Drive past the paper, please," Medill asked. "I'd like to show Mr. Pohlman a little of the city before we go to the hotel."

There was a great deal of mutual respect between Medill and Pohlman. To say they were friends, however, would be somewhat of an exaggeration.

"Do you really believe you can convince them to go along with the White House?" Pohlman intended for his question to reflect his doubt.

"That's why I asked the President to involve you, Ernst." Medill smiled. "The top editor for the New York Associated Press should be able to help me do that."

There were few men whose pure journalistic ability was more universally admired than Ernst Pohlman's. During the war he was an AP "special," what later was called a correspondent. His speed and accuracy were legendary. His account of the battle of Shiloh, and his story of Gettysburg from the vantage of Cemetery Hill, the most exposed point, were considered classics.

As a Prussian army captain, Pohlman initially was an observer. A natural and gifted writer, Pohlman became so intrigued by the war and the people waging it that he resigned his commission and joined the AP. His accurate accounts of battles were attributable to his military training and his knack for being where the action was. Generals and their staff officers, watching Pohlman dash on horseback from one hot spot to the next, often complained that he had more information about the fighting than they did.

Even Abe Lincoln came to depend on Pohlman's accounts of the fighting. On several occasions Pohlman was invited to the White House to brief the President on what he had seen. As a mutual respect and trust developed between the two men, Lincoln asked Pohlman about the performance of Union generals. More than one military career was enhanced or diminished after the discussions.

The landau turned off Madison Street onto Dearborn and stopped in front of the *Chicago Tribune* building.

"Will you be going in, Mr. Medill?"

Medill looked up at the building where he'd been editor for more than a dozen years.

"No, driver. Let's go to the hotel."

The landau turned toward Potter Palmer's grand and expensive Palmer House at State and Quincy streets. Medill often said he loved Chicago for many reasons, but primarily because it was a great city for the news business, and he had helped mold the *Tribune* into one of the nation's best written and edited papers.

Medill also had a finely developed sense of the devious side of politics. He almost single-handedly achieved the nomination of Abe Lincoln. He manipulated the convention in the best tradition of Chicago politics by giving away jobs in the new administration. During the critical negotiating, Lincoln was sequestered in the Iroquois Hotel, his visitors carefully screened.

When Lincoln learned how he won the nomination, he refused to make the appointments. Medill's support for Lincoln became at best lukewarm.

He still squirmed when he recalled what occurred when the '63 draft riots broke out in several cities. Medill headed a group that went to Washington to protest the draft call for six thousand Chicagoans. The city of one hundred fifty-six thousand had already contributed twenty-two thousand to the war.

Lincoln heard them out, then said, "Gentlemen, after Boston, Chicago has been the chief instrument in bringing this war on the country. You called for war until we had it. You called for emancipation and I have given it to you. Now you come here begging to be left off from the call for men, which I have made to carry out the war—a war which you have demanded. You ought to be ashamed of yourselves. And you, Medill, are acting like a coward. You and your *Tribune* have had more influence than any paper in the Northwest in making this war. You can influence great masses, and yet you cry to be spared at a moment when your cause is suffering. Go home and send us those men."

The delegation went back to Chicago and sent Lincoln the six thousand men.

The quality of service at the Palmer House was something the rich and famous from two continents had come to expect and appreciate. The manager was especially attentive to the former editor-in-chief of the city's favorite newspaper, who had been named by President Grant to the Civil Service Commission.

"Mr. Medill, welcome to the Palmer House. Your suite is ready, and the other gentlemen have arrived. At your convenience, I will inform them of your arrival."

"Thank you. Have them come to my room at two o'clock. Our meeting will probably take the rest of the afternoon. Please have a light lunch brought up at half past two."

"Of course, Mr. Medill."

At two o'clock precisely, there was a light tap at the door to Medill's suite. When Pohlman opened the door, he recognized one of the two men as Melville Crawford, editor of the *Louisville Courier-Journal*. He presumed the other man was Henry Bradley, editor of the *Atlanta Constitution*.

Medill stepped around Pohlman to shake the hands of the two editors. "Come in, gentlemen; please come in," Medill said. "I've ordered refreshments, which should arrive shortly."

It was clear to Pohlman that the editors were apprehensive about the meeting, primarily because they didn't know precisely why they had been invited to attend. Pohlman also suspected that Medill's reputation as a crusading editor who had opposed the rebellion, and the South's cause in general, meant that he would have to tread lightly with these men. Pohlman knew Medill faced a delicate piece of work this afternoon.

"Joseph," Pohlman said, "since this is your meeting, why don't you begin."

"Before we proceed," Medill said, "let me suggest that the meeting be informal, and that we address each other accordingly."

Medill paused for a moment, then began.

"As my message to each of you indicated, you have been invited to this meeting at the request of President Grant. The only stipulation he and I ask is that you not report or otherwise disclose the content of our discussion today until October sixth. Unless I can have your word that you will agree to the stipulation, gentlemen, the meeting cannot continue."

Medill looked expectantly at the two editors. Neither immediately responded. Then Bradly shifted uncomfortably on the couch.

"Mr. Medill...Joseph," Bradley said, shaking his head. "How can you, considering your experience as an editor, expect us to agree in advance that we will not report what is said here today?"

Crawford also shook his head in agreement and turned to Pohlman. "Have you agreed to the stipulation?"

"Yes, he has," Medill answered, "and he did so before knowing precisely what would be involved."

Bradley, glancing at Crawford, pursed his lips. "I am disappointed, Mr. Medill, that you would ask me to come here from Atlanta to attend a meeting at which, to quote you, 'something vital to the well-being of the nation will be discussed,' then expect us not to write about it until a certain date. That request is not only unreasonable, but I find it difficult that anyone—especially a former editor who I am certain took pride in his journalistic integrity—would ask such a thing."

"Gentlemen, please. I understand your concerns. I also will admit that, as an editor, if someone had come to me with such request I might have hooted him out of my office."

"Ernst, both Melville and Henry are understandably concerned about the request that nothing be written about this meeting until the sixth. You and I have met separately with the President and have agreed to the restriction. Isn't that correct?"

Pohlman hesitated a moment before answering. "That is true, Joseph," Pohlman responded, a German accent evident in his speech. "But there is a caveat that these gentlemen should be made aware of. I agreed, but with my own stipulation. And that was if the information I received was, in my judgment, of grave and immediate importance to the well-being of the nation—and that assessment would be mine alone to make—then I would release the story immediately."

"And what was Grant's response to that?" Crawford asked.

"He agreed to the terms."

"Why do you suppose he trusted you to hold the story?"

Medill answered before Pohlman could. "Obviously, gentlemen, the President was confident that Ernst would see why the information must be held confidential for a period of time."

The room was quiet for a long moment.

"Let me add this," Pohlman said. "The premature release of the story may complicate the President's political future. There is even the possibility that the story may put the President's life at risk. But he told me he views the risk as acceptable if he realizes his objective."

It was apparent that Bradley was agitated by the uncertainties of the situation. "Frankly, Ernst, I don't give a damn about Grant's political complications. Some of his actions—perhaps I should say, inaction—have created more complications than the man obviously is capable of handling. But if you say there is some risk to his life, then I will at least listen before making a judgment.

Bradley turned to Medill. "In order to protect the integrity of the *Constitution*, and my own as its editor, I will agree, but only under the same terms Pohlman gave the President. I alone will decide whether to hold the story."

Crawford hesitated, then nodded agreement. "I also will agree under the same circumstances. I must add, however, that if I decide to print the story immediately, I also would feel obligated to my readers to report the circumstances and objectives of this meeting, obviously including the fact that we were asked to withhold the story."

"One last thing," Pohlman said. "Obviously, if any one of us breaks the news embargo—assuming you agree to the embargo after you hear what Joseph has to say—then each of us is free to write the story." The other editors nodded agreement.

"Agreed." Medill sighed deeply, apparently recognizing that this was as good an agreement he would get. "Now we can begin." He leaned forward on the couch, resting his fingertips on the low table separating him from Crawford and Bradley.

"President Grant is deeply concerned about the bitterness that still exists between the North and South. He feels there must be a dramatic gesture to heal the wounds."

Medill reviewed a litany of problems with which the nation still struggled in the aftermath of the war. When he told them about the reunion planned by the senior officer corps of the Army of Northern Virginia, and the possibility that Lee might attend, Bradley shook his head.

"I am aware of the reunion plans," he said, "but I seriously doubt that General Lee will attend. His health has been failing. I also doubt it because he has very carefully avoided any public discussion of the war. In fact, many of his friends who served with him say that he won't discuss the war even with them. But more importantly, what does that reunion have to do with our being here, whether or not General Lee attends?"

"I think I'm beginning to understand now what's troubling the President," Crawford said, smiling. "He would like to prevent the reunion from taking place because of how the Radical Republicans will react to it, especially if General Lee does attend. I presume he would like our papers to avoid covering the reunion, or that we write editorials in opposition to such a gathering."

"No, gentlemen," Medill said. "The President does not object to the reunion; in fact, he wants it to take place, and he hopes that General Lee will be there."

"You're toying with us, Medill," Bradley said. "Get to the point of all this."

"As we speak, gentlemen," Medill said, "one of the President's aides is meeting with General Lee. He is carrying a request from the President asking Lee to attend the reunion."

Medill paused for a moment, wondering what reaction to anticipate. "Further, the President is asking General Lee to invite him to attend."

"*What?*" Crawford was incredulous. "Grant wants Lee to invite him to the reunion?"

"The President hopes that he and General Lee can stand in front of the veterans of the South's most famous and effective army, and that together they can declare that the bitterness on both sides must be ended."

The room was very quiet. Then Bradley slowly shook his head in disbelief. "I can't believe it," he said. "Grant must be a fool. If he's not killed by a radical, he'll be run out of Atlanta on a rail. The only thing worse I can thing of would be to have Sherman stand on the other side of Lee while expounding on the tactics and wisdom of his march to the sea."

Bradley paused and looked intently at Medill. "Joseph, does the President intend to bring Sherman to the reunion?"

"I don't know," Medill said. "The President made no mention of any role that Sherman would have in the matter. If I learn otherwise, rest assured I will counsel the President not to bring any of his general staff, obviously including Sherman."

Crawford seemed awed by what Grant hoped to achieve. "Yes, Grant may be a fool," he said, "or it is a master stroke that could ensure his political future. Will the veterans know Grant is coming?"

"No. We understand that Lee, if he goes, will address them, and we will urge that his remarks support the President's theme of unity and harmony. We will ask Lee to prepare the veterans with an introduction that will explain Grant's presence."

Bradley asked, "Will Grant go if Lee doesn't?"

"No," Medill said.

"What will happen if Lee attends but refuses to invite Grant?" Pohlman asked.

Medill pursed his lips. "That, of course, is the key question. Grant understands that Lee still has hard feelings about the war and his treatment immediately following. Grant unsuccessfully sought Lee's help, we all know, on two occasions—once at Appomattox when Lee refused to use his influence to get other Confederate armies to surrender, and more recently when Grant invited him to the White House, hoping for at least a symbolic gesture that the bitterness was over. So the answer to your question, Ernst, is that I don't know what will happen if Lee turns down the request."

Medill paused dramatically to look at each man. "But I think I can, with some confidence, say that I have the feeling that if ever Lee were to make the kind of gesture that the President is certain the nation desperately needs, he will make that gesture in front of his beloved Army of Northern Virginia. He will do so, if for no other reason, than to hasten the time when his men who suffered so much can finally be rid of the war. So, I personally feel that Lee will issue the invitation."

"Why?" Bradley asked.

"Pardon me?" Medill asked.

"Why should Lee do it? Why should he be the one to risk so much?" Bradley's voice was rising. "Look what happened to General Longstreet when he openly supported the Grant Administration. He is a hated man in the South, and he has lost whatever respect the North had for him as a soldier."

Crawford said, "Understanding the realities of politics, as we in this room do, what possible benefit can there be for Lee to take such a risk?"

"The most noble benefit of all—what could be the most significant step since the end of the war to unite the nation," Medill said.

"Do you really think that such a meeting will change anything?" Bradley's tone bordered on sarcasm. "If you do, your thinking—or Grant's—is simplistic."

"No, my thinking represents reality," Medill said evenly. "And that reality is that Lee, more than any other man, has the universal respect of the nation—despite the noise and smoke generated by the radicals. And, yes, there is risk for Lee in such a meeting with Grant. But if Lee can take personal risks for the glory of war, he can take them for the greater glory of peace."

Pohlman thought Medill had gone too far, and he braced for an outburst from both editors. Instead, Bradley smiled, shaking his head.

"Medill, you're beginning sound like some of the editorials you wrote in the late fifties. My observation still stands: your motives for Lee's participation are simplistic, especially considering the complexity of the problems involving Reconstruction. Unless you have something better, I see no benefit to continuing this meeting."

There was a knock at the door, and an usher wheeled in a cart. The usher turned toward the four men, bowing slightly. "With the personal complements of Mr. Palmer, gentlemen. Fried Lake Michigan perch, boiled potatoes, and fresh corn on the cob. The wine is a delightful French white. Shall I serve your meal?"

Medill thanked the usher, tipped him generously, asked him to leave, then hurried back to his seat on the couch.

Although Pohlman knew that Medill was eager to resume the

conversation, he leaned forward to speak. "I can personally recommend the perch. They are tasty and the chef here removes nearly all of the bones.

"But before we sample the cuisine, however" Pohlman said, "I would like to make this point in support of at least part of what Joseph has said. Think back, gentlemen, to a year or so after the war. Do you recall the movement in Virginia to elect Lee governor? That proposition was greeted with enthusiasm throughout the South. Virginia has always taken a leadership role among the states, especially among southern states. Where is she now? Only Lee could restore leadership to the South. Only he could do it then; only he can do it now. Now, think back to the sixty-eight presidential election. One of the North's most prestigious newspapers called for Democrats to nominate Lee for President—contending that Lee would be a better President than Grant."

Pohlman cleared his throat. "Mr. Medill's point, perhaps made with too heavy a hand, is that General Lee, even now, has enormous influence in this country, perhaps more than any other man. He is in a position to mold public opinion on the issues if he would but step forward. Instead, it appears to many that General Lee has retreated behind the shield of a small college. The impression among even some of his most ardent supporters is that he is an aristocrat who, defeated in battle, chooses not to become soiled with the more mundane aspects of post-war politics."

Pohlman leaned back in his seat. "I must agree with Joseph to this extent: General Lee is a leader who the nation will follow. The symbolism of Lee and Grant standing together will be too powerful for even the hard-headed radicals to blur or distort. If substance will follow—and Lee can help provide the substance—then a giant stride will be taken to heal this nation. For that reason, and that reason alone, I have agreed to what the President asks."

The room was quiet for a very long moment.

"All right, Joseph, you've made your point," Bradley said, his voice now subdued. "That still leaves the basic question of why we've been asked to come here. What precisely are we being asked to do?"

Medill thought for a moment of how he had planned to answer the question. "The President, as I'm sure you know as well as anyone, is keenly sensitive to the power of newspapers to influence public opinion. He hopes that you gentlemen will report this event—the reunion—with a depth far greater than you might otherwise. He asked that I make clear, however, that his request should in no way be viewed as an attempt by the President to direct media coverage of the reunion, should any of you choose to cover it with the depth he's hoping for. Finally, we hope you will consider carrying Ernst Pohlman's coverage of the event."

"We have great respect for Ernst, but we would prefer to cover it ourselves," Bradley said.

Medill nodded. "I understand, but Ernst has had an inside track on this story and he has excellent contacts that include the President."

Crawford asked, "Have you or anyone else in the Administration had this kind of meeting with other newspaper editors?"

"You are the only editors with whom such meetings have—or will be—held. I recommended you three to the President because of the reputation you have for quality journalism. There also were geographic considerations. The *Courier-Journal's* office is only a few blocks from the Mason-Dixon line. Who better can represent the border states? The *Constitution*, in addition to its outstanding reputation, is located in the city that, for obvious reasons, always will have a special significance for the South. The rapid growth of Atlanta also represents the new emergence of the South's economic power. In the case of the New York Associated Press, we felt that who better than Ernst could report for the Eastern press?"

What Medill didn't say was that he would not have discussed the story with any Eastern newspapers because of the long-running feud he'd had with them when he was an editor. Although Horace Greeley's *New York Times* did not escape his wrath, it was with James Bennett's *New York Herald* that he had traded editorial broadsides. Bennett promoted Grant as "the people's candidate" during the '64 election. Medill wrote that Bennett and his paper should not be permitted to "paw and slobber over our Illinois general." Medill added that unless the *Herald* kept its "unclean and treacherous hands off of him, it may expect to get tomahawked." Bennett, who not only was wildly eccentric but was considered mad as well, replied that the *Tribune* was the "sewer into which goes everything too dirty for its New York namesake to print."

Conspicuous by its absence was any reference by Medill to the Western Associated Press, which operated as a separate agency from its eastern counterpart. Although Medill had no serious problem with the journalistic quality or the politics of the Western AP, he obviously felt that the *Tribune* could best serve readers in the Northwest.

"There is one point I personally would like to make clear," Pohlman said, looking directly at Medill. "I told the President that I would report to our newspaper clients what is said and what occurs in Atlanta, whether or not my accounts are favorable to the President or his mission." Looking now at the two editors, he added, "I am confident that the President understands that if we agree to report the event in depth—or support it editorially—we will do so objectively."

Bradley and Crawford nodded agreement.

"Frankly," Bradley said, "whether or not the President understands that point, that's how it shall be, as far as the *Constitution* is concerned." Bradley looked at Crawford for a long moment. Crawford's nod was almost imperceptible.

"Based on what you just said about your objectivity, Ernest, we agree to use your coverage of the reunion."

Medill sat back on the couch, obviously pleased with how the meeting had gone. As he had presumed before the meeting had started, it couldn't have succeeded without Pohlman.

"Well, gentlemen, let me again ask that you not mention the possibility of the President attending in your pre-reunion coverage prior to October sixth." Medill paused. "However, if General Lee refuses to invite the President, we have no objection to your telling your readers that the President had hoped to attend and his reasons for doing so."

Medill stood. "Now, I suggest we pause for some refreshment. I also hope you will permit me to be your host for dinner tonight, so that we can continue our discussion of this interesting development."

Pohlman excused himself, saying that he would be back in time for dinner. He went immediately to his room where he wrote a message to be telegraphed to his New York office. In it, he asked one of his editors to contact the White House and arrange for an interview for him with the

President. He also asked that an interview be arranged with Lee as soon as possible, although he knew that Lee disliked reporters and rarely granted interviews. He asked that complete profiles of Grant and Lee be prepared, specifically including details of the years spent by both men at West Point and their service together in the Mexican war. He also wanted a narrative of the key problems involving Reconstruction, and what actions the best minds in the nation thought were required to solve them. Finally, he asked for written summaries of the battles during which the two men faced each other, and the tactics each employed.

Pohlman was not at Appomattox on that Palm Sunday when Lee surrendered. But he did arrive the next day, in time to see Lee and Grant when they met between the lines, flanked by eighty thousand Union troops and hardly more than twenty-eight thousand Confederates. Still in Pohlman's files were detailed notes of the dozens of interviews he had that day. His had been the unique experience of talking to men in blue and gray, often standing together. Everything in those files, the summaries that would be prepared, and the interviews that he planned to schedule, would provide the grist for what Pohlman was planning.

Pohlman fully intended to honor his agreement to hold the story. He also knew that such a story would not remain confidential for very long. Someone would learn about it. When the story did break, Pohlman would be ready. He envisioned a series of main stories about plans for the reunion, the events during the reunion, and whatever results there might be. The main story would be accompanied by profiles of Lee and Grant.

When the story broke, Pohlman intended to assign a team of writers to get the reactions of the most influential people in the North and South.

Pohlman hoped the reunion would be successful for both Grant and Lee, as well as the nation. But no matter how it turned out, whether good or bad, he would tell the nation.

Chapter 9

September 8, 1870
Georgetown
7:30 p.m.

The sun had been down for more than an hour as the victoria, its top raised against the cool night air, bounced over the rutted road from Georgetown to Washington City.

"My lord!" Mattie complained to the driver after the carriage wheels dropped into a massive pothole. "Nelson, you drive like a muleskinner."

"I'm sorry, ma'am," Nelson answered from the raised front seat, "but the rains have ruined this old road—besides, it's too dark to see good."

Mattie leaned back, still holding tightly to the hand strap in the swaying carriage.

A messenger had arrived earlier in the evening with a note from Brewster, the banker who handled Rachel's investments. Just yesterday Rachel had said she would stop doing business with him because of something that had happened a couple of nights earlier at a party. Mattie knew something bad happened that night because she had never seen Rachel so angry—or so frightened. The message from Brewster asked Rachel to meet him in the Jefferson Hotel restaurant. He said it was extremely urgent.

"What do you suppose that pompous ass wants to talk about that's so all-fired important?"

"I don't know," Rachel said, "but it can't be anything good."

Rachel remembered the meeting with Gould, how the man's eyes could cause pain that was almost physical. And Fisk—it was clear what he wanted. She remembered that Gould had said, *When the time is right, you will receive an assignment from us.* Perhaps that time had arrived.

In the days following her meeting with Gould and Fisk, Rachel had decided that she would defy them, no matter what the cost. Tonight she would try to convince Brewster to let her liquidate at least some of her investments, preferably converting them to gold. If he agreed, then she would leave Washington and move back to Richmond.

Rachel realized that if Gould and Fisk wanted to find her, there was no place she could hide. But she was counting on the fact that they would not follow if she left behind most of her money. After all, they had threatened her with financial ruin if she didn't cooperate, so their hold on her would be broken if she abandoned the bulk of her fortune.

Still, Rachel knew how dangerous the two were, and she would have to move cautiously. If she could recover at least a third of her money, her situation would not be hopeless. Perhaps she could even find a way to sell the house without Brewster finding out about it. Even if she got fifty cents on the dollar for the house, it would be better than just walking away from it.

The victoria pulled up in front of the Jefferson. A ramp extended down from the boardwalk to the street, so that ladies could more easily step down from their carriages without getting mud on the hems of their dresses.

"I'll wait with Nelson," Mattie said, "but we won't be far if you need us. Nelson may be getting old, and maybe he don't see too good anymore, but he still can break a man's back—especially one as puny as that jaybird Brewster's."

When Rachel seemed hesitant to leave the carriage, Mattie reached across and touched her hand. "I don't know what you've gotten yourself into," Mattie said softly, "but you don't have to go in there."

"Yes, I do. If things go as I hope they will, we will be going back to

Richmond very soon." Rachel hesitated for a moment longer. "But I am worried. I'll explain on the way home. I don't think I'll be too long."

The doorman assisted Rachel down from the carriage. Brewster was waiting for her in the foyer and helped with her coat.

"Hello, Roger," she said coolly.

"I'm glad you could come, Rachel. I have a table, there in the corner, where we can talk."

It was evident that Brewster was very nervous. As he led Rachel to their table, he stumbled over the leg of a chair, jostling a naval officer having dinner with his wife.

"I'm very sorry," he said, holding the palms of his hands out as if he expected the officer to strike him. "Please, forgive me." The naval officer looked at Brewster, then at Rachel, and shook his head in disgust.

When they were seated, Brewster ordered brandy. "Nothing for me, thank you," Rachel said.

Brewster fiddled with the silverware until the usher brought the brandy, which he swallowed in two gulps.

"Bring me another, please."

Rachel, concerned by Brewster's nervousness and by how he was drinking, didn't wait for him to bring up the reason for the meeting.

"Roger, why am I here?"

Brewster ran one hand through his thick, brown hair, his eyes darting around the room.

"Roger, what in hell do they want me to do?" Rachel's voice was louder than she had intended it to be, causing Brewster to grimace and nervously sweep his eyes around the room.

"Please, Rachel, give me a moment to collect my thoughts...and for heaven's sake, please keep your voice down."

When his second drink came, he sipped it, then leaned back and took a deep breath.

"It is so...so incredibly crazy that I still don't believe it." Brewster's mouth opened and closed in several false starts. Then, for the first time since they had sat down, he looked directly into Rachel's eyes. "They're going to kill him," he said in a low monotone.

"What did you say?"

"They are going to *kill* him!"

"*Who*, for God's sake?" Rachel leaned closer to Brewster, reaching across the table to tug at the sleeve of his jacket, as if she could pull the words from him. "Who is going to be killed?"

"Grant…the President." Brewster's lips trembled, as if overwhelmed by the mental image his words created. "They are going to *kill* the President of the United States."

Rachel stared in disbelief, then slowly shook her head in confusion. "Are you saying Gould and Fisk are going to do it?"

Brewster reacted immediately to the two names, his body going rigid. "No!" he blurted. Then said more softly, "No…at least I don't think so."

"Tell me the truth, Roger, do they want me to play any role in this thing?"

"Your name was mentioned, but not by Gould or Fisk. Do you remember those two men with Gould and Fisk, the ones who were with them when they talked to you?"

Rachel nodded. "Who are they?"

"I don't know, for certain. They handle special assignments, mostly for Fisk, and especially rough things like union trouble. I've seen them occasionally, but I don't know much about them."

"How are they involved in this?"

"Two days ago they came to my bank. They withdrew a huge sum of money they had in a joint account, more than twenty five thousand dollars. While they were waiting for the money, they told me to get out of my office because they wanted to discuss business privately."

Brewster toyed with his brandy snifter, turning the glass slowly, seemingly mesmerized by the amber fluid. "I, of course, left immediately and waited in the outer office. But I noticed that the transom over my office door was open, and that if I stood nearby I could hear almost everything they said. One of them, Hollis Connor, did most of the talking. The other man's name was Charles Wells, an Englishman who has lived for many years in this country."

Brewster described Connor as highly intelligent and very aggressive. He said Connor was the kind of man who was shrewd enough to use his influence with Fisk to develop his own investment opportunities without appearing as a threat to either Fisk or Gould. Fisk was said to like Connor because of his explosive temper, his intimidating physical strength, and because he would do whatever he was told. Connor often bragged that he was using his money to buy vast tracts of land in his native Texas. Brewster said he overheard Fisk say that neither Connor nor Wells received salaries for their services to Fisk or Gould. Their reward was the opportunity to ride the coattails of the financial giants.

The Englishman made a fortune during the war running the Union blockade of southern ports to supply the Confederates with arms and other supplies. Wells would have delivered supplies to the Union side, had the price been right. Both men earned a great deal of money in various financial deals with Fisk and Gould.

"Wells said something about having second thoughts about their plan, which made Connor very angry. Connor said they were committed and that there would be no backing out. It was clear that Wells was frightened."

"Roger, get to the point. What did they say about Grant?"

"Well, I could hear Connor walking about the room as he talked. I could tell that he was getting angrier by the moment with Wells. He talked about how much money they had made in the gold market. You've heard the story of how Gould and Fisk convinced Grant's own sister that she and her husband use their influence to keep Grant out of Washington while they manipulated the gold market. In fact, Rachel, you benefited from the arrangement even though you didn't know how they were controlling gold prices. You see, they got control of the Treasury Department in order to—"

"I know, Roger," Rachel said, exasperated. "I know that when the price of gold kept climbing, and investors were betting that it would fall, Gould and Fisk somehow kept government gold supplies from the market to keep the prices up. They made their money—and I guess I did, too, based on your advice," she said sarcastically, "because you, Fisk, and Gould knew the price would not be going down. Now, I know all of that, so I want you to tell me immediately what they said about Grant."

"Well, I don't remember the exact words that Connor used, but he talked about the confusion in the gold market when Grant was out of

Washington for just a few days. Connor said something like, 'Just think what would happen if Grant were removed—removed permanently—from Washington.' He said the market would be in chaos. It certainly would fall very quickly and, most importantly, they would know about it in advance.

Rachel sat quietly for a moment while she considered what Brewster had said. She was desperate to learn how she might be involved, but she realized she would have to take Brewster through his story a step at a time. "But you didn't actually hear them say that they would kill Grant, did you?" Rachel asked.

"Well, no…no, I didn't. But what else could Connor have meant?" Brewster paused for a moment, suddenly remembering something. "Wait…there was one other thing Connor said. It had to do with Grant going to Atlanta sometime soon. That seemed very important to them."

"Think, Roger. Did they say why he was going to Atlanta?"

"No, I don't think so."

"All right. Now, how did my name come up?"

"Wells asked Connor whether he knew whether Gould and Fisk still intended to use the woman. Then Connor laughed, saying, 'Of Course'. But that's all they said about it."

"My God, Roger, are you telling that's all you know?"

"I'm sorry, but if anything more was said, I didn't hear it."

A movement at the door of the dining room caught Rachel's eye. Mattie was standing just outside of the doorway, obviously concerned. Rachel waved, indicating that she would be a few minutes more. Then she turned to Brewster.

"Roger, I want part of my money immediately, perhaps two hundred thousand dollars. I want it delivered as soon as possible, and I want it in gold."

Roger shook his head. "I'm sorry, Rachel, but that won't be possible. Gould told me that you can't withdraw more than five thousand a month without his personal permission."

"Without his *permission*?" Rachel's voice was so loud that the naval officer turned to look at them, causing Roger to cringe.

"Rachel, *please*! Keep your voice down. You had to know that they weren't going to let you have your money until you've done whatever they wanted of you. Besides, I'm getting out. I'm severing all connections with Connor, and Gould, and all the rest of them before something terrible happens. Perhaps I'll spend several months in Europe. Maybe by then it'll all be over."

Rachel felt a surge of anger. "You can't go until you get my money. You helped get me into this mess, and you have to help me get out of it."

"No, Rachel. Your only interest was in making as much money as you could. I admit that I may have contributed to your problem, but it was your greed that got you into this."

Rachel was stung by Roger's words. Her mind raced, trying to find a way to convince Brewster that he should help her. "Look, I'm willing to leave most of the money behind. I don't care who gets it. You can have the New York properties I just bought. But I have to get my son out of Washington."

Tears welled into Rachel's eyes. Her fingers wound the table napkin into a tight ball. "Roger, I am not greedy." She regretted the tears, the quaver in her voice, how defensive her words sounded. "You don't understand. That damn war took everything—my husband's life, my father's mind, my son's future, everything we owned. I saw Yankee soldiers blow up daddy's plant, then they burned our house to the ground. All of that happened while you were growing dull and fat in your father's New York bank."

Rachel wiped her eyes. She leaned back in her chair to take a deep breath, trembling momentarily as she exhaled. She was in control again. "You know, Roger, I swore that I'd make the Yankees pay for what they did. At first I thought violence was what I wanted. For a time, I suppose I actually wanted to kill someone—anyone, as long as he was a Yankee. Then I realized how crazy that was. It wasn't long before I saw the poetic justice in making the Yankees pay for what they had done—and make them pay in Yankee gold.

"My goal, Roger, was a half-million dollars, which is about what my investments amount to at the moment. With that much money, I intended to start rebuilding my father's plant. I don't know how much longer my father will live, but I want to be able to buy the finest carriage available and drive him into Chase Foundries so he can see it operating again. I am convinced that seeing his plant running again will help cure his troubled mind. That plant is also my son's future."

There was a long pause before either of them said anything. Rachel looked toward the doorway of the dining room and noticed that Mattie had moved several steps into the room, her progress stopped by a hotel manager.

Brewster neatly folded his dinner napkin and placed it beside his empty brandy snifter.

"All right, Rachel. I suppose it's possible that you can get at least some of the money. I'll telegraph the bank in the morning and order that your money be transferred to a bank of your choice. The transfer can be kept confidential, but only for a few days. Fisk will find out eventually, so you'll have to move quickly to find a more secure place for your money."

Rachel gave Brewster the name of a bank in Richmond, then reached across the table and patted Brewster's hand. "Thank you, Roger."

"Well, I've already transferred most of my personal assets to a bank in London. I'm sure Fisk and the others will find a way to take over my bank. But if nothing else, Rachel, I am a good banker. Perhaps when I come back I will explore the possibilities in California."

Roger came around the table and helped Rachel to her feet. They stood for a moment at the table.

"Roger, what should we do—what can we do—about the threat to Grant?"

"Nothing," Roger said, vigorously shaking his head. "It would be too dangerous to say anything to anyone. Besides, since Lincoln's assassination, the President's security is not such a casual thing. But it's not our worry. I urge you to say nothing about it."

"Roger, why did you come here to tell me all this?"

Roger hesitated a moment. "Despite what you may think, Rachel, I am not a bad or evil person. I have regrets that I involved you. I don't precisely know what they will ask you to do, but I have reason to believe that they want you to influence someone—by means appropriate for a beautiful woman—someone who is highly placed in the government."

"Who?"

Roger lowered his voice to a whisper. "I can only guess, but I suspect it might be the Secretary of the Treasury."

"Do you mean that old fool, Stoval?"

"Yes. That would be logical if they expect to control the price of gold should a plot against the President succeed. The same scheme worked for them before, and they probably feel that the government wouldn't expect them to try it again. I do know that if you cooperate, you will earn an enormous sum of money."

Rachel considered what Brewster had said. "Thank you, Roger. I realize that this meeting posed a considerable risk for you."

For the first time during the evening, Roger smiled. "It would be wise if we avoided contacting each other in the future. I wish you well, Rachel."

When Rachel stepped into the carriage, it was obvious that Mattie was agitated. "Rachel, I can tell you've been crying. What did that jaybird say to you?"

Rachel just shook her head, her mind still churning with all that she had been told. *I have to do something about the threat to the President's life. But what? Who can I tell? I can't go to the police.*

"Honey, say the word and I'll have Nelson go in there and feed that puny bastard his own privates, and he probably wouldn't even gag once on 'em."

Rachel noticed that the gray-haired Negro was standing at the side of the carriage, apparently waiting for a command from Mattie.

Perhaps it was the stress and tension of the evening. Perhaps it was the sight of Nelson solemnly standing ready to carry out Mattie's ludicrous threat. Rachel couldn't help herself. She started to laugh, fully, from deep within herself.

"Child, what is it?" Mattie, concerned, glanced at Nelson.

"It's okay," Rachel said. "It's okay. Mattie, after all these years, I still am amazed at the words that can come out of your mouth." Rachel leaned closer to the carriage window. "Nelson, please drive us home. You won't be going in there to feed anyone his privates."

Chapter 10

September 9, 1870
Lexington, Virginia
7:10 a.m.

The goshawk wheeled in a tight circle over the road three hundred feet below, the efficiency of its short wings aided by the cool, heavy air. The hawk's slate blue plumage and its white and brown breast feathers were shabby and matted. It had just completed the long journey from Canada to Virginia, as it had each fall for the last four years.

Heavy woods, broken by occasional small clearings, stretched away from either side of the road. The hawk had spotted a plump grouse darting across one of the clearings nearest the road. Banking more steeply, the hawk kept the clearing in sight because its incredibly sharp eyes could see the grouse hiding in brush. Twice the goshawk started to swoop down to the treetops to ambush the grouse when it left its hiding place. But each time the hawk wobbled indecisively, then resumed its circle.

There was the distraction on the road. It was a man. He was alone, walking slowly. The man looked up, shielding his eyes against the early morning sun. He was fascinated by birds, envying their grace and freedom.

Bundled in a tattered Confederate greatcoat, he had to stop every so often to rest. He was carrying a basket of withered apples, the last of the crop. He hoped to get at least a few cents for them in Lexington. He needed the money because his horse had died two weeks earlier, and he somehow had to save to buy one before it came time to work his small patch of ground.

Robert E. Lee and his secretary, Clarence Hooper, saw the man standing in the road ahead, and they could tell that the man was a veteran. Hooper, who had been a major on Lee's staff, knew the general would stop and talk to the man. He always made time available for any of the veterans.

When Lee became president of Washington College five years before, he made it a point of taking daily rides on Traveler. Normally, the rides were in the late afternoon when the press of duties at the college would ease somewhat. It was something the general always enjoyed, even though he had noticed that the aging Traveler had in recent months become a hard trotter. As the general's health deteriorated, the rides became less frequent.

Lee squinted, the sun backlighting the man ahead, making it difficult to see him clearly. But when the man's stance became more erect, Lee knew that the man had identified him. When Lee reined Traveler to a stop in front of the lonely figure, the man removed his hat, holding it to his chest. Lee saw the man's shoes were badly worn, his beard ragged.

"Good morning, General Lee, sir. I'm Sergeant Nathanial Hardin, Longstreet's First Corps."

Longstreet. The name stung Lee for a moment. No one close to the general used it, even though James Longstreet had been Lee's most trusted and dependable general, his confidant, his right hand until the very end. The First Corps had been the strong backbone of the army. But within two years of Appomattox, Longstreet became a Republican and joined Grant to attempt to rebuild the South. Longstreet's motives were pure. He wanted to quickly rebuild the South, and he knew that could only happen by building a strong link with the North. But for many, he'd moved too quickly. Longstreet was now referred to by many Southern newspapers as "the most hated man in the South".

Lee looked down at the pitiful figure standing in the road. These were hard times for most of his soldiers, especially those trying to scratch a living from small farms. He knew many of them were starving. The general felt a great sadness at the thought that so many of his men had been hungry for so long.

"Good morning, Sergeant Hardin." Lee also removed his hat, then reached down to offer his hand.

Hardin looked up into Lee's face, framed by the silver hair and beard gently tousled by the light breeze. Hardin wiped his weathered hand on his coat before reaching out to clasp the general's hand.

"Where did we serve together, sergeant?" Lee thought the man looked familiar, but there were so many faces during those years, the nameless faces of young men who too often paraded through his mind when the slept.

"Why, General Lee, I was with you danged near the whole time, sir. That is, 'cept for a month or so it took me to get over catchin' a piece of Yank shrapnel right here." Hardin smiled as he patted his buttock. "I got back in time for Appomattox."

Then his smile faded and he lowered his eyes, obviously regretting having mentioned the name. He reached out to touch Traveler's muzzle, then gently stroked the animal's neck.

Lee remembered the face of the young soldier who on that final day had desperately held Traveler's bridle. Lee had gathered his troops to announce his intention to surrender the Army of Northern Virginia to Grant. The soldier, his voice breaking with emotion, his eyes welling with tears, pleaded with him not to surrender.

"We can still whup 'em, general! Don't give up! We can still whup 'em for you!"

Could this man have been that soldier? The eyes, Lee thought. He remembered the fierce pride and spirit in those young eyes. But any fire in this man's eyes had long since burned out. No, this couldn't be the same man. Besides, he seemed much older.

Lee straightened in the saddle. "Well, sergeant, we must continue on. Good luck to you."

"Wait, general." Hardin picked up his basket of apples. "I'd be honored if you took these apples. They don't look none too fresh, but they'd be fine for cookin'."

Lee hesitated a moment. Many of his former soldiers left gifts of fruit and vegetables for him at the college, for which they always refused payment.

"Yes, Mrs. Lee would appreciate some good cooking apples, but I won't take them unless you permit me to pay a fair price."

"No, sir," Hardin said firmly. "I won't take no money from you, general. I just want you to have 'em."

Lee nodded and smiled. "Thank you, sergeant. I appreciate the gift." Lee glanced at Hooper and carefully replaced his hat.

At that moment, Lee heard a whistling sound and looked up. He glimpsed a goshawk hurtle across the road just over the tree tops, banking sharply, the sun reflecting the luster of its blue feathers. A heartbeat later he heard the hawk's screech. Lee continued to look in the direction of the sound for a long moment. Then he lightly touched Traveler's flanks.

Hooper moved the chestnut closer to Hardin and reached down for the basket, then pressed a silver dollar into Hardin's hand. "That money is not for the apples, sergeant. Think of it as a small token of General Lee's appreciation for meeting a former comrade-in-arms."

Hooper wheeled the chestnut and trotted away before Hardin could respond.

Hardin watched the tired old general ride away on a horse that was nearly spent. He watched until Lee was out of sight.

Gripping the dollar tightly in his right hand, he turned and began to retrace the four miles along the lonely road to his farm.

"Dammit, general," Hardin, his throat tight, whispered hoarsely. "You didn't have to give up. We really could have whupped 'em for you."

Chapter 11

September 10, 1870
Pedlar Mills, Virginia
9:20 a.m.

It sounded to Jessie McLaws like someone was trying to break down her front door. When she pulled the lace curtain aside to look through the small oval window in the door, she saw a huge cavalry soldier standing on the porch. She opened the door and the soldier took a step backward and removed his weathered campaign hat. The full, gray-flecked beard seemed to add to the man's enormous bulk.

"Pardon me, ma'am," the voice boomed. "Sergeant Major Barlow. I'm told that I can find Colonel John Spencer here."

Jessie was too startled by the blue uniform and the size of the man wearing it to answer immediately. Behind the sergeant, a dismounted cavalry squad was in the street, each man holding the bridle of his horse. One man was still in his saddle on a handsome black stallion. He was in civilian clothes, the collar of his coat pulled up around his face.

"Yes, sergeant, the colonel is a guest here, but at the moment he's trying out a new horse. I expect him back shortly." Jessie held the door wide for Barlow. "You are welcome to wait for him inside."

Barlow turned to the street and nodded to the civilian, who

immediately dismounted and walked to the house. He stepped past Barlow and Jessie. In the hallway, he paused and turned toward Jessie.

"Where is the colonel, Mrs. McLaws?" Jessie was about to answer, when Spencer rode up. He dismounted and walked into the house, stopping in mid-stride when he saw the civilian. Spencer started to speak to the civilian, then remembered that Jessie was present. Spencer turned to Barlow.

"Welcome, sergeant. You made good time. I lost my horse the other day, and I was trying one of Mrs. McLaws's. I told her the army would pay top dollar for the animal."

Spencer was aware that Barlow was examining him closely. Both of the colonel's eyes were blackened. His face still was badly bruised and his lips were cracked and swollen. His left wrist was heavily bandaged.

"And the army will keep your promise, colonel," the civilian said as he removed his hat and overcoat.

Jessie looked closely at the man's face. It was familiar—the finely chiseled features, the closely cropped beard, the quick, bright eyes. She slowly stepped to within a couple of feet of the man.

"You are very wise, sir. Skulking about as a civilian is no doubt the safest way for you to travel through any southern state, especially Virginia."

Spencer saw the set of her jaw harden as she added, "You are not a welcome guest in this house, so please do me the favor of remaining in your...your disguise. I do not want my neighbors to learn that General William Sherman was a visitor in this house."

Sherman smiled and bowed slightly. "I sincerely regret, Mrs. McLaws, that my presence in your home is so unsettling for you. But this is an official army investigation into the deaths of two men who attacked an army officer. I can understand that you do not wish the people of this community to learn of my presence. That also is my wish. In fact, madam, I am ordering you not to divulge my presence now or at any time in the future."

"You needn't be concerned about that, general."

Despite the fact that Sherman looked and sounded like he was not offended by Jessie's remarks, Spencer knew that the general was not accustomed to anyone addressing him in such a manner, especially a woman. Considering Sherman's trigger temper, and what he'd seen of Jessie's, Spencer speculated on what appeared to be the makings for a classic confrontation.

"I presume, general, that your presence also has something to do with the colonel's letter to General Lee."

Sherman's head snapped toward Spencer, his expression reflecting the struggle to control his temper. "Mrs. McLaws," he asked evenly, "have you mentioned this letter to anyone else in town?"

"Of course not," she replied quickly. "Let me say that the circumstances following the shooting in the stable were such that Colonel Spencer had no choice but to disclose—to me only—that aspect of his mission."

Sherman's anger was now apparent to everyone. "I will be the judge, Mrs. McLaws, of what choices the colonel had." Still holding his coat draped over his arm, Sherman walked the length of the hall, examining a couple of the rooms, then returned to where Jessie, Spencer and Barlow were standing near the door.

"The first thing I want to know is where the bodies of those two men are buried?"

"Behind the stable," Jessie answered.

"Did anyone search them before they were buried?"

"Yes, sir," Spencer replied. But we didn't find anything that looked very important."

"By *damn*!" Sherman exploded. "Everyone in this house seems determined to make decisions for me. Where are the articles that were found on the bodies?"

"I have them in a bag in my room, general," Spencer replied.

Sherman turned to Barlow. "Sergeant Major. Select the men to dig up those bodies. I want every stitch of their clothing removed, although after this much time you'll probably have to cut their clothes from their bodies. I personally will direct the examination of their bodies and clothing. I want to see the weapons they carried. I also want you to bivouac the troops behind the stable and set up my tent in that same field." Sherman looked at Jessie. "I'll be spending the night there."

"Yes, sir." The small frame house shuddered as Barlow stomped through the hall door and onto the porch.

"Now, Colonel Spencer. I want to talk to you privately. We'll walk to that field behind the stable."

Sherman put on his coat and stepped onto the porch. For the few moments Spencer and Jessie were alone, Spencer could tell that she wanted to tell him something. He knew she'd been unnerved when Sherman walked into the house, and she still was upset about his insistence on delivering the letter.

Sherman's temper had cooled somewhat by the time he and Spencer were in the field. From a distance, they watched the four troopers digging up the bodies.

"What in God's good name possessed you to tell that woman about the letter? Were you trying to impress her?"

"No, sir, that wasn't it at all. I had to tell her about the assignment because she threatened to contact local authorities about the killings. You ordered me not to disclose my presence to anyone."

"Well, the fact that I'm wearing civilian clothes should indicate that I still want our presence to be confidential. I hardly would be personally involved in the routine investigation into the deaths of a couple of bushwhackers. Let's at least hope that people in this area are accustomed to seeing small cavalry units on patrol."

Sherman and Spencer remained out of earshot of the troopers while they walked slowly through the knee-high grass. "Explain to me, colonel, why you thought you could trust her?"

Spencer shrugged. "I can't answer that, sir. I just know that I can."

"Does the woman know anything…anything at all…about the contents of the letter?"

"No, sir. She knows nothing about that."

"Well, colonel, let's hope that your intuition is on the mark."

Sherman nodded to the two graves. "What do you suppose that was all about?"

"No one I've talked to around here has ever seen them before. The brand on the horses is the same as the one on the horse I rented in Lynchburg. One of them had a railroad ticket stub from Baltimore in his pocket. But as to why they would try to kill me? I can only assume that someone didn't want me to deliver that letter."

"Why? What makes you think it wasn't just attempted robbery?"

"Because they very clearly wanted to kill me."

Activity at the gravesite attracted their attention. They saw Sergeant Barlow wave as the troopers lifted the canvas covered bodies from the graves. Spencer could see that the corpses were stiff.

"I suppose we had better get this over with," Sherman said.

The canvas had been folded around the bodies of Silas Morgan and Choka. Even though Sherman and Spencer had seen the worst of what war can do to the human body, they braced themselves when the canvas was removed.

"Good God almighty!" The soldier who had pulled the canvas away from Choka's body lurched backward so quickly that he fell.

"Christ, his face is gone," one of the other soldiers said.

Spencer had seen Choka's ravaged head in the shadowed stable. But what he saw in daylight was shocking. The buckshot had blown away most of the flesh from Choka's face. An oozing black mass seeped from the empty eye sockets and nose cavity. All the front teeth had been knocked out, and the jaw, partially torn loose, was resting at an angle on Choka's chest."

Sherman looked at Spencer. "Shotgun?"

"Yes, sir. Mrs. McLaws got him just as he was about to pull the trigger on me."

Sherman, nodding understanding, leaned closer to examine Choka's head with almost clinical interest. "Yes, I've always believed the shotgun had great potential for close fighting," Sherman said, as if recalling a recommendation that had been ignored.

"It would help, colonel, if you told me everything you can remember about the events that occurred here almost…let's see…it must be about thirty six hours ago now."

Spencer hesitated a moment while he collected his thoughts. Then he began to relate the events in detail, beginning with the rental of the roan. It was a description of the facts that was nearly devoid of any emotion. While he talked, Sherman watched as the four soldiers began to cut the clothes from the bodies.

"Which one was the shooter?"

"The one without the face fired the first shot with his Winchester. But there was something strange about him, general. He had more than one chance to kill me after that first shot, but he didn't shoot."

"Why do you suppose he didn't?"

"Well, I don't know exactly, but it was clear that these two didn't get along. I remember this one was called Choka—or something that sounded like that—by the other man. Choka must have been a foreigner, because the big one called him a hunky and threatened to kill him if he didn't shoot me."

Sherman leaned closer to the big man to examine the gaping knife wound in his chest. "Where's the knife?"

"It's in the back of the house, sir, with the Winchester and the handgun the big one carried."

"I'll want to see all of that." Sherman spoke to the men who were cutting the clothes. "I want all of the seams checked to make sure nothing is sewn in them. And check their boots carefully."

One of the troopers attempting to cut away Choka's gore-soaked shirt jumped up suddenly and ran into the field where he dropped to his knees and vomited. Barlow waved the men away from the bodies.

"Let's take a break, men. Take ten minutes for a smoke."

Everyone moved away from the bodies, except for Spencer and Barlow. He saw that the big man was still wearing his boots. He remembered the knife sheath.

Spencer tried but couldn't pull the boots free because the man's feet were so stiff. Barlow reached into his own boot and pulled a short, thick-bladed knife. He kneeled next to Spencer. "Colonel, we'll have to cut them boots free."

Barlow cut the boots from the top to the ankle, then tugged them off and handed them to his colonel. Spencer examined the sheath inside the boot. He had hoped to find a secret pocket sewn inside one of the boots. Then he checked the heels to see if they were hollow. Disappointed, he started to toss them into the grave when he remembered something.

The knife blade. It was six inches long. He had reason to be very certain of that. He examined the sheath again. Yes, it was longer than six inches, perhaps almost two inches longer. He took Barlow's knife and cut the stitches that held the sheath to the boot.

Spencer turned the sheath over in his hand. It was well worn and appeared to have been made from the top of an old boot. The leather had been folded over to form the sheath and was stitched along one edge.

There was a small lateral seam a couple of inches from the tip of the sheath. Spencer could feel metal under the seam. He tugged, but it wouldn't pull apart.

"Hand me your knife again, sergeant." Barlow kneeled next to Spencer. Sherman had walked up behind them. Spencer cut the stitches along the edge near the tip of the sheath, then carefully peeled the leather apart.

There was a metal capsule in the tip of the sheath. Spencer examined it closely, then twisted the capsule. Apparently threaded into a metal ring sewn to the leather, the capsule unscrewed like the top of a fruit jar.

When he removed it, Spencer could see a white piece of paper folded into the capsule. He turned the capsule over and tapped it into his palm until the paper fell out. Spencer turned and handed the paper to Sherman.

"Well, well." Sherman carefully unfolded the three-inch square of paper. He read the note and, without comment, refolded it and put it into his shirt pocket.

"Colonel, what are the chances that your Mrs. McLaws will provide us with a couple of cups of coffee?"

Barlow moved away to check on his men. Spencer didn't respond immediately. "Well, general, I'm sure it can be arranged. Do you want the men to continue their work?"

"Yes. Tell Sergeant Barlow to check everything. Tell him to report to us in the house when they've finished."

Spencer noticed that Jessie couldn't bring herself to be more than civil to William Tecumseh Sherman. She placed the coffee cups on the dining room table and told Spencer she would be on the back porch washing clothes. Her daughter, Amanda, would be helping.

"What do you know about the woman?" Sherman asked a few moments after she left the room.

"Well, sir, while we were waiting for you to arrive, we had an opportunity to talk. Her father was a doctor, a surgeon, in Louisville. They lived in France for more than a year where he studied new medical procedures. When they returned to Kentucky he began teaching at a medical school in Louisville, which is where she met her husband. When the war began, her father became an army surgeon. She said her husband could have completed his training, but decided to fight for the cause. She's bitter about that. He was an artillery captain. Her father died of consumption in sixty-four. Her husband died in the closing days of the war. She moved here to find his body and return it to Kentucky. She wrote to members of his unit, hoping they could tell her where it might be. But she said she can't find anyone else to contact, so she's considering going back to Kentucky."

Sherman nodded as he sipped his coffee. Spencer noticed the general's eyes were drawn to the sideboard in the dining room, an eighteenth century French heirloom. "Do you know her family name?" Sherman asked.

"Harrison, sir."

"When I first walked into the house, I noticed a bookshelf in the sitting room off the hallway. Several of the titles were medical books authored by Dr. Michael Harrison.

Sherman lighted a long, thin black cigar, and slowly exhaled, as if he were savoring the rich, blue smoke. "Her skill and timing with a shotgun aside, colonel, it appears that your trust was well placed."

Spencer was not aware of it, but he had just received the most generous and elaborate apology that Sherman was capable of offering. The general finished his coffee and pushed and cup and saucer aside.

"Now," he said as he reached into his pocket for the note and handed it to Spencer, "we should discuss the implications of this message."

Spencer unfolded the paper. The writing was cramped, small, and hardly legible:

> *Col. John Spencer arriving Lex. 9.8 by rail from Balt. to Lynchburg. Use whatever means to prevent arrival. Robbery must appear to be motive. Arrive Atlanta on 10.4., Georgian Hotel. H.C.*

Spencer refolded the note and placed it on the table, pushing it slightly toward the general.

"What do you think, colonel?"

"Whoever these people are, they know…they know everything, it seems, including about Atlanta." Spencer shook his head in confusion. "I can't explain how the security of the mission was breached, sir. But it's clear we have to convince the President that he can't go to Atlanta."

"We can try, colonel; we can try. But the President is determined to carry out his plan while Lee is alive."

Spencer glanced through the window to see Barlow walking across the street to the house. He noticed that Barlow was carrying something and rose to open the door.

Barlow stood at the head of the table and held out a rolled piece of linen. "A money belt, colonel," Barlow said as he placed the fabric on the table. "There's more than one hundred dollars in it. The big one was wearing it around his waist under his shirt."

"Be seated, sergeant major," Sherman said, as he opened the pouch and pulled out the bills. The dining room chair, seeming too fragile for Barlow's size, creaked as he settled gently into it.

Sherman replaced the money in the pouch and folded it neatly, turning in his chair to place it on the sideboard. "I think it appropriate that Mrs. McLaws should receive that money for her inconvenience. That, of course, would be in addition to the cost of the horse, which I will pay before leaving."

Sherman placed the palms of his hands on the table in front of him, as if he were going to stand.

"Gentlemen, let's review what we know about the two dead men. It's clear they were killers hired by some unknown person or persons to stop you from delivering that letter. The ticket stub tells us that at least one of them came to Lynchburg from Baltimore. We can assume from the note that the big man's initials are SM, and that he's taking orders from HB. The smaller man may be a foreigner whose name was Choka, or something sounding like that. Just before he died, Choka admitted to the colonel here that he had been paid to kill him. We also know, based on the note, that the big one was ordered to meet HC in Atlanta—at the Georgian Hotel—after he killed you. What else?"

The room was silent while each man considered the evidence.

Barlow cleared his throat. "It may not be important, general, but the one without a face probably was in the army."

"Whose army?" Sherman asked.

"A lot of them foreigners who came over during the war ended up in our army—but I'd say they both were in the Union army, sir."

"How do you know that?" Sherman asked.

Barlow reached into his overcoat pocket and withdrew his handkerchief. He unfolded it and placed it in the center of the table. Sherman and Spencer leaned closer. It was a .58 caliber Minnie ball. The tip of the conical, inch-long bullet was badly deformed. The bullet was glazed with a pinkish material.

"Where'd you find that?" Spencer asked.

"When we got the clothes off the big one, I noticed what looked like a scar from an old bullet wound just below his ribs on the right side. I rolled him over and found that the bullet didn't go through him."

"You mean you actually opened him up to dig this bullet out?"

"Yes, sir."

"What in the world did you hope to find out by doing that?" Sherman wasn't squeamish about what Barlow had done. He just couldn't imagine what the sergeant had hoped to discover.

"Well, first off, general, I wanted to see if the bullet was still in him and what kind of bullet it was."

"But sergeant, both sides used that same bullet for a while," Sherman said. "He could have been a Confederate soldier."

"Yes, sir. But the Rebs used it longer than we did. What I think is most important is that he survived a wound like that. We generally had better doctors, and more of them, than they did. I found the bullet within an inch of his spine, which means the doctors thought it best to leave it be, rather than try to cut it out. It takes a good doctor to know when not to try to dig a bullet out. If they'd tried, chances are he'd either be dead or paralyzed. All in all, sir, I'd have to say that he was one of our boys."

"How about the one without a face?" Spencer asked.

"I'd say he wore blue, colonel, because most of those foreigners came to our side."

Sherman glanced at Spencer and smiled. "All right, sergeant. I'll accept your interpretation of the evidence. If you are correct, and we find more clues to their identity, military records might help. Have your troopers dig new graves at the far edge of that field and bury the bodies deep."

"Yes, sir." Barlow folded the bullet into his handkerchief and started to leave.

"Sergeant Major?"

"Yes, general."

"Very good work."

"Thank you, sir. Barlow hesitated, confused about how to react to the compliment, then quickly left the house. Sherman chuckled. "An amazing man, your sergeant major. I often have wondered why you didn't select an officer to assist you. Now I understand."

"I have never worked with a man who is more competent or conscientious. Most important, general, he scares hell out of most everyone he meets."

Both men laughed.

"Well, colonel, will you be sufficiently recovered to leave for Lexington in the morning?"

"Yes, sir. I'm anxious to complete this assignment so that I can get back to the White House."

"Do you want Barlow with you?"

"Yes, sir, I do. But I'd feel better if he were with the President. Besides, if they're going to try to ambush me again, I don't suppose that even Barlow would be able to prevent it."

Sherman pursed his lips in thought. "Yes, perhaps you're right. I'll assign more men to White House security. I'll leave for Lynchburg in the morning, and I'll take the horses the dead men rented back with me—and pay for your horse."

"If I may ask, general, where did you get the squad?"

"Colonel, among the privileges accorded the general-in-chief of the army, is the use of a personal military train. I brought the men and horses, including my own, down from Baltimore."

At that moment, they could hear Jessie and her daughter come into the rear door. When Jessie, with Amanda hiding behind her skirt, came to the dining room door, both men got to their feet.

"It's nearing dinner time, gentlemen." Jessie was smiling. "Although you have chosen to sleep in your cold and uncomfortable tent tonight, general, you are welcome to have dinner with Colonel Spencer and me."

Spencer was amused to see that Jessie's offer had obviously impressed the general. Sherman bowed slightly in a gesture that appeared a bit too formal and which he executed somewhat awkwardly.

"Well, yes, thank you for the generous offer, Mrs. McLaws. I accept, of course."

Jessie permitted a longer than necessary silence. She was pleased to see that the urbane and pugnacious General Sherman could be even slightly rattled by what he must presume was a simple country woman.

"How about your sergeant major? Unless I take at least the edge off what must be an enormous appetite, I'll worry about his spending the night near my horses."

Spencer laughed. "Sorry, Jessie. He'll want to stay with the men."

"Well, it will be more than an hour before dinner is ready. Perhaps you men may want to give those horses a little exercise."

Chapter 12

September 11, 1870
The White House
10:20 p.m.

Although members of the White House staff considered Abner Babcock to be a highly competent secretary to the President, they also considered him to be a pain in the neck.

It wasn't just that he was tall and so painfully thin that his clothes always seemed much too large. It mostly was because he was fussy, nervous and had the maddening habit of talking to himself, especially when he was faced with an important decision. The telegraph message he held in his hand, as he stood outside the door of the President's sitting room, certainly required a decision that was important. So, of course, he was talking to himself.

The President was meeting with Robert Simmons, a top official of the Union Pacific Railroad, and he had asked not to be disturbed. Yet, the sealed envelope Babcock held was from General Sherman and it was marked urgent.

"There should be a procedure developed for a situation like this one," Babcock said as he started to knock on the door, then backed away several steps. He tapped the envelope against his baggy trouser leg while he considered the possible consequences of interrupting the President. Then he considered the range of possible consequences if he failed to interrupt the President.

"That's what I liked about the army," he said. "There were rules and procedures for every conceivable situation."

Finally, Babcock screwed up his courage and knocked on the door. For a moment there was no response. Then the door opened and Grant stood there, the exaggerated sadness in his left eye an indicator of his displeasure. Babcock noted the trail of cigar smoke, like the wake of a ship, leading from the door back to the couch behind him.

"I know that you didn't want to be disturbed, sir," Babcock said as he handed Grant the message, "but this was delivered by the army telegrapher. It's from General Sherman, and it's marked urgent and confidential."

Grant nodded and closed the door. Babcock stood outside the door for a moment, breathed deeply, then hurried back to his office on the first floor.

"Excuse the interruption, Mr. Simmons," Grant said as he opened the letter. "My staff could benefit from training by a railroad man in matters of scheduling and efficiency."

Grant quickly scanned the message:

U.S. Grant, President 9.11
White House

Attempt made on Spencer's life. He was injured, but should be arriving Lexington as you read this.

Two assassins dead. Evidence clearly indicates plot. Strongly recommend you cancel Atlanta plans. Will personally continue investigation. Have ordered additional military and Pinkerton security for White House.

Suggest avoid leaving White House until I arrive. Sending Barlow ahead.

Spencer acquitted himself well.

Cump
Lynchburg, Va.

Grant, still standing near the door, pondered the note for a long moment. He regretted putting Spencer at risk. Now his plan had involved his old friend, Cump, which may pose political and personal danger for his general-in-chief. But at least Spencer would have the benefit of the resources and protection that he knew Cump would make available. Maybe they would be able to protect each other. For an instant, the President considered abandoning his plan to meet with Lee. Yet, despite the risk to people who were important to him, Grant knew that he couldn't give up. The possible benefits of success with Lee more than balanced the potential risks. Sherman and Spencer would have to handle whatever was involved in this conspiracy business.

"Ah...Mr. President. Is there a problem?"

Grant had completely forgotten about Simmons.

"My apologies, Mr. Simmons." Grant returned to the couch. "No, no problem. The situation is in good hands. But something important has developed that requires my immediate attention, and I would like to continue our discussion at a later time, perhaps after lunch."

Simmons reluctantly gathered his papers. "Yes, of course, Mr. President. But I am anxious for you to hear my proposal on expansion of the railroad land grant program."

"And I am anxious to hear about it." Grant walked Simmons to the door. "Please see Babcock for an appointment immediately after lunch. Again, Mr. Simmons, my apologies."

When Simmons was gone, Grant sat on the couch and considered Sherman's message. Who were the assassins and who hired them? Could it be related to his plans to meet with Lee?

Grant stretched his legs out in front of him, resting his head on the back of the couch.

As a general, he had been accustomed to being in the center of action, controlling the situation. He could analyze the problem, develop the strategy and knew which of his men were the most capable of carrying out his commands.

In fact, one important new dimension that Grant brought to warfare was the development of a strong staff and the delegation of responsibility. He had surrounded himself with competent men he could depend upon.

Grant also knew that Lee had tried to make too many decisions himself, even those involving the more mundane aspects of top command. One man, even a man like Lee, just couldn't do all of that very well.

But politics? Why didn't the same principles work in government? He would never understand the kind of men who now surrounded him. To Grant, the nation's problems were clearly defined. But the solutions were clouded by the intrigue and self-serving motives of the politicians and businessmen.

How then could he help Sherman and Spencer through the danger they faced? Grant smiled ruefully. He held the nation's highest office, yet he knew there was little more he could than sit and watch.

That's one reason why he wanted Lee's support. He understood Lee, probably much better than history would recognize. Grant knew that Lee never truly wanted the South to secede from the union. In fact, from the very beginning Lee must have known that he couldn't win. The best Lee could hope for was that the North's resolve would weaken as the casualty lists grew. Lee knew that early on the Union generals would be too concerned with personal ambition and politics to fight well. Lee's tactic was to bleed the North until he could win concessions. If he could embarrass Union generals in the process, so much the better.

But there were two men who haunted Lee in the final phase of the war. Lee realized that Lincoln, once the decision to fight had been made, would fight to the finish to preserve the union. What concerned Lee was that Lincoln gave his generals a completely unfettered hand to wage war. The tactic did not work early in the war because Lincoln could not find a general who would or could fight—with or without presidential constraint. Lee realized that if Lincoln did find such a man, that general could focus the North's advantage in men and resources against him. It wasn't long before Lee realized that Grant intended to be that kind of general.

Grant felt certain that Lee would join him now in the effort to unite the country. Lee would do so because he was a fighter. Grant suspected that if there were one quality he had that Lee respected, it was his ability to doggedly pursue an objective.

Grant wondered whether Cump was right about the British. The Brits helped the Confederates get through Union blockades and provided other support, perhaps hoping that an America destabilized by war might make it possible for Britain to regain control of its former colonies. Perhaps. Do they believe I am a President weakened by scandal, making the government ripe for a takeover? Perhaps by Lee? But why, if Sherman is correct, do they want to meet with Forrest?

Before he dozed off for his mid-day nap, Grant thought about the concern Spencer and Cump had for his life. The one thing he didn't worry about was his personal safety. He never had. Grant was not a completely fearless man, but he did not fear death. Yes, he would permit Cump to increase White House security, for the simple reason that his friend wished to do so.

But a threat on the President's life? No, he wouldn't worry about that because he didn't think it likely. Grant took pride in the fact that he was not a worrier.

September 11, 1870
Brockton Estate
Georgetown

Nelson liked the tack room. It was at the rear of the stable, and he would look forward to the little chores that always were required to keep the saddles, harness and other gear in top shape. One of the things he liked most was the smell of leather. Since Mattie didn't permit him to smoke his pipe in the house, the tack room was also the place where he could relax in a comfortable old chair and light up.

Nelson had been with the Chase family for more than thirty years, ever since Mr. Chase himself bought him on the block in Charleston. He was only maybe twenty years old then. The early years had been hard. Most of the time he'd worked in the fields, but for a few years he'd worked in the Chase Foundry, where his great physical strength was needed to manhandle the big guns that were made there.

Five years after the war, Nelson still was confused by all the talk about slaves being free. He'd always been treated well by Miss Rachel, but most white men treated him the same. In some ways, the war had made things worse for Negroes.

In fact, the worst beating he'd ever received occurred just after the surrender. The Chase property had been several miles east of Richmond. He'd been sent into town on an errand for Mattie. When he'd walked out of a store, he saw two white men escorting a woman crossing the street toward him. Rather than step in front of them, he paused. But he couldn't help noticing the woman. She was young, beautiful, with hair that shimmered like gold in the sunlight. Perhaps he had stared a moment too long. One of the white men, who was short and paunchy, grabbed him by the front of his shirt.

"You takin' a fancy to white women, are you, nigger?"

The small man pushed him against the wheel of a wagon, then struck him with the back of his hand.

Nelson could smell the whiskey on the man. He could remember every detail of the flushed face, the sneer, the hate in the man's eyes.

A small crowd gathered.

The man looked around at the other white faces, while he held onto Nelson's shirt.

"We have here, ladies and gentlemen, one of Lincoln's niggers who thinks he is free now to boldly stare at a white woman. You gentlemen standing here—mark my words. Your women will not be safe when bucks like this one roam the streets."

The man reached for a thin steel rod he saw in the wagon. Nelson recalled vividly the sound the three-foot rod made as it arched through the air before each blow.

Mr. Chase was angry when Nelson returned home, his shirt soaked with blood from a large cut that had nearly taken off his left ear. But it was the kind of anger a man has when his property has been damaged. Only Mattie and Miss Rachel seemed concerned about him.

He still hated white men. It was a deep, seething hatred. He made up his mind that no man would ever whip him again.

But life had been better the last couple of years. He even had a little money saved. The only thing he regretted was that he'd never had his own woman. He'd had women many times, but never a wife. He'd had an eye for Mattie, who he thought was the most beautiful creature he'd ever seen. But he'd always been a field nigger and she'd always worked in the house.

Besides, she could have a white man if she ever wanted one. He'd seen the way they looked at her. But after all these years, he still wondered what it would be like to bed her. Nelson leaned back in the old wooden chair, his eyes half closed, enjoying the rich flavor and aroma of the tobacco he'd cured himself, and he thought of Mattie writhing in his arms.

That was probably why he didn't hear the two men when they rode up.

Hollis Connor and Charles Wells dismounted and quietly walked their horses to the stable door. Connor paused for a moment at the entrance when he caught the aroma of Nelson's tobacco. He motioned Wells to be quiet, then drew his pistol.

Nelson's chair was facing the door. Although he didn't hear them, something he felt made him open his eyes. He knew better than to move quickly when he saw the two white men, one of them holstering a gun. Nelson had that special insight that most Negroes have about white people. Although it was obvious that both of these men were trouble, Nelson knew that the one with the gun was especially dangerous—and not just because of the weapon.

Connor smiled. "Well, we seem to have interrupted your nap." The smile faded. "Who's in the house?"

Nelson didn't respond.

"Talk to me, nigger, or I'll blow your lazy black ass out of that chair. Are there any men in the house?"

Nelson's eyes narrowed, his jaw clenching the stem of his pipe. He looked from one man to the other.

"Hollis," Wells said nervously, "we're wasting our time. He's not going to give us any trouble."

Connor smiled again and nodded. "I suppose you're right. It's just that I don't like this nigger's attitude."

If Nelson had been a few years younger, and perhaps if his eyesight were better, he might have been able to anticipate what happened next. But Connor's boot was only inches from Nelson's chest when he saw it coming.

As the blow crushed the air from his lungs, Nelson could hear his ribs snap, the jagged bones cutting into his lungs. He was catapulted backward into a tangle of leather in the corner of the small room. The last thing he heard before lapsing into unconsciousness was Connor laughing.

Wells was amazed at how gracious Connor could be. When Mattie answered the door, Connor removed his hat and bowed slightly. "Pardon our calling unannounced, but we have business with Mrs. Rachel Brockton."

Holding the door only partially open, Mattie immediately recalled what Rachel had told her following the meeting with Brewster in the Jefferson Hotel.

"May I tell her who is calling, please?"

"Mr. Wells and Mr. Connor."

Mattie's expression didn't change, but she didn't invite them into the foyer.

"I am sorry, gentlemen," Mattie said, "but Mrs. Brockton, her son and I were about to leave to do some shopping in the country. She may not be able to see you, but I will tell her that you are here."

Mattie found Rachel in Johnny's room, helping her son straighten his room.

"They're here, Rachel," Mattie said excitedly. "Those men Brewster told you about. They're on the front porch and they want to talk to you."

"Do you mean that man Connor and his partner?"

"Yes, yes. It's them. What are you going to do?"

Rachel reached over and patted Johnny's head. "It appears we have no choice at the moment except to talk to them. You stay here with Johnny, and I'll go down and see them."

"You can't go down alone. Let me get Nelson. He should at least be in the house with us."

"No. I don't want any trouble. I'm sure that they're here just to talk, so I might as well see what they want. Remember, you stay here with Johnny."

Rachel drew on all the self control she could muster while she walked down the steps and opened the front door. She knew that she could not show fear.

Rachel invited Connor and Wells into the parlor and asked them to be seated. "How can I help you gentlemen?"

Rachel clearly remembered Connor being present during her meeting with Gould and Fisk.

"You know why we're here, Mrs. Brockton."

Rachel was puzzled at first, then she could feel the surge of fear as she realized what Connor implied.

"Yes, Mrs. Brockton. We are aware of the conversation you had recently with Mr. Brewster. You two had a pleasant meeting in the Jefferson Hotel, as I recall."

"Where...what has happened to Roger?" Rachel could feel her composure slipping away as she thought of what might have happened to the banker. She knew that if Brewster had been correct about these two plotting to kill the President, they would not have hesitated to kill Roger. How much had Roger been forced to tell these two about their conversation? If they suspected she knew about the plot against Grant, they probably would kill her and everyone else in the house.

"You should be aware, Mrs. Brockton, that although Brewster managed to divert some of your cash to your new bank, we have halted the movement of any more of your funds." Connor smiled. "I would say that of your half-million or so in assets, we have control over nearly three hundred thousand."

Rachel felt a great sorrow for Roger. She desperately wanted to know what they had done to him, but she also realized that she was afraid to find out. She was aware that Connor and Wells were watching her reaction.

"And, finally, Mrs. Brockton, we also are aware that you are willing to sacrifice some of your money in hopes we wouldn't involve you in our little plan." Connor laughed sarcastically. "Really, Rachel, I'm surprised you could be so naive as to think we would trade your services for a few thousand dollars."

Rachel's mind raced. She felt a rising panic as she realized she was being drawn into the plot. She fought for control of her emotions. She knew she had to resist.

"I am sorry, Mr. Connor, but I have no intention of providing you with any services—as you put it—for any price. It is true I am planning to move back to Richmond. If Mr. Gould feels I am indebted to him because of the money I've made, apparently with his help, then he is welcome to all of it. Except, of course, for my original investment."

Rachel got up from her chair and took several steps toward the foyer, then turned and looked at the two men. "I must ask you to leave this house immediately," she said as firmly as she could. "We have nothing more to discuss."

The door behind Rachel opened so violently that it crashed against the stop. When she spun in alarm, she saw Nelson stagger into the foyer. He was bent over slightly, holding his left arm close to his chest. In his right hand he held a length of heavy steel rod, which was part of what once had been the axle of a carriage. As Nelson grimaced in pain, Rachel could see that his mouth was bloody, a pinkish foam around his lips.

Rachel stepped toward Nelson, but she could see that his eyes were locked on Connor. She could hear someone running and knew that Mattie would be coming down the stairs. She thought of Johnny and hoped he would remain in his room.

Rachel moved closer to Nelson. He gently, but firmly, pushed her aside, taking agonizingly short steps toward Connor. She saw that Connor and Wells were on their feet.

"Nelson!" Mattie shouted as she hurried down the staircase. "What are you doing?"

Nelson paused for a moment as he turned to look at Mattie. His eyes softened, and he shook his head slowly. Mattie could read his eyes. She could see the frustration, the anger, the fear. She moved close to Nelson, putting her hand gently on his shoulder.

"Nelson." Her voice was soft now. "Please stop. Don't do it."

Nelson tried to say something, but the words were choked off by a fit of coughing that sprayed red spittle onto the polished oak floor of the sitting room. His breath rasping through clenched teeth, Nelson again focused his attention on Connor and shifted his grip on the steel rod. Mattie could see Nelson's eyes harden, she could near him grunt in pain as he raised the rod menacingly over his head.

"Woman, control your nigger or I'll kill him."

Rachel was surprised by how calm Connor's voice sounded, and it frightened her. She saw that Connor had drawn his gun. He held the weapon close to his right leg, the barrel pointed at the floor.

Wells, obviously unnerved by Nelson, moved back behind the couch. "Hollis, let's get out of here. Put the gun away. We can talk to her later."

Nelson also saw the gun. He knew he would have to cover the remaining twenty feet or so as quickly as possible. But his pain-clouded vision no longer saw Connor. Nelson was back on that Richmond street, pinned to the wheel of a wagon, while the little man with the florid face whipped him in cadence to the cheers of the crowd.

The shot deafened everyone in the room. When the bullet struck Nelson just below his left eye, his head snapped back violently. For several seconds Nelson remained standing, his head tilted back slightly as if he were examining the ceiling. The only sound was the snap of the hammer on Connor's Colt as he thumbed it back to fire again.

But then the steel rod clattered to the floor, gouging a deep groove in the wood. Nelson, his arms rising as if to reach for whatever his lifeless eyes had seen above him, fell over backward, his head thumping heavily against the floor.

A scream pierced the stillness that followed, and Mattie ran to Nelson and knelt beside him. Rachel, unable to move or speak, felt rooted to the floor. She saw Connor lower the hammer on the revolver and holster it. He stepped around a low table and walked up to her.

"If you decide to go to the authorities about this, keep in mind that he obviously intended to attack me. You must realize that the word of two reputable businessmen would carry considerably more weight than that of a crazed nigger."

"You provoked him," Rachel said, glancing at Nelson's body, the anger surging within her. Mattie was holding Nelson's hand to her cheek, her eyes welling with tears. "He was hurt when he came into the house."

"Nonsense. I've never seen the man before."

"But why else would he—"

Connor held up his hand. "What should be clear to you now is that you have no alternative but to cooperate with us." Connor placed his hands on Rachel's shoulder, tightening his grip until her lower lip quivered.

"A week from this Saturday, a small, intimate party will be held for

Secretary of Treasury Horace Stoval. He is a man with a weakness for attractive women like you. I am confident that you will show him every consideration. Do I make myself clear?"

Rachel tried to pull away from Connor, but he tightened his grip until she was forced to nod her head and sob, "Yes, damn you!"

Connor released her, stepped back and smiled. He glanced at Wells and started to leave, pausing for a moment to look down at Nelson's body.

"Mrs. Brockton, "he said without turning. "A carriage will arrive for you at precisely eight. I will be in it, and I will give you more detailed instructions during the ride into town. I trust that you understand the consequences for others in this house if you attempt anything foolish."

Connor turned to look at Rachel. "Mr. Brewster has already paid the price for your foolishness."

"Hollis, you didn't have to kill the black," Wells said as he and Connor cantered along the desolate road toward Washington. "You know that he wasn't in any condition to hurt us."

Connor laughed. "I know you wouldn't have been hurt hiding behind that couch."

"You know what I mean, Hollis. If Fisk or Gould find out what we're doing, we'll have hell to pay. This whole scheme is too risky, even for them."

"Where's your backbone, man? We've only killed a worthless old nigger. Why, I'd venture to say that we've done the woman a favor. Now she won't have to take care of him in his old age—the way she has to take care of that idiot father of hers."

Wells shook his head. "I still don't think it will work."

"Listen, my timid friend," Connor said lightly, buoyed by the events in the house. "It could not have worked better. We've frightened hell out of her. She will be at the party. And old Stoval will make a fool of himself trying to get her into his bed. And at the precise moment that he is slavering over that delicious body, you and I and our newspaper friend will burst into the room. He will be mortified. He views himself as dedicated to public service, his family, and his church. Yes, from that point on, Stoval will be ours."

"But what if—"

"Enough!" Connor angrily reined to halt and moved his horse as close as possible to Wells' animal. He reached across to grab the front of the other man's coat. "Damn you, if you back out on me now you will regret it. Our plan is working. Morgan must have taken care of the army colonel by now, and I know Washington will suspect he was killed by the Klan."

Wells shook his head in confusion. "But if you want Grant to be in Atlanta so you can kill him, why did you have the colonel killed? He was carrying the letter to Lee that would have set the whole thing up."

Connor obviously felt too good to remain angry. He released Wells, smoothing the man's rumpled coat.

Connor patted Wells on the shoulder. "Look, my friend, Grant's desire to meet with Lee not only reflects the man's stupidity, but also offers the perfect opportunity for our plan to succeed. I can assure you that they will suspect that the Klan killed the colonel, because Grant's people know that more than a half-million of my colleagues would howl at the thought of Lee and Grant in the same room."

Connor felt very good now. "Look, Charles, even if that colonel isn't dead, the attempt alone will get the Federal hounds sniffing in the wrong direction. And if that fool Silas Morgan is caught, he only knows the initials of my name, which will be useless to the government. He's been told only that he's working for a group of Republican Radicals that objects to any effort to help the South in any way. So even if Morgan is taken alive and talks, he only has to tell them what he knows to help our cause."

"But won't Grant cancel his plans to attend if he suspects there will be violence?"

"No, Grant is not only stupid, he is also stubborn. He will contact Lee again, and I'm confident they both will go to the reunion. When Grant goes to Atlanta, he will be meat for our table."

Although Wells still was shaken, Connor laughed as he spurred his horse into a trot.

"The only real risk in our plan is that old Stoval's heart may give out when he sees what Rachel has to offer. Think of it, man. Why, I almost regret interrupting such a high point in the old man's life."

Chapter 13

September 18, 1870
Washington College
Lexington, Virginia
8:20 p.m.

"His name is Colonel John Spencer, general, and he says he has a message from President Grant that he must personally deliver. However, sir, the man is dressed in civilian clothes, and he looks like he brawled his way here from Washington City."

Robert E. Lee chuckled softly. He had just completed his morning prayers and was sitting quietly in the chapel when Hooper came into the church and sat next to him. He knew that Clarence Hooper was totally dedicated to him and was the most efficient secretary imaginable. He had served him capably as an aide for two years during the war.

The school's budget didn't provide for a secretary to the president, so Hooper simply volunteered to serve the general, without pay, for one year. He came to visit Lee one day to pay his respects. When Hooper saw the general's workload, he convinced the general to let him stay and help. Hooper's father had retained his wealth in the closing days of the war by moving his business to Galveston Island in Texas. He had since made a great deal of money in the shipping business. Hooper not only volunteered to serve as Lee's secretary, he convinced his father to contribute five thousand dollars to the school.

But what Lee liked best about Hooper, at times what he appreciated most, was his sense of humor—plus the fact that, despite his wealth, efficiency and obvious dedication to his former commander, Hooper could be downright irreverent.

"Well, Clarence," Lee whispered, "we can't keep a U.S. Army colonel waiting, can we? Show him to the office and I will be down in a few minutes."

Lee was in a playful mood. The pains in his chest and left arm were all but gone. Although he visited with students in the classrooms as often as his health and schedule permitted, Lee spent most of his time handling administrative chores in the spartan, fifteen-by eighteen-foot office in the basement of the chapel he helped design. It had been dedicated three years earlier.

Spencer, who had been waiting at the chapel entrance, was escorted by Hooper down the twenty-four steps of the circular cast-iron staircase. When he entered the office, he was surprised that there was no rug on the random-width pine board floor. There were no curtains on the two windows and no paintings or prints on the plain white walls.

Hooper gestured toward one of two wicker bottom chairs at the large circular table that Lee obviously used as his desk. Lee's chair was the largest and was covered with leather. Behind Lee's chair was the largest object in the room. It was a bookcase—although only one of the shelves held books—that at one time had been a sideboard.

Spencer stepped closer to the bookcase. The largest volume was a dictionary by Webster. There were grammar books in French, Greek and English. There also was a volume of Downes' Algebra, which didn't surprise Spencer because he knew that Lee had been an engineer for most of his forty years as a soldier. All of the books were worn from frequent use.

In the far corner there was a cast-iron stove, and a leather couch sat under the windows. There were three pictures on the mantel: one was of a man Spencer didn't recognize; another was a photo of a Confederate family; and a print of George Washington.

When Lee came into the room he smiled and warmly shook Spencer's hand. Lee was surprised by the man's bruised and lacerated face. Hooper may have been correct that the colonel had brawled his way across Virginia.

Lee asked Spencer to be seated at the table, then moved to his leather chair.

Spencer had rehearsed what he would say, based on the advice he received from Sherman. But the words would not come. He found it difficult to believe that he finally was meeting with Lee. Back-lighted by the window behind him, the old general seemed unreal, an apparition. The violence in Pedlar Mills, the long hours on horseback and his final moments with Jessie, when she shyly said she hoped he would stop on his way back from Lynchburg—all of those thoughts rushed through his mind.

Spencer reached to rub the indentation on his forehead, near the streak of silver hair.

"Clarence," Lee said to his secretary who was seated on the couch. "I suggest we have some coffee before we begin. Do you agree, colonel?"

"Yes, sir, I would like that very much."

Lee nodded to Hooper, who left the room.

"You look familiar to me, colonel. Have we met previously?"

Spencer smiled. "Yes, we have, general, but I'm surprised you would remember. Most recently, I was in charge of the security detail when you visited the White House about a year ago."

Lee nodded. "And was there a previous occasion?"

Spencer hesitated. "Well, sir, I was with General Grant at Appomattox."

"Ah, yes. I see. You were his aide then?"

"No, sir. Actually, I was on General Sheridan's staff, but in the final hours I was assigned to General Grant." Spencer obviously intended to avoid mentioning that he led the cavalry scout unit that spotted Lee's retreating army and made it possible for Sheridan to encircle the Confederates. Or that when Lee's surrender seemed imminent he guided Grant to Sheridan's headquarters while dressed as a Confederate colonel.

"And your current assignment?"

"Still White House security and intelligence, general."

"What does that assignment have to do with your visit today?"

Hooper entered the room with a tray of coffee cups. He served the general, then offered Spencer a cup. Spencer had planned to prepare Lee by discussing Grant's proposal before giving him the letter. But now that he sat across from him, Spencer felt that he wouldn't say anything until he saw how Lee reacted to the letter. He placed the cup on the edge of the table, then reached to an inside pocket for the letter and handed it to Lee.

"The President asked that I convey his personal compliments, General Lee. He requested that you read this, and that I report to him any comments or decisions you make regarding its contents. I also am authorized to discuss any questions you may have."

Lee seemed hesitant to open the letter. He turned it over several times, looked at Spencer and Hooper, then finally tore off the end of the envelope.

Spencer reached for his coffee while the general read. Over the rim of his cup, he studied Lee's face for any reaction. He still was in awe of the man. Rather, he was in awe of the general. His emotions were mixed about the man.

During the war Lee had often been elusive when the Union generals would finally decide to face him. When the North hesitated to plan, to consolidate, to ensure that all the political contingencies were covered, Lee would appear as if by magic, to pounce, seemingly from every point of the compass.

Spencer wondered about the man. Lee was the epitome of honor and dedication. But were those qualities too narrowly focused? Was he slavish to his perception of honor? How did the man balance the defense of honor against the cost of more than a half-million lives, all of them American? What if Lee had refused to lead, to fight? Would someone else have taken his place? Would someone else have taken his place as effectively? Perhaps Stonewall Jackson. Probably Longstreet. Would the outcome have been different?

Even during the fighting, when Spencer witnessed the waste and stupidity of it all, he realized that the war was a giant rolling boulder that would thunder and crash until its momentum was spent.

Spencer reflected on the three previous occasions when he had seen the man sitting across the table. The last time had been the awkward, stilted meeting in the White House. The first time had been when Lee walked out of the red brick home in Appomattox, slamming one gauntleted fist into the other after signing the surrender.

But that second meeting, between the lines of blue and gray on the morning following the formal surrender, was the one Spencer most vividly recalled. He remembered the tens of thousands of faces on both sides watching expectantly, still not believing that it was over. Spencer's horse was to the right and slightly behind Grant's *Cincinnati*. He could see Lee clearly and hear every word either man spoke. That's what struck Spencer—they were surrounded by more than a hundred-thousand men and the only sound were the words spoken by Lee and Grant. It was as if each of the thousands of men watching was holding his breath.

Lee was resplendent that morning. The sun, still low, seemed to focus its warmth on the man in gray, complementing the silver hair and beard and *Traveler*'s light gray coat.

That was the moment. Even in defeat Lee still was the legend, his honor and skill and daring established on dozens of battlefields. Spencer felt that when Lee surrendered his Army of Northern Virginia, he could have halted the bloodshed for all Confederate troops throughout the South, as well as for Union soldiers. Instead, when Grant asked him to urge all Confederates to surrender, Lee said that only Jefferson Davis could issue such an order—even though most of the Western world knew that, more than any man, Lee was the South's leader.

Spencer noticed that when Lee read the final page, he began to carefully re-read the letter. There had been no reaction that he could see. Nothing. Spencer could not understand how the man could fail to reveal at least a hint of a reaction.

Spencer could feel his anger growing. He dreaded the thought of reporting to the President that Lee had once again rejected his request to help end the bitterness. Spencer made up his mind not to accept Lee's rejection. He would argue the President's case with tact and consideration for what Lee had been, and continued to be, in the eyes of most people. But he also would be firm.

Lee carefully folded the letter, tucked it into the envelope and carefully placed it in front of him on the desk. The general turned his chair slightly so that he could see through the window behind him, his eyes tracking a small group of young men leaving the chapel. Spencer thought the old man looked exhausted. After several moments Lee turned from the window.

"Colonel, one of my regrets is that I have not realized my hopes of writing a history of the campaigns." Lee traced his forefinger along the edge of the envelope. "I urged other general officers to write their memoirs and, as I am sure you are aware, some of them have done so. But my writing was complicated by several factors. My material for the history is meager. I have copies of most of my reports through the Gettysburg campaign, but most of the reports after that were burned in the retreat from Petersburg. And, of course, the archives of the Confederate War Department were seized and the Federal government has not made the documents available to me."

Although Spencer was mystified by the direction of Lee's conversation, he immediately realized how eagerly a book by Lee would be received by the entire country.

"I have attempted to overcome that difficulty by writing to the general officers with whom I served to ask for whatever records they might have. The response has been encouraging, but not adequate to fill the void."

Lee was silent for a moment, still fingering the envelope. "My objective in writing such a history, Colonel Spencer, is to accurately establish the comparative strength and resources of the Union and Confederate armies. If the truth were known so soon after the war, it would not be believed. I thought that writing such a history would be the only tribute I could pay to the courage of the officers and soldiers who accomplished so much with so little."

Lee paused while he grimaced and rubbed his left arm for a moment, then reached for his coffee cup. When he set it back on the desk, he looked closely at Spencer.

"My concern during all these years has been for the people of Virginia, the people of the South." Lee shook his head slowly. "All those young men who fought so well, and all those who are gone forever."

Spencer could see that Lee's pain stemmed from more than his words. The general pressed his hand to his chest, his eyes squeezed shut. Hooper was on his feet immediately, quickly coming around the table to Lee's side.

"General Lee?" Hooper put his hand on Lee's shoulder. "Perhaps you should lie down, sir."

Lee took a deep breath as the pain seemed to pass. He looked up at Hooper, smiled, and shook his head. "No…no, I'm fine now."

Lee, obviously shaken and pale, waved Hooper away, his hand fluttering. "Please, Clarence, it was just a passing thing. I am much better now."

Spencer was alarmed. Both Grant and Sherman had told him that Lee's health was failing, but he had not imagined the situation was this serious. He had to admit, however, that his principal concern was whether Lee's health was good enough to make a long trip to Atlanta, even if he agreed to go.

"General Lee," Spencer said, rising from his chair, "perhaps I can come back tomorrow to continue our discussion. I'm sure I can find accommodations in town."

"Nonsense." Lee seemed agitated and embarrassed by the concern. "Please keep your seat, colonel." He turned to Hooper, who still was hovering at his side. "Clarence, the colonel will need accommodations for the night. Will you see to it, please?"

Hooper hesitated, obviously reluctant to leave the room, but finally agreed. "Yes, sir, I'll take care of it. But as long as Colonel Spencer is spending the night, I suggest that the discussion today be brief and that you continue it tomorrow." As Hooper left the room he caught Spencer's eye and almost imperceptibly shook his head. Spencer thought the aide looked angry.

"Please, colonel, resume your seat," Lee said. "I would appreciate continuing our conversation for a few minutes more."

Spencer took his chair again, still concerned about the old man's health.

"Now, where was I? Oh, yes, my memoirs." Lee paused while he organized his thinking. "You must understand that I do not wish to write them for my benefit...to in any way attempt to glorify my conduct of the war. My only wish is that due credit be paid to all those in the South who fought so gallantly against such huge odds."

Despite Lee's condition, Spencer felt his anger growing. The old general should be concerned about the future of his soldiers who survived the war. Spencer had long ago become weary of the *Gallant South*.

"Excuse me, general. Those of us who fought against you are intimately acquainted with how well the Confederate army performed. I don't mean to be impertinent, sir, but I would think that we should put the war behind us. As you said, general, perhaps more time must pass before such a book can be written."

Lee's face was impassive for a moment, then he grinned broadly. For the first time Spencer was aware that the general was not only an imposing figure, but he was a handsome man as well.

"I am sixty-three years old, colonel, and you have seen the evidence that my health is...shall we say, precarious? Among the limited resources available to me to write such a book, colonel, time may be the most limiting of all."

"Excuse me, general, but it seems clear to me that our national history will eventually record the accomplishments of the Confederate soldier. It is the immediate future that is in doubt at the moment. I'm sure that you recognize the President's concern about the present course of Reconstruction. For many in the North, you have as much or more prestige than the President. President Grant is convinced that you and he together can redirect the nation's preoccupation with the bitterness of war. General Lee, the President needs your assistance."

Lee moved forward in his chair to lean his elbows on the table. Spencer heard Hooper enter the room and take a seat somewhere behind him.

"Colonel, you speak of the future, but the future is not mine. Somewhere I have read that each age is a dream that is dying. My dream—"

"I am sorry, general, but I don't believe that your personal dream is one which will carry this nation forward. It dwells on the past and frankly, sir, the only value in the past is the lessons it offers for the future. We must leave it and move on."

Spencer heard Hooper move from his chair to the side of the table. "You indeed are impertinent, colonel. I suggest that you either apologize or leave at once."

Spencer ignored Hooper, keeping his eyes locked with Lee's, although he could see with his peripheral vision that the aide's face was flushed with anger.

"General, no disrespect was intended, sir. But I've made many trips through the South in the last five years. And although there has been some improvement, there still is too much poverty and hopelessness, especially among the young men who left their farms and families to fight for the Confederacy. These are among the people of concern to the President. These are the people who will guide the South's future—more importantly, the nation's future."

Lee slowly pushed back from the table and rose from his chair. He took a step toward Hooper and patted him lightly on the shoulder. Then he turned to look through the window. A group of perhaps a dozen young men were gathered in front to the chapel.

Spencer stood, walked around Hooper, and stepped to within a few paces of the general. They both stood quietly for a moment, watching as several of the students paused to circle around one young man who was showing them something in a textbook.

"General Lee," Spencer said softly, "the fact that you have dedicated yourself to this school is evidence that you recognize the role young men like those will play in the nation's future. The President is convinced that if you invite him to stand at your side during your army's reunion, the burden that those young men must carry will be lightened considerably."

Lee recalled the meeting on the road south of Lexington when he was riding with Hooper. What was that man's name, the one from whom he'd bought the basket of apples? Mrs. Lee said the apples were so withered they couldn't be used, even for cooking. Yes, his name was Hardin, Sergeant Hardin, but Lee couldn't remember the first name. Hardin had obviously been carrying those apples a long way, and he obviously desperately needed the few pennies they might have brought. Lee remembered the ragged Confederate great coat, the badly worn shoes, the tired eyes. A man's eyes could tell a lot. Lee pondered on the message that was in Hardin's eyes. Hardin obviously was proud of his service. Didn't he say that he'd been with the Army of Northern Virginia for almost the entire war? Yes, he had been proud.

But what hope did he and all the other Hardins have for the future? The pathetic sight of the man trying to pull himself to attention, the ragged clothes and shoes, the basket of spoiled apples at his feet—all of it kept replaying in Lee's mind.

When a man loses hope for the future, he loses everything. Lee turned to look at the young man next to him. Here was a young man with hope and determination in his eyes. It was clear that he would do all he could to leave with what Grant wanted. But Grant wanted too much.

"Colonel Spencer, perhaps...perhaps we can continue this conversation in the morning. I find that I am very tired."

Spencer, for the first time, noticed how much Lee had aged since he'd last seen him. The general's hair was completely white now, and the shoulders were becoming stooped.

"Of course, general." Spencer hesitated a moment, then added. "General Lee, I hope that you and Mr. Hooper will understand that the President makes his request with the full understanding of the difficulties it poses for you. You also must appreciate that hard-headed radicals in the North and South may pose a risk to the President's personal safety—and perhaps your safety, as well. The President is convinced, however, that the potential benefits of his proposal are worth any risk. And if I...if I have too vigorously advocated the President's position, sir, I sincerely apologize."

Lee's expression softened. "I would say, colonel, that General Grant...the President...was well represented here today."

"Thank you, sir." Spencer, concerned about Lee's ability to make the trip to Atlanta, suddenly remembered the military train that Sherman had brought to Lynchburg. "One more thing, sir. I recognize that the trip to Atlanta might be uncomfortable for you. I'm certain that arrangements can be made for a private train to take you, and whomever else you choose, to Atlanta." Spencer wasn't certain how he would explain to Sherman the commitment he had just made, but he would worry about it later. Spencer couldn't tell what impression, if any, had been made on Lee. But at least Lee had not rejected Grant's request. Although the general had said nothing that could be considered encouraging, Spencer felt that the next morning's discussion could be productive.

"What time shall we meet in the morning, general?"

Lee looked at Hooper, who grimaced. "General, your schedule for tomorrow is full, but I would say about eight-thirty. You will have no more than about an hour to spend with the colonel."

"Thank you, general." Spencer nodded toward Hooper. "Mr. Hooper." Spencer turned to leave.

"Colonel." Lee came from behind the desk to stand near Hooper. "Mrs. Lee has always said that breakfast is her favorite meal. She contends that we should endeavor to start each day with a good meal and, whenever possible, we should share our table with pleasant company. Will you consider an invitation to join us?"

Spencer was so surprised that he was concerned that Lee would misunderstand his delay in responding.

"Thank you, general. Of course I accept."

"Fine. About seven thirty?"

"Yes, sir."

"After breakfast, colonel, if weather permits, perhaps we can take a short walk. I'd like to show you the grounds. That will give us an opportunity to talk."

Spencer nodded and left the room. When he was gone, Lee handed Grant's letter to Hooper. Lee turned back to the window, anticipating Hooper's reaction.

"Impossible! The man can't be serious. Does he realize what he's asking?" Hooper paced the room, holding the letter at arm's length, slapping it periodically with the back of his right hand. "General, I recommend that you authorize me to immediately send this colonel and his letter packing."

Lee, his hands clasped behind his back, didn't respond. Hooper could see the general's reflection in the window, the expression one of deep thought.

"General, you can't be seriously considering this ridiculous request from Grant?"

Lee turned slowly. "No, Clarence, I am not seriously considering the President's request."

"Thank goodness, sir. For a moment I thought—"

Lee turned back to the window. "What I am considering, Clarence, is the request made by that young officer. If the war taught us nothing else, it was that the desire to succeed can overcome what may appear to be impossible odds. That young man isn't a tavern brawler. We have no way of knowing what obstacles he overcame to deliver that letter you are batting about. He may even have risked his life to do so."

Lee took his seat at the desk. "I must prepare for the vestry meeting this evening, Clarence, so if you will excuse me."

Hooper sighed heavily, theatrically. He folded the letter and placed it on the desk, then left the room.

Lee knew that if he attended his army's reunion, his presence would ensure the absence of two of his most famous generals. George E. Pickett, Lee knew, now hated him. Pickett was heard to say of Lee, *That old man had my division massacred at Gettysburg.* Lee blamed faulty intelligence for the disaster, but down deep he regretted ordering Pickett's division to charge Cemetery Hill. Neither would James Longstreet be there—both because of Lee's presence and because he would not be welcome in the South.

That's what concerned Lee about Grant's request for help. Longstreet made the decision to support Grant's presidency, and it had cost him the friendship and respect of his colleagues.

Lee had dedicated his very soul to his beloved Virginia. The thought that she might turn on him in the short time he knew he had left created a surge of panic.

But this young colonel, Spencer, was unsettling. In almost so many words, Spencer said that Lee was so consumed with the past that he could not see beyond his own mortality. Could that be true? The unshakable foundation of Lee's character was his religion. He believed that his mortality was preparation for that moment when he met his maker.

The world would not end when General Robert E. Lee went to his grave. Lee knew that. But before his life ended, was it really his destiny to ensure the legacy of bravery and determination of the Confederate soldier? Yes, Spencer was unsettling—as were the Sergeant Hardins.

September 20, 1870
Pedlar Mills, Virginia
2:20 a.m.

Jessie McLaws was certain she'd heard it. Perhaps she'd only dreamed it, but it sounded like a voice. It must be two or three o'clock in the morning.

There. She heard it again. It was a man's voice, and there was fear in it. Jessie threw back the covers and sat up in bed. She got up and opened her bedroom door and listened for a moment. Then she walked across the hall to Amanda's room. The child was soundly asleep.

Jessie thought of lighting a candle, then decided against it. She felt her way the few feet to the end of hall where Spencer was sleeping in the guest room. He'd stopped late yesterday afternoon on his way back from Lexington. He was leaving in the morning for Lynchburg, rather than Washington City, as he'd planned. A message for him had arrived early yesterday. After he had torn open the envelop and read it, he said that General Sherman wanted him to ride to Lynchburg to board the general's train. They were going to Richmond.

"John?" Jessie called softly from outside the door. There was no answer. She started back to her room, then stopped. She was certain that she heard a low moan.

She called louder this time. "John. Are you all right?" She waited a moment then went back to Amanda's room and found the candle. She lighted it and opened Spencer's door.

She could see Spencer sitting on the edge of the bed. His back was to her. He was leaning forward, his head in his hands.

"John? Is anything wrong?"

Spencer turned slowly to look at Jessie. In the flickering light she could see that his face was bathed in perspiration. He was breathing heavily. His eyes looked as if he were in pain. She came around the end of the bed, holding the candle closer to see Spencer. "What is it, John? Are you ill?"

Spencer took a deep breath. He looked up, smiling thinly. "No. I'm better now, thank you. I'm...I'm sorry I woke you."

Jessie felt Spencer's forehead. She gently forced his head back so she could see his eyes.

"Please, Jessie. I'm fine now." Spencer seemed embarrassed. "It was just...just that dream again. I guess I'm like a child—I have them every so often." He pressed his fingertips to his temples. "I have these headaches that always come with the dreams."

With his feet still on the floor, he leaned back against the pillow, his left arm over his closed eyes.

Jessie left the room, returning a few minutes later. "Here, John, take this." She held out a cup of water and a white powder in a small silver cup.

Spencer raised to one elbow, took the medicine and lay back on the pillow.

Jessie also had brought a towel and a cool wet cloth. She told Spencer to put his legs on the bed. Then she began to gently wipe the perspiration from his face and chest.

She knew about the dreams some of the veterans had. Nellie Thomas, who lived across the street next to the stable, said her Michael would sometimes scream in the middle of the night. She said she had to hold him tightly, like a child, until the fear went away.

Jessie folded the wet cloth and placed it over Spencer's closed eyes. She lightly massaged his forehead, her fingers pausing when she felt the indentation at his hairline.

No, John Spencer, you and all the others are not having the nightmares of little boys.

Spencer slept fitfully while she sat on the edge of the bed, lightly massaging his neck and shoulders. Then, after a long while, she could feel the tension drain away.

Jessie didn't know how long she sat there. The candle had been out for what seemed like an hour. The blackness outside the window had gradually turned to the blue-gray of dawn.

That's when she noticed his eyes were open. Spencer reached for her hand, gently pulling her to him. Jessie lay down beside Spencer, her arms encircling him. They held each other closely for a long, long moment. Then Spencer pulled back to look at her. There was more light now. Jessie's face was framed by her long auburn hair splayed out over the pillow, her eyes soft and glistening.

Spencer kissed her lightly, his lips brushing her eyelids and the small pulse beat at the base of her throat. They loved each other slowly, savoring the moments of pleasure and discovery, and they were astonished at how secure each felt in the arms of the other.

Hours later, before Spencer was to leave for Lynchburg, they held each other as they stood in the hallway near the front door.

"What if I asked you to come to Washington," he whispered in her ear.

Jessie stepped back and looked at Spencer closely. "I…I really don't know. Since I can't find out where my husband is buried, I thought I would go back to Kentucky." She stepped forward and leaned against Spencer. "Of course, that was before I met you," she said softly."

"I'll find a place for you and Amanda to stay. When I've completed this assignment, we'll plan what we can do after that. But I want you with me."

Jessie smiled and hugged him.

Finally, Spencer stepped out onto the small porch and mounted the chestnut for the ride to the train station.

September 22, 1870
Linden Row Inn
Richmond, VA
10 a.m.

General Sherman and John Spencer, in civilian clothing, were escorted into the elegantly furnished parlor of the Linden Row Inn, a four-story hotel built in the 1840s in central Richmond. When they were seated, a waiter brought in a tray containing an elegant porcelain coffee decanter and three cups, which he placed on a low table between two couches.

They had arrived in Richmond near midnight the night before aboard the *Pioneer II*, Sherman's personal three-car train. During the journey to

Richmond, Sherman explained that he had arranged a meeting with Nathan Bedford Forrest, former lieutenant general of the CSA. Sherman explained that although Forrest, as head of the KKK, had ordered the organization to be dissolved, Sherman wanted to be convinced that the Klan would not be a threat to the President.

"What isn't clear to me, sir, is that if the general ordered the group to disband, why do you still consider the Klan to be a threat?"

"Yes, well, although my people tell me that the national organization has indeed been dissolved, there is clear evidence that many local Klan groups exist in several states. What I am more concerned about is—"

Both men saw a tall, slightly more than six feet, and broad-shouldered man enter the parlor.

"This is our man," Sherman said softly, as he and Spencer rose.

Nathan Bedford Forrest deliberately walked toward the two men, his dark gray eyes focused on Sherman. Spencer noticed that the two men stood for a long moment, each assessing the other, before Forrest extended his hand.

"One of my regrets, General Forrest, is that during the war you and I did not personally meet in the field."

Forrest's stern expression softened slightly. "With due respect, general, I would say that was your good fortune."

They stood for a long moment, each gripping the other's hand. Spencer could see Sherman's jaw muscles flexing. Finally, Sherman said, "This is Col. John Spencer of my staff." Forrest nodded toward Spencer, but didn't extend his hand.

Sherman gestured toward the facing couch. "Please be seated, general. Would you like coffee?"

"No, thank you, and I am no longer a general. Please call me Bedford." Forrest cleared his throat. "General, I have an important business meeting in two hours. Your message did not indicate how long this meeting would take. And the only thing your message said regarding the subject of this meeting was a vague reference to the wellbeing of the nation."

"I can assure you that we will need only an hour or so of your time."

"Then let us begin, sir," Forrest said.

Spencer wondered whether the meeting would produce any new information. Forrest, his mood accentuated by his dark goatee, mustache, and deep-set eyes, seemed on the verge of losing his temper.

"So we shall. A British delegation of senior military officers and government officials recently visited the President," Sherman began, "ostensibly to ask the President to escort them to West Point."

"I take it you believe that was not their true mission."

Sherman leaned forward, resting his elbows on his knees. "I believe the officers indeed wanted to visit West Point, as they have frequently in the past. However, I have information that one of the Brits, whose name I do not have, made a special trip to visit with you in your home in Memphis."

Spencer was surprised that Forrest didn't hesitate. "Yes, that is true. His name is David McLean. He is a member of the government, but he did not disclose in what capacity."

"And what was the nature of his business?"

For a long moment, Forrest looked at Sherman, then at Spencer. "He wanted to know what influence I might still have with the Klan."

"I would like to know that, as well. But, first, why did he want that information?"

"He did not divulge that, but I told him I had severed all ties with the organization."

"Have you really."

Spencer thought the tone of Sherman's response was more than a bit sarcastic. "General Forrest," Spencer said, feeling it presumptuous to use Forrest's middle name, "may I ask a question?"

Forrest extended his right hand and made a 'continue' gesture.

"Did this Mr. McLean give you any indication that he was supportive of the Klan?"

Forrest was thoughtful for a moment. "I asked him directly why he wanted such information. His response was vague, noncommittal. He then asked if I would give him the name of the most influential leader of any of the existing local Klan units."

"Did you, sir?" Spencer asked.

"I did not, for the simple reason that I do not have that information."

Forrest leaned forward and spoke directly to Sherman. "And if you continue to question my honesty, General, then I will consider this meeting to be concluded."

"I am confident, sir," Spencer said quickly, that General Sherman's focus is to ensure the safety of the President. His intent was not to impugn your honesty."

For the first time, Forrest smiled broadly. "As a member of your staff, General, what exactly does this young man do for you—aside from trying to settle the dust you raise?" Forrest then took the porcelain pitcher and filled the three cups.

Sherman held up his hands in a gesture of surrender, then reached for his cup and saucer. "In less than two hours earlier today, my young colonel determined the identity of the British official who visited your home. And, yes, it was a test to see if you would tell us the truth."

"Frankly," Forrest said, "I presumed you knew his name. Now that I have passed your honesty test, what is this all about?"

Sherman hesitated a long moment. "Bedford, I believe that the English are attempting to use the Klan to undermine the government, and the Klan may even pose a threat to President Grant's life."

"To what purpose?" Forrest seemed surprised, perhaps disbelieving.

"There is a small faction in the English government—unsupported by its leaders and the British people—who want this country to revert back to becoming a colony of that government. I believe McLean represents that faction.

"After all, they supported the Confederacy during the war and, after an incident on the high seas, sent thirty-thousand troops to Canada as a threat to invade this country. Fortunately, President Lincoln resolved the issue."

"Yes," Forrest said, "the English supported the Southern cause, but their government knew the British people did not support slavery. But why do you believe they would make such an attempt now?"

Sherman hesitated.

"Could it be, General Sherman, that the British recognize that the current President does not have the full support of the people, that Reconstruction was an utter and complete failure, and that the President is being rendered ineffective because of scandal?"

Spencer could see Sherman's jaw muscles working again. "If I may, sir," Spencer said to Forrest, "we have drifted from the focus of this meeting—the Klan. We are asking for whatever support you can provide to ensure that any threat by the Klan is neutralized."

Forrest sipped his coffee, looking at the two men. "Most people," he began softly, "have a distorted view of the Klan. It was formed in '66 as a purely social organization by six former CSA veterans in Pulaski, Tennessee. They helped widows and orphans of our dead soldiers."

"But it became more violent after you took over," Sherman said.

"Understand that I was never an official member of the group. My support, my full support, was prompted by the Klan's opposition to Reconstruction. I have—"

"And to controlling the blacks," Sherman said.

Forrest sighed. "Yes, I admit that I was quoted as being opposed to black equality." He leaned forward and slowly ran his forefinger around the rim of his cup before he picked it up. "Let me just say that my views regarding that issue have moderated in recent years." Then he said more firmly, "And let me make clear that I never advocated or supported the violence, much of which, by the way, committed by other groups and blamed on the Klan. The violence is why I asked the Klan to disband and why I no longer have anything to do with the organization."

"Sir," Spencer said, "back to my question: are you willing to support our effort to safeguard the President?"

Forrest smiled. "You indeed are a persistent young man. The answer is yes. We all have seen far too much violence. But, let me make clear that I will decide how I will cooperate."

"Agreed," Sherman said quickly. "First, we must know if the English contact you again, for whatever reason."

Forrest nodded.

"I have reason to believe," Sherman continued, "that the Georgia Klan may pose the greatest risk to the President. I have information that you personally went to Georgia a couple of years ago and helped establish a powerful, state-wide organization."

Again, Forrest nodded.

"Then are you willing to investigate the organization and provide me with the names of its key people?"

Forrest hesitated only a moment. "Yes."

"I am specifically interested in learning more about a man named Hollis Connor. I suspect he is part of the Georgia Klan. Do you know him?"

Forrest shook his head.

Sherman withdrew a small sheet of paper from a pocket and handed it to Forrest. "If you find anything regarding Connor, you can contact me at any time. If you decide you must travel to Georgia to investigate this matter, I will personally reimburse your travel and lodging expenses."

Forrest's dark eyebrows rose. "Thank you, but if travel is required, I am capable of handling such expenses."

"One last question, Bedford," Sherman asked. "Have you seen General Lee in recent years?"

"I have never had the privilege of meeting General Lee. Why do you ask?"

"Just curious, I guess." Sherman rose and extended his hand. "Thank you for your time, Bedford. I hope to hear from you soon."

Forrest firmly took Sherman's hand. "If I have anything to report, rest assured you will hear from me."

Forrest turned to leave, then paused. He looked back at Spencer for a moment before stepping around the low table to stand in front of him.

"You remind me of a young colonel who was on my staff. He was a very good man who I think of often. He died at Chickamauga."

Forrest shook Spencer's hand, then turned and walked form the parlor.

Sherman and Spencer took their seats as they refilled their coffee cups.

"Well, colonel, was our time well spent?"

"Yes, sir, I believe it was. I presume you singled out the Georgia Klan because if the President and General Lee meet, it will be in Atlanta."

Sherman nodded. "Although my trust in Forrest is enhanced, I still didn't trust him enough to mention the possibility that General Lee and the President will meet at the reunion."

When they finished their coffee, Sherman said, "Before we return to our duties, why don't we see if the quality of the food in this place is equal to the décor."

Chapter 14

September 23, 1870
Associated Press Offices
Washington City
9:40 a.m.

"Mr. Pohlman, there is a woman in your outer office asking to see you."

Billy Spires, the young Associated Press clerk had opened Pohlman's office door just wide enough to stick his head in.

Pohlman, editing a story by one of his new reporters about a series of Cheyenne Indian raids on Central Pacific Railroad crews in the far West, didn't look up from the copy. "And what does she want to see me about?"

"She wouldn't tell me, but she says it's urgent and, frankly, sir, she seems rather upset."

Pohlman sighed. The last three or four paragraphs of the story were badly mangled. He waved Billy into the room. "Give this to Mr. Chapman, please, and ask him to rewrite the sections I've indicated." He handed the copy to the boy. "You can ask the woman to come in."

Always fastidious about his clothes and personal appearance, Pohlman had a habit of making judgments about people based on how they dressed. He felt that the selection of clothes and how they were worn could almost always provide some clues about personality, even character. Pohlman was impressed by the woman who stepped into his office. Her dress was emerald green, trimmed in black. The jewelry and other accessories were expensive, but understated.

"Good afternoon, Mr. Pohlman. I am Mrs. Rachel Brockton. Thank you for seeing me on such short notice. There is a matter I wish to discuss with you which is of the utmost importance."

Pohlman noticed that the woman was indeed nervous, her eyes darting about the room. He moved around the desk to help Rachel into a chair. He knew of Rachel's reputation as a young woman who had made a great deal of money on Wall Street. It was said that she was shrewd, calculating, driven to become the wealthiest woman in the country. The story was that her objective was within reach.

"How can I help you, Mrs. Brockton?"

Rachel had been unable to work out everything in her mind before arriving. She knew of Pohlman's reputation as one of the nation's finest journalists. She had heard his name mentioned often at parties and business meetings, and he was known in social and business circles as a gentlemen with integrity.

She had decided to come to Pohlman, rather than go to the authorities, because her evidence was based only on what Roger Brewster told her, on what he had overheard. Most importantly, she didn't want to be linked in any way to the investigation. Rachel hoped that Pohlman would investigate whether there was a plot to kill President Grant. Perhaps he also could find out what happened to Roger. Rachel hoped Pohlman could do all of that and still protect her anonymity.

"Mr. Pohlman, if my name is linked in any way with what I am about to tell you, my family and I will be in great danger. Before I proceed, I must have your assurance that, if you choose to investigate the validity of what I am considering telling you, there must be no reference to me."

Pohlman had become accustomed to such requests, especially from influential people in Washington. He gave Rachel his standard response, even though he was intrigued by what she had to say.

"Mrs. Brockton, it is not possible for me to give such assurances without more information. All I can do is assure you that if it is not necessary for you to be involved in your story, then I will not use your name. But that will be my decision to make. That must be clear."

Although she knew little about how journalists functioned, Rachel had anticipated such a response. She had all but made up her mind that she would tell Pohlman at least most of the story.

"Mr. Pohlman, I apparently have no choice but to defer to your good judgment, as long as you keep in mind the potential risk to my family and me."

She paused for a moment, then began. "I have reason to believe that there is a plot to kill President Grant. And I believe the attempt on his life will be made when he visits Atlanta sometime soon."

Pohlman didn't react to what he'd heard. He was scheduled to interview Grant the next afternoon. He planned to discuss the President's plan to attend the reunion of Lee's army, although Pohlman would hold the material until the release date. Pohlman knew when he'd first heard of the plan that keeping it secret would be almost impossible.

"Tell me what you know about the President's plans to visit Atlanta."

"I know nothing about his plans. My knowledge of this matter is based on a conversation overheard by another man who related it to me."

Pohlman took a couple of sheets of copy paper from a desk drawer. "I suggest that you start from the very beginning, Mrs. Brockton, and tell me everything you know about this matter."

Rachel paused while she tried to decide just how much to tell Pohlman, then began with the meeting she had with Gould and Fisk, mentioning the presence of Connor and Wells. Pohlman took comprehensive notes while Rachel talked. She told him how Brewster was used to help her make money. Then she related what Brewster had overheard when Connor and Wells came to the bank. She nearly broke down when she described how Nelson had died.

"Did you tell any of this to the police?"

"No. No, of course not. I was afraid of what Connor might do."

Pohlman wrote a memo in the margin of his notes to remind him to learn more about Connor and Wells.

"Are Gould and Fisk involved in the plot to kill the President?"

"I don't know. Connor didn't mention either name, but Roger seemed to believe that they were not. He had the impression, in fact, that Connor—he is the viscous one—and Wells were acting alone."

"Did Brewster say what motive, what reason Connor has for killing the President?"

"The implication is that Connor wants to try to control the gold market, as Gould and Fisk did. Roger recalled overhearing that Connor said something like, 'Just think what would happen if Grant were removed—removed permanently from Washington.' Connor said that the market would be in chaos. It certainly would fall very quickly and, most importantly, they—Connor and Wells—would know about it in advance, and they would be able to act on that knowledge."

"Think carefully now, Mrs. Brockton. Did Brewster say anything more about Grant going to Atlanta? Did he indicate in any way that he knew why the President was going there?"

"No, I have told you all I know about that."

"Did Brewster give you the impression that Connor knew why Grant was going there?"

"If Roger knew, he didn't tell me. I am concerned about Roger, Mr. Pohlman. He took great personal risk to help me, and I am afraid that something horrible has happened to him. Is there anything you can do to find out if he is safe?"

"Perhaps, Mrs. Brockton. Perhaps. But why would you be concerned about what happened to him, considering what you've told me about how he helped involve you in all of this?"

Rachel's expression reflected the pain and anguish she felt. "I'm afraid, Mr. Pohlman, that Roger fell victim to the same temptations that trapped me. He is basically a good man, and I know that he regrets involving me in this mess, and that he was willing to give up a great deal of his fortune to get out of it himself. Please help him if you can."

Pohlman looked over his notes. "What specifically does Connor want you to do for the secretary of the treasury?" Pohlman, who knew about Stoval's reputation with women, suddenly realized what he had asked, his face flushing with embarrassment. "Please forgive me, I...ah...I suppose the answer is obvious."

Rachel couldn't help smiling at Pohlman's discomfort. "Judging from what I've been told about how Gould and Fisk manipulated the market," Rachel said, "my guess is that Connor intends to blackmail Stoval."

"To what purpose?"

"Well—again it's only my guess—but Connor and Wells probably hope to prevent Stoval from taking any action that would stabilize the gold market when—if—Grant is killed. With the President dead, and the Secretary of the Treasury under their thumbs, the market will indeed be in chaos."

Pohlman set aside his notes, folding his hands on his desk. "Mrs. Brockton, what do you intend to do about Connor's demands?"

Rachel responded in almost a whisper. "I really don't know. I am certain, Mr. Pohlman, that I have no intention of meeting Mr. Stoval, under any circumstances. Nor will I permit anything to happen to my family by refusing Connor's demands. I don't know how I will accomplish all of that, but I will."

Pohlman felt a growing empathy for the woman. He knew that her father had been a man of power and influence in the Confederate government. He also began to realize that Rachel's reputation as a woman who was cold, shrewd and aloof may have been the result of the disappointment of men who failed to interest her in something other than business opportunities.

It was also clear to Pohlman that he had a major news story, which he could develop while helping the woman. What he knew of Fisk and Gould convinced him that, while they could be devious and ruthless, they more than likely were not involved in the plot to kill Grant—they were too smart for that. But they did apparently hope to repeat their successful manipulation of the gold market.

It also seemed clear that they hoped to use this woman to somehow put Stoval into a comprising situation that would put him in their control. Based on what he had just heard, it was clear that Connor worked for Gould and Fisk, and that in all probability Connor and Wells had simply gotten greedy and were operating on their own.

"Tell me, Mr. Pohlman. Do you think Connor can succeed in his plot against the President?"

Pohlman replayed in his mind what the country went through following the assassination of Lincoln. He remembered the shock, the sorrow, the anger, the chaos.

"I really don't know, Mrs. Brockton. What worries me most is that Connor appears to be mad. And he's obviously ruthless. I personally feel that his plan to manipulate the market is foolish and not well thought out. And that concerns me because his instability may force him to become so frustrated, so desperate, that he will try to kill Grant anyway."

"What do you plan to do with the information I have given you?"

"I have someone in mind who can help us, but I'll have to contact him first to see if he can see us. Can you return to this office in an hour or so?"

"Yes, for course. I had intended to see a stone mason to prepare a grave marker for Nelson. I will return in an hour." Rachel picked up her gloves and bag and prepared to leave the office.

"Mrs. Brockton." Pohlman came around the desk to stand near her. "You are a courageous woman. Although I am confident that I can find the help you need, the safety of you and your family will be uncertain until this matter is resolved."

"Thank you—and, yes, I understand all of that. I will be back at eleven o'clock."

Pohlman walked Rachel to the street. As he returned to his office, he asked the copy boy to follow him. He sat at his desk, rapidly writing a note.

"Billy, take this note to the White House and ask to personally deliver it to Colonel John Spencer. Wait for a response. Now go, son, as quickly as you can."

What concerned Pohlman about his story was that he couldn't see how he could report the plot to control the gold market without revealing Grant's intention to go to Atlanta. Even if he could write about it, the story would put Grant in a bad light because of Stoval's involvement. That didn't necessarily bother Pohlman, despite his high regard for Grant's personal integrity. But Pohlman knew that still another scandal in Grant's Administration would more than likely ruin whatever chances for success Atlanta offered. Lee probably would withdraw his invitation.

Pohlman stood behind his desk, looking down at the paper scattered over the top of it without really seeing any of it, his hands thrust deep into his pockets. He knew that he had an advantage on the story that no one else had. He would have to protect that. He decided he wouldn't break the story before the reunion. The reunion, and what Grant hoped to accomplish there, was the big story. Connor, Gould and the others would be a dimension to the story that no one else would have. Yes, he would give Grant the opportunity to try one more time to work with Lee.

September 19, 1870
Washington College
Lexington, Virginia
9:20 a.m.

General Lee could clearly see that Clarence Hooper still was very angry.

"Please reconsider, General." Hooper was walking with Lee toward the main campus building where Lee had promised to spend some time with the engineering students. "Aside from the fact that the trip to Atlanta will be long and arduous, I am compelled to question the wisdom of appearing with Grant before the men. You must recognize the repercussions from such a meeting."

Lee had never seen Hooper so agitated, even during the closing days of the war. "Yes, Clarence," he replied calmly, "I am aware of the hazards."

"But, General, you have worked so hard in these last five years to avoid any public discussion of the war or the issues it involved, or the issues that have arisen since the war."

Hooper was almost pleading, seeming to reach for any argument that might persuade Lee to change his mind. "You are admired and respected by people across this nation, and you have worked miracles with the college. Why would you risk everything just to help Grant overcome the terrible mistakes he and his predecessors have made?"

"I have explained, Clarence, that my intention is not just to help the President." Lee paused near an ancient oak whose huge and knarled branches shaded a portion of the path leading from the house to the main building. He reached out to touch the rough bark. "Yes, I admit, Clarence, that I was persuaded by that young colonel. He and I walked down this same path this morning, and we paused at this tree."

Earlier, after breakfast, Lee and Spencer had strolled casually, stopping in the shade of the giant oak. Their conversation was equally casual—the fields of study offered by the college, and the challenges the army faced in the far west.

Spencer was eager to hear what Lee had decided about Atlanta, but he knew that Lee was a deliberate man who would not be rushed.

"Colonel, I did not sleep very well. The President's letter was on my mind." The old man smiled. "In fact, I admit that I got up from my bed during the night to read it once more."

In the short time they had been together, Spencer was developing a new appreciation for the man. If he were in Lee's place, Spencer considered, he too might have sought the kind of escape this little college offered. *I was only a soldier and I still have difficulty putting the war behind me,* Spencer thought. *How much more difficult would it be had I been the general who directed tens of thousands of men to fight, and to die? How many nightmares would I have created?*

"Colonel," Lee said, "you believe that what the President wants will help unite the country." It was a statement, perhaps an accusation, rather than a question.

"Yes, sir."

Lee nodded slowly, reaching out to lightly touch the oak's rough bark with his fingertips. "The question, colonel, is for what purposes will the nation be united?"

"Sir?"

"When the war broke out, I had to decide which side I would serve." Lee looked into Spencer's eyes. "I did not make that decision capriciously; it was indeed difficult, but my actions were guided by my belief that I owed my allegiance to the South—for many reasons, including my disagreement with some of the policies that represented the thinking in the North. You are asking me to abandon everything I fought for, everything I believed, everything my men suffered and died for." Lee shook his head briskly. "That would be the ultimate defeat."

Lee added, in almost a whisper, "You and President Grant are asking for the impossible." Lee sighed heavily. "What you are assuming, Colonel, is because the war was lost, my views must now coincide with those represented by Washington City."

Spencer felt a sinking feeling. Lee still was the unreconstructed rebel, after all. Spencer felt the anger surge and he considered ending the conversation and leaving. Then he thought of Grant, and what the effect would be on the man if he had to report still another failure to get Lee's help. Judging by what he'd seen of Lee's health, there would never be another opportunity.

"General Lee, I can say with confidence that President Grant does not expect you to abandon your beliefs. That was neither his objective nor his expectation. The President does not seek your support for his administration or his policies. In fact, knowing the President as I do, and the great respect he has for you, he would welcome the opportunity to hear your views. He merely is asking that all sides work together to soften the bitterness so that we all can help the nation move ahead. The President is convinced that you are the one man who can help him pull this country together."

"And he thinks that he and I standing before my corps of officers will accomplish that?"

"The process, general, must start there, for obvious reasons."

Lee looked out across the campus. "I am afraid the reasons are not so obvious to me."

Spencer didn't respond for a long moment. He believed now that he had nothing to lose.

"General Lee," Spencer said firmly, "the reasons will become apparent and obvious the moment you can put Appomattox behind you and look to the future."

Spencer immediately felt regret for his words. He saw Lee's expression harden.

"Sir, I sincerely apologize. I had no right—"

Lee stopped Spencer with a raised hand. Then, unexpectedly, the old general smiled and looked closely at the young man. "Colonel, you obviously suffered those injuries recently. Are they in any way connected with your being here?"

Spencer hesitated. He wondered how much he should reveal to Lee. He certainly would say nothing about Sherman. "Sir, I was ambushed on my way here. There is some evidence to suggest the attack was an effort to prevent me from delivering the President's letter."

"Were there other casualties?"

"Two men died. The investigation is continuing."

"Do you know who these men represented?"

"No, sir, not at this time."

"And you have reason to believe that Grant, the President, may be in some danger?"

"There is that possibility."

Lee walked away for a short distance and stood with his back to Spencer. The old man looked off into the distance and, as Spencer watched, Lee rubbed his left arm. After a minute or so, Lee turned and walked back to Spencer.

"Colonel, you may inform the President that I will be in Atlanta for the reunion. I will comply with the President's request."

Spencer was at a loss for words. He merely looked at Lee and nodded. Finally, he asked, "General Lee, may I ask what convinced you to make that decision?"

For the first time since their conversation began, Lee laughed. "Let me assure you, colonel, that it was not simple capitulation. You mentioned a train yesterday. Please make whatever arrangements you deem necessary. You may make those arrangements known to Mr. Hooper."

Lee held out his hand. Spencer grasped it and held it for a long moment.

"Have a safe trip home, Colonel Spencer."

Later that morning, as Lee and his secretary stood near that same ancient oak tree, Clarence Hooper decided that Lee did not look well. The old man looked pale and very tired. "General, why don't you speak to the engineering students later. I think we had best head back to the house."

Lee didn't protest. He turned and slowly started toward the house, then stopped and turned toward Hooper.

"Is it possible, Clarence, that I have not made the best use of these five years—that I should have played a greater role, a more active role, in helping our people recover from the war?"

Hooper hesitated. He recognized long ago that one of his principal values to Lee was that he always spoke his mind, and he did so frankly and candidly. But he wasn't even certain that Lee was expecting a response.

"General, I don't know how to answer that question." Hooper's voice was low and soft. "What I do know is that you should have no regrets about what you have accomplished with this school. You have managed to attract financial support from the North—why, even Cyrus McCormick of Chicago has contributed ten thousand dollars to the school. And more and more young men from northern states are enrolling."

"I have no regrets about what we have accomplished here, Clarence." Lee paused and looked back at the campus. "You are aware that I firmly believe that the outcome of the war was the will of God, even though I believe that He gave us guidance to wage war against such impossible odds."

Lee turned and continued walking to the house. "But I suppose, Clarence, that I am uncertain about how I have conducted myself these last few years. Perhaps the gesture that Grant wants is appropriate. If I have made a mistake, if I should have worked harder to help our people deal with defeat, then perhaps I am even obligated to stand with him before the men. I will tell them that we are gathered as veterans of a terrible conflict, which now is behind us, and that we must get on with building the future."

Hooper, obviously still angry about Lee's decision, spoke with more emotion then he intended. "But, general, why should we help *him*? After all, he beat us, then helped create the mess the South is in now."

Lee smiled, resting his hand on Hooper's shoulder as they walked slowly. "You're wrong, Clarence. He did not beat us—he just won. And he won because we chose not to pay the price that continued fighting would have demanded. No, he didn't beat us. You must never think that."

"I'm sorry, sir. I just don't see how you can cooperate in any way with the man."

The two men entered the house, pausing in the foyer. "Perhaps I will take a short nap, Clarence. But I may alleviate some of your concerns if I tell you this: I will ask to meet privately with General Grant shortly before we appear before the men. I will tell him then that if he expects my support, he must be prepared to accept that support with two provisions. First, I will make it clear to the men that I do not categorically endorse the Grant Administration—only the concept that the nation can not move ahead until we put the bitterness of the war behind us.

"And second," Lee continued, "Grant must realize that since I am abandoning my reluctance to speak publicly about the war or any other political issue, it would be unrealistic of him to think that I will speak out only on this one issue."

Lee was smiling broadly now. In fact, it had been a long time since Clarence could remember seeing the general so animated. "If he views himself as our shepherd, Clarence, then he must not think that the South will meekly join his fold."

Lee rubbed his hands together. "Clarence, you have a piece of work to do. You may even choose some of our most capable Southern students to assist you. Before I meet with the President, I would like to have a report on issues critical to South. That report must indicate the position of the President and Congress on those issues, as well as what we feel our position should be. I would suggest that the report be developed as soon as possible."

Lee started for his bedroom, then stopped and turned back to Hooper.

"We lost once, Clarence, because we lacked the will and the resources to continue the struggle. General Grant must be made to understand that if the South is indeed part of the United States, he must be prepared for a South that will play a full and vigorous role in the governance of this nation."

Lee smiled at the expression of shock on Hooper's face. "Now, now, Clarence. Don't worry. I have merely decided not to go my grave without one last fight.

"Oh, and one other thing. General Joe Johnston is in charge of arrangements for the reunion. Please contact him and ask that he not tell anyone about our plans to attend. I know you won't mention anything about the President. I understand there will only be a couple of hundred of our senior officers attending, and I would like my appearance there to be a surprise."

Lee considered whether he'd forgotten anything, then he chuckled. "Certainly we know that General Grant's appearance will be a surprise."

Both men laughed as Lee turned toward his bedroom.

Chapter 15

Office of White House Security
The White House
September 26
10:20 a.m.

Rachel was exhausted. The small office assigned to Colonel Spencer on the first floor of the White House was confining, and much too warm. It was the second time within a few hours that she had told her story, and the heat, the tension, and the ceaseless questioning confused her at times and made her feel light-headed.

One thing she was aware of—she didn't like this Colonel Spencer. When she told him about he plot to kill the President, he became cold, suspicious, his questions penetrating and almost harsh. His reaction to what she told him about the meetings with Gould, Fisk and Brewster made her feel unclean, as if she were a participant in the plot. Spencer showed no sympathy for Nelson's murder or the threats made by Connor if she didn't accompany him to the party tomorrow night for Secretary of the Treasury Stoval.

The room now was quiet. Pohlman had asked someone to bring her a glass of cool water. Thank goodness for Ernst Pohlman, Rachel thought. He had been thoughtful and considerate, a gentleman throughout this ordeal.

Rachel could hear a hall clock ticking, and the floor creaking as someone walked past the door. Two or three minutes passed. It was as if everyone were drained of energy. Rachel was conscious of how heavy her eyelids were becoming. She was certain she could instantly fall asleep.

Spencer had leaned back in his chair, seemingly weighing what he'd heard. Rachel noticed that Spencer had turned his chair slightly and appeared to be examining a small painting on the wall. It was a night scene of two old Plains Indians huddled around a small campfire. Both old men were staring into the fire, the flames harshly lighting their heavily wrinkled faces. Rachel noticed that Spencer fingered the slight indentation high on his forehead, edged by strands of hair that were more white than gray.

Spencer's mind had been racing while Rachel's story unfolded. He couldn't shake the image of Choka's face dissolving in the roar of Jessie's shotgun. Were those two men who tried to kill him involved in what this woman said was a plot against the President? Were Connor and Wells still working for Gould and Fisk? Someone would have to talk to Gould and Fisk, but Spencer knew that it would have to be handled very delicately. If they weren't involved, he would have to learn more about Connor and Wells—especially Connor, it appeared.

Then Spencer pushed back his chair and walked to the door. He spoke briefly to an aide, then returned to his desk.

"It is obvious, Mrs. Brockton, that you and your family must leave your home and relocate, at least temporarily, to more secure quarters."

"And where to you propose to send us, colonel?"

"Arrangements are being made now. You obviously will not be meeting Mr. Connor tomorrow night. I will be waiting for him."

Spencer turned to Pohlman. "Ernst, I hope you agree that a story at this time would jeopardize the investigation."

Pohlman smiled. "I will not write a story at this point, but I will accompany you tomorrow night for your meeting with Mr. Connor."

Spencer didn't respond immediately. "Well, we both know I can't stop you. If anyone understands the risks involved, you certainly must."

"One other thing, John. I was scheduled to interview the President tomorrow at lunch. I had intended to ask him about the Atlanta trip.

However, in light of these developments, I will postpone that interview until we see what transpires tomorrow night."

There was a sharp knock at the door. When Spencer called for him to enter, Sergeant Major Gideon Barlow filled the door frame.

Pohlman stood to shake Barlow's hand. "Good afternoon, Sergeant Major. It's good to see you again."

Spencer nodded a greeting to Barlow. "Sergeant Major, this is Mrs. Rachel Brockton. We must temporarily relocate Mrs. Brockton and her family from their home in the Georgetown area. I have asked Corporal Samuelson to check on the availability of two unoccupied private residences, which might serve our purposes, at least for a week or two. Requisition the carriages and men you'll need, and plan to leave with Mrs. Brockton within the hour."

"Yes, sir."

"And sergeant, it will probably be dark when you leave Mrs. Brockton's home, so be sure you're not followed. Assign whatever number of men are required to remain as permanent guards at the new residence."

Barlow nodded. "Mrs. Brockton, will you be ready to leave within a half-hour?" he asked.

Rachel seemed flustered. Events were moving too quickly. "Why, yes, I suppose so. But my father—he's ill, and I don't think he can travel very far."

"That won't be a problem, ma'am," Barlow said. "I'll bring along an army doctor and an ambulance. We'll make sure your father is comfortable."

Rachel looked questioningly at Pohlman. "Don't worry," Pohlman said, "you can be confident that Sergeant Barlow will take every precaution."

Rachel looked at the towering cavalryman, his great black beard streaked with gray. He epitomized all that she had learned to hate and fear about the Union army, the kind of men who permitted her husband to die and who destroyed her father's plant."

Rachel merely nodded her head.

Barlow looked at Spencer. "Will there be anything more, sir?"

"That's all for now, sergeant. See me when you get back tonight, no matter how late. We have another job tomorrow night."

Barlow turned to leave. "Good seeing you again, Mr. Pohlman."

Spencer looked at Rachel, then Pohlman. "You know, Ernst, she is the only person we have who can identify Connor and Wells. She will have to come with us to Atlanta, if we don't get them before that."

Pohlman shook his head. "John, I am not sure that would be a good—"

"Listen, colonel!" Rachel leaned forward in her chair, her face flushed in anger. "Don't refer to me as a *she*, as if I were not in this room." Rachel rose from her chair.

"*Damn* you men! You bully your way through..." Her right hand fluttered as she searched in her anger for words. "I am not going to Atlanta, colonel, and I don't want that gorilla sergeant of yours around me."

The gush of anger was ebbing quickly. Although she meant every word she said, Rachel began to feel embarrassed by her outburst. "I am...I am perfectly capable of moving my family to safety without your help...or the help of any other man."

Rachel's words now were measured, her voice more controlled. "It may not fit your perception of the role of women in this new society, gentlemen, but I believe I have adequately demonstrated that I am capable of making decisions more complex than deciding which dress to wear each morning."

When Spencer, confused over what had provoked Rachel's anger, looked at Pohlman, he thought he saw a trace of a smile before the journalist began to busily thumb through the pages of a notebook in his lap.

Spencer was never comfortable around spirited, independent women who, on the one hand wanted to be treated as if they were helpless creatures who required constant attention and assistance, then a moment later thought they were in every way the equal of men. How do I handle a woman like this one, Spencer thought, who plays both roles simultaneously?

The woman obviously expected an apology, but Spencer wasn't aware of what he had done wrong. "I apologize, Mrs. Brockton, if I have...ah...said something that offended you." Spencer noticed that Rachel's eyes, still reflecting her anger, were boring into his. "You must appreciate, ma'am, that my first responsibility is the protection of the President." The woman's face was impassive, and now Spencer's anger began to surge.

"The hard fact, Mrs. Brockton, is that although I appreciate the information you have provided, I don't have the time to worry about any discomfort or inconvenience, real or imagined, that you may experience because of this situation. So let me be clear about this: You will be going to Atlanta, if the need arises. Whether or not you do so under military arrest will be a matter for you to decide."

Pohlman closed his notebook and leaned forward in his chair, as if he were preparing to leave. "John, perhaps we all can discuss this at a later time when—"

"Colonel Spencer." Rachel now was seething with anger. "You represent the kind of arrogance and disregard for human values that I have come to expect from Union officers. I, of course, will comply with your *orders*." Rachel rose abruptly. "Unless you object, I prefer the company of the statuary in the foyer. I presume your hulking sergeant is capable of finding his way there when he is finally ready to leave."

"I think that would be wise." Spencer also stood. "Perhaps among your problems, madam, is one that I have noticed with some Southern women. You are living in the past. The Union army no longer exists; I am an officer—arrogant or otherwise—in the United States Army. Good day, Mrs. Brockton."

Rachel slammed the office door so hard that the picture of the two old Indians was jarred from the wall. The glass frame shattered when it hit the floor, the shards slithering around the boots of the two men.

Pohlman had been surprised to see that Spencer, whom he had first met during the war, had lost his temper. He had always considered the man to be a very competent officer, one who had a reputation for courage and daring, yet who was sensitive to the well-being of his men. But Spencer was, Pohlman mused, typically American in his misunderstanding of women. It was clear to Pohlman that both Spencer and Rachel were so consumed by their current fears and responsibilities that neither recognized the fact that they both were caring, sensitive individuals. Yes, the trip to Atlanta would be very interesting indeed.

"John, I think you will find that Mrs. Brockton will be very helpful and cooperative. It is just that she has had some frightening experiences, and she is concerned about the safety of her son and father."

Spencer walked over to the shattered picture frame. "Well, Ernst, since you apparently will be a member of this traveling circus, I suggest that she be your responsibility—until I need her to identify Connor and Wells." Spencer picked up the oil painting, which had been badly cut by the broken glass.

"Permit me to have that repaired for you. I have a friend who can do wonders with damaged canvas."

Spencer smiled thinly. "Well, as long as you are so intent on playing the peacemaker, I would very much appreciate having it repaired."

Spencer removed the canvas from what remained of the frame and wrapped it in newspaper.

Pohlman paused at the door. "It will be a few weeks before it is repaired. And John, unless you object, I would like to accompany Sergeant Major Barlow this afternoon."

Spencer hesitated a moment before answering. He had noticed that Rachel appeared to be comfortable with Pohlman. "That might not be a bad idea. I don't think Barlow will have enough troopers with him to help handle that woman. Besides," Spencer smiled as he shook his friend's hand," you seem to have a talent for talking to such free-thinking ladies without inciting them."

Pohlman laughed. "Actually, she is probably more like your Sergeant Barlow than she realizes. I am curious to see how they get along this afternoon."

"Yes, that should be interesting." Spencer suspected that Pohlman was interested in the woman.

"One last thing, John: Will I be privy to your meeting tonight with Barlow? I presume you will plan how to deal with Connor tomorrow night."

The relationship between the two men had always been open and honest, primarily because of their mutual respect, but also because neither could ignore the fact that each of them had easy access to the President. Both men could wield some influence with Grant. So they realized that, in certain matters of common interest, it was to their advantage to cooperate.

"Perhaps, Ernst. But General Sherman is in town and I'd better ask him first. I'm about to send a messenger to his hotel to tell him what information the woman gave us, and my plans for tomorrow night. I'm sure he will want to see me immediately. I'll ask him about you, and I'll leave a message for you at your hotel."

"Fair enough. If I don't see you tonight, I of course will want to know the details of what transpires tomorrow night."

"I'm sure that General Sherman will agree to that, but you know that I must get his approval for that as well."

Pohlman nodded his understanding. "Good luck, John. I'm sure I will see you Sunday."

When Pohlman was gone, Spencer quickly drafted a message to Sherman, indicating only that he had an important witness regarding a security matter, which could be related to the incident at Pedlar Mills. He explained that he was relocating the witness to more secure quarters. He requested a meeting with Sherman as soon as possible.

"Corporal Samuelson!"

The young, tow-headed soldier almost immediately stepped into Spencer's office. "Yes, sir?"

"Deliver this confidential message immediately to General Sherman's hotel. Wait for a response."

Spencer knew that the corporal would put the message in Sherman's hands within twenty minutes. He also was certain that Sherman would want to meet with him as soon as he read the note, so he began trying to anticipate how events would develop and plan strategies.

If the woman's story is true, there was a good chance that Connor would be arrested tomorrow night. If Connor were behind the plot, then perhaps all immediate danger to the President would be averted.

The most complicated element was the possibility that Gould or Fisk, or both, were behind the plot. Spencer could not imagine that they were, but investigating two of the most powerful men in the nation would be a challenge in delicate diplomacy.

Spencer also was certain that Sherman would try once more to convince the President to cancel the Atlanta trip, which now was only about ten days away.

It was clear to Spencer that the best hope of protecting President Grant was to arrest Connor when he showed up at the Brockton home. If he failed, and if the Brockton woman was telling the truth, then the President might be in great danger. Pohlman thought that Connor was crazy, which might be true, considering the way Connor had killed that Negro. That would make Connor unpredictable, and very dangerous.

For the first time since being assigned responsibility for the life of the President of the United States, Spencer knew fear and doubt. He must find Connor. To lose him would mean that from the moment Grant stepped from the train in Atlanta, he could be the target of a bullet fired from hundreds of windows, doorways or rooftops. If he failed, Spencer knew it would be impossible to guarantee the President's safety.

Chapter 16

September 26, 1870
Brockton Mansion
Georgetown
7:35 p.m.

Henry Gilmore knew that snakes were more active at night, and it was almost dark. He hated them. And he feared them more than any other creature. So far he hadn't seen a snake and didn't even know if any were around. He feared them because an Eastern Diamondback had bitten his brother, and Gilmore didn't want to die that way.

Gilmore had been hiding in a weed-choked drainage ditch no more than fifty yards from the Georgetown mansion. He'd been well paid to watch the house. His orders were that if he saw the family moving out, he had to follow them, then report their new location to a contact at the Jefferson Hotel in Washington City. He didn't know the contact, or the man who hired him, but it was the easiest way to earn fifty dollars that he'd ever heard of.

Gilmore had spent most of the last three days watching the house from a small grove of trees. When he saw the two carriages and an ambulance arrive earlier in the afternoon, he left his horse in the grove and moved into the ditch. He was intrigued by the fact that the carriages and the ambulance were driven by soldiers, with an escort of six more on horseback.

For more than an hour he watched as the soldiers carried luggage and personal belongings and strapped them to the carriages.

"They're using the goddam Union army as house movers," Gilmore said under his breath. "I suppose that's something they can handle."

A New Yorker, Gilmore had been drafted during the closing months of the war because he had failed to raise the three hundred dollars he needed to pay someone to take his place. During training he'd been assigned to share a tent with a German who spoke very little English. Gilmore didn't like foreigners, especially the German who excelled at soldiering. What amazed and angered Gilmore was that the German seemed to like soldiering.

One night, when the two men were alone in the tent, Gilmore goaded the German into a fight, which Gilmore quickly discovered had been a serious mistake. Gilmore did not intend to kill him, but the German wasn't intimidated when Gilmore pointed his rifle at him. The gun went off when the German tried to bat it away.

Gilmore told investigators that the German had gone berserk. He said he tried to frighten the German with the gun, but it went off accidentally. The war ended before the investigation concluded, and the authorities dropped the murder charge. Gilmore was discharged as unfit for military service.

There was just enough light left for Gilmore to see two soldiers carry a stretcher from the house to the ambulance. Then he saw a black woman and young white boy get into one of the carriages. A few minutes later an expensively dressed white woman came out of the house, pausing on the porch to talk to a tall civilian. They were joined a moment later by a huge sergeant.

Although Gilmore couldn't hear the conversation, it appeared that the woman was upset about something. She seemed angry with the sergeant.

"Atta girl," Gilmore chuckled softly, "give that big bastard hell." Gilmore saw the sergeant nod, then walk to the edge of the porch and call for two men to dismount. The sergeant talked to the two men for a moment before they walked back to their horses, got their saddle bags and entered the house.

It was clear to Gilmore that the woman had demanded that the house be guarded while they were gone. That might be important information for his contact.

Gilmore remained in the ditch until they began to drive away. He knew that he could catch them on the road. Besides, if he waited until they were gone he wouldn't have to crawl back through the weeds and risk bumping head-on into a goddam snake.

Barlow didn't know how Colonel Spencer felt about it, but he was glad that Mr. Pohlman had come along, for whatever reason. Barlow cold tell when he met Mrs. Brockton in the colonel's office that she was upset about something, but he'd never met a woman who could be so demanding. His orders didn't provide for assigning guards for this house, but it was clear that the woman wouldn't leave if he didn't. He was certain the colonel would understand when he met him later tonight.

Barlow had eight miles to cover. He had been instructed to take Mrs. Brockton to the home of Major Gerald Millikin, a close friend of Colonel Spencer's, who now was on special assignment in London.

Millikin, the bachelor son of the wealthy U.S. Senator from Delaware, had often urged Spencer to use the house, a large, fashionably redecorated farmhouse on the outskirts of Washington. The house was more often vacant than occupied because of the many foreign assignments the young major received, most of which were arranged by his influential father.

Barlow had sent one trooper out about a quarter-mile ahead of the column. He told the other men to stay close to the carriages and ambulance, and he dropped back several hundred yards to watch the road behind them. Barlow walked his horse behind a giant oak and waited, listening for any sound. He waited five minutes, trotted a few hundred yards in the direction of the column, then pulled off the road to listen for another five minutes or so.

Barlow had moved twice when he'd heard the rider approaching. Although it was very dark now, Barlow could tell that the horse was moving at an easy trot. When the rider passed, the sergeant pulled onto the road, staying just close enough to see the other man. Stopping a man on a lonely road at night involved considerable risk, so Barlow wanted to make sure that the rider wasn't just a local resident coming home late.

When the rider got close enough to the column to see it, he reined to a halt and watched. Barlow still wasn't convinced the man was trouble. In these times, the rider was exercising good judgment in not riding up abruptly to a column of men moving in darkness. Still, Barlow opened the flap of his holster to have the LeMat ready.

The rider nudged his horse to a walk, keeping the column just in sight. He stayed near the edge of the road where the shadow cast by the quarter moon was deepest, which is where Barlow followed.

Barlow watched the man for almost a mile, working his way to within about forty yards of him. That's when he decided it was time to talk.

"You, there! Halt and identify yourself!" Barlow's deep voice boomed in the still night air, carrying all the way to the column.

"Who the hell wants to know?" Gilmore reached into his saddlebag for his Navy Colt, and spun his horse to head off the road cross-country.

"I am Sergeant Barlow, United States Army. I ordered you to halt—halt or I'll fire!" Barlow didn't draw the LeMat. In fact, he didn't want to shoot unless forced to. He was moving up at a gallop and wanted both hands free until the last second.

He cocked the Colt, twisted in the saddle and fired two shots.

Barlow was close enough to see that the man was going to fire. He leaned forward against his horse's neck, closing one eye to save his night vision after the muzzle flash. Barlow felt a sharp burst of heat on the right side of his face. He wasn't aware of it yet, but the first bullet had neatly clipped off his right earlobe.

Barlow spurred his Appaloosa and forced it to swerve into the side of Gilmore's animal. The two horses thundered through the underbrush just off the road, with Gilmore's horse to the left and slightly ahead of Barlow's.

Gilmore tried to point the Navy Colt, but Barlow was too close. The sergeant reached out and grabbed the weapon away and flung it into the darkness. Barlow then twisted in his saddle to reach across with his right hand to grab the back of Gilmore's coat collar. With a powerful sweep of his arm, Barlow yanked Gilmore out of his saddle. For a few seconds,

Barlow held Gilmore suspended, like a rag doll bouncing against the side of the Appaloosa, the man's boots dragging through the underbrush.

Then Barlow heaved Gilmore across the neck of his horse until the man lay balanced like a turtle on its back. As Barlow reined in his horse, Gilmore was screaming in pain as his back was pounded by the front of the saddle.

"Why damn you, you're gonna break my back," Gilmore whined. "Lemme up…lemme up, goddam your miserable hide."

Barlow balanced Gilmore by pressing his left hand against Gilmore's chest, letting the man's lower body weight act as a counterbalance.

As the Appaloosa to made its way carefully back to the road, Barlow noticed that several lanterns were lighted. When the big sergeant rode into the circle of light, one of the young troopers asked, "Did you shoot him, Sergeant Major?"

Barlow noticed that Ernst Pohlman and Mrs. Brockton had stepped down from their carriage. The woman walked up close to Barlow's horse. "Is it necessary for you to torture the man that way, sergeant?"

Gilmore turned his head and recognized the woman as the one who had been arguing with the sergeant on her front porch. "He's a killer, lady." Gilmore's voice was high-pitched, strained more by fear than discomfort. "And he's crazier than hell. I was just ridin' along when he attacked me and all I was doing was—"

Barlow shoved down hard with his left hand against Gilmore's chest. Gilmore screamed as he fell head first onto the road. He moaned softly, then lay quietly.

"You!" Barlow pointed to one of the troopers. "Ride out there and find his horse, then tie him to it. Mrs. Brockton, I suggest that you get back in your carriage, ma'am, so that we can move on."

One of the troopers held his lantern up high to look closely at Barlow. "Sergeant Major, there's blood all over your right shoulder and on the side of your neck. Were you hit?"

Barlow looked down, then removed his glove to feel his right ear. He was surprised to discover that part of his ear was gone. Mrs. Brockton stepped closer. "The surgeon is in the ambulance. Have him dress that wound, sergeant."

"I will, ma'am, in due time. But right now I want this column moving. Put those lanterns out. There may be more bushwhackers out there."

Barlow wheeled his horse around and trotted up to the ambulance. The surgeon, an experienced army doctor, suspected that he might be needed when he heard the shots.

"Just give me something to sop up this blood, doc. I've already ruined a good blouse." Barlow grabbed a handful of bandages and turned toward the rear of the column. He pointed to another one of his men. "You stay here with the prisoner until that trooper comes back with his horse. I want both of you to guard him. The rest of you get moving—do it now!"

Barlow waited until he was sure the carriages were under way, then he turned back down the road. He walked the horse for what he thought was about fifty yards, pulled off the road near a tree and listened. He tried to read his watch in the dim light, but couldn't.

Off in the distance, toward the column, he could hear the trooper leading Gilmore's horse back. Barlow felt the warm blood trickling down the side of his neck. He reached up and tenderly touched his ear, then dabbed at it with the bandages. He could feel the pain now. Barlow thought of trying to bandage the wound, but didn't know how to do it without looking foolish.

Barlow chuckled. "Well, I've always been ugly as a goat, so I don't suppose losing a piece of ear is gonna make much difference." He estimated five minutes had passed, so he moved another fifty yards closer to the column to pause and listen.

Barlow noticed that his horse had settled down and was breathing evenly again. He'd had the animal for about eight years and hated to run him hard. An Appaloosa with a spotted rump was an unusual cavalry mount, especially this one. It had a nervous tick that caused the hide on its rump to ripple in spasms, prompting one old gunnery sergeant to comment: "Gideon, that ole' horse looks like it's fixin' to jump right out of its skin."

Barlow reached out and patted the animal's neck. "Jitters, old friend, we may be getting a little long in the tooth for this kind of thing. Yes, sir, it looks like it's gonna be a long night for both of us."

September 26, 1870
The White House
9 p.m.

In all of their years together, General Sherman had rarely lost his temper with the man he most admired. His temper had not only flared, but Sherman had called Grant a fool—perhaps not in so many words. But close enough, and Sherman felt the regret of it in the pit of his stomach.

The White House sitting room was quiet, neither man quite sure of what to say. Finally, Sherman broke the silence.

"Damn it to hell, Sam," his voice soft and conciliatory now, "maybe I am being too cautious. But you can't deny that there may be something to the woman's story. It's just too risky to go to Atlanta."

"Are you going to talk to her tomorrow?"

"Yes. Spencer is having Barlow take her to a farm east of the city, one that Senator Millikin bought for that spoiled kid of his." Sherman looked at his watch. It was nearly nine o'clock. "He ought to be there within the hour."

"What do we know about this Hollis Connor?"

"Right now, not nearly enough to suit me. But it's clear, at least to me, that he was behind the two who tried to kill Spencer. We also know that he's a killer, based on what Spencer told me earlier. It seems to me that Connor killed the Brockton woman's servant just to scare hell out of her."

Grant rested his cigar in the ashtray and vigorously rubbed his eyes. Sherman thought he looked tired, too tired to argue about something so complicated that clear decisions seemed impossible.

"How about Gould or Fisk—are they involved?"

"I seriously doubt it, Sam, for a couple of reasons. Although it appears that Connor did some work for them—probably for Fisk—I doubt that they would try to fool with the gold market again. But I'm not taking any chances. After I talk to the Brockton woman, I'm going to New York and talk to them myself."

"Now, Cump, you're certainly not going to come right out and ask them if they are involved?"

"Why, hell no, Sam, I'm not going to do that. I'm just going to ask them a lot of questions about Connor, without telling them why I want to know—except maybe to tell them that Connor is wanted for questioning in a matter of national security. I figure that if by some chance they are involved, they'll call it off if they see we're on to something. Hell, those two probably have better contacts and more resources than we do. If they're not involved, they can probably find Connor for us quicker than we can."

"And what about Stoval? How is he involved?"

"Sam, I regret having to say this—again—but I don't understand why you keep that fool to head up Treasury. No, I can't imagine he's involved. It's just that Connor must know that old Stoval acts like a stud bull around pretty young women. But I'd guess that some of those young ladies would tell us that the old fool does more pawing and snorting than charging."

Grant chuckled and reached for his brandy snifter, cupped the glass in his hand and gently swirled the amber fluid. He looked at his friend and smiled.

"Cump, I hope the issue of my going to Atlanta is resolved. I am going. If you are concerned about Connor, then you handle him. But I am going—I must—if for no other reason than, as President, I can't be prevented from moving about this country because of threats from a man like Connor. And please consider these two requests: I believe it would be a mistake for you to accompany me to Atlanta—for obvious reasons—nor would it be wise for you to send down a whole division of troops to protect me."

Sherman stopped his pacing. He slumped into an easy chair opposite Grant, drumming his fingers nervously on the armrest.

"Mr. President," Sherman said with mock formality, "you are the most stubborn cuss it's ever been my misfortune to come up against. You're a hard man, Sam Grant, but if that's the way you want it, so it shall be. Now, would you at least consider asking your man Babcock to refill these brandy glasses?"

Nearly four hours later, Sherman was standing on the front porch of the Millikin farm house, less than three miles due east of the White House. He stood at the railing, smoking a small cigar, looking out at the rolling countryside that now was nearly invisible because of the clouds that masked the quarter-moon. Spencer and Barlow stood behind him. They knew the general was agitated because of how rapidly he puffed on the cigar, the red glow blinking like a signal lamp.

Sherman turned to face them. The hat, dark blue great coat and the beard blended with the darkness. But they could see the eyes, which always radiated energy.

"What do we know about him?"

"Very little, sir." Spencer held his note pad in front of him, even though he couldn't see it. "His name is Henry Gilmore, and he lives in a rooming house on Eighth Street in the city. We found that out from papers he was carrying. He's not able to talk very well, but even if he could I suspect he's the kind of hired hand who wouldn't be able to tell us anything."

"You've sent some people to search his room?"

"Yes, sir. Three of my men are there now and should be back before sunup."

Barlow clearly was miserable. Gilmore couldn't talk because he'd suffered a concussion when his head had hit the road. The surgeon had treated Gilmore, but he said the man probably wouldn't be able to talk for a day or more. The sergeant also was upset because he had to meet his commanding officer and General Sherman while wearing a blood-caked uniform. The surgeon had dressed Barlow's wound, and the sergeant didn't like the huge bandage that covered the side of his head.

Barlow had sent a man ahead to alert Spencer and to ask him to come to the farm house. Spencer then contacted Sherman. Barlow had sent another trooper to his quarters to bring him some clean clothes, but events had moved so quickly that he didn't have an opportunity to change.

"General Sherman, sir," Barlow said. "I realize that I shouldn't have dropped Gilmore on his head like that, sir. I guess I just lost my temper."

Sherman removed his cigar, examined the glowing tip, then hurled it in a long fiery arc that ended in a splash of sparks.

"Sergeant Major, if the bastard had fired at me, I would have blown him out of his saddle. Don't concern yourself over it. You did a good job tonight, a damned good job. What concerns me, gentlemen, is that we may have lost an opportunity to get Connor. I'm sure that Gilmore was to report to Connor if the woman left the house. Who knows how long he'd been watching the place? I'm also sure that he was told to report in each day. Since Connor won't be hearing from him today, my guess is that Connor won't call on the woman to take her to that party."

"I'm sure you're right, general. But I still think Sergeant Barlow and I should stay at the house tomorrow night—I guess I mean tonight—just in case."

"Yes, I suppose so. We might get lucky. We're certainly due for some good luck."

"If you agree, general, I'll keep Gilmore here under guard until he's able to talk."

Sherman started for his horse, the reins held by a young trooper. Although they couldn't be seen, four other soldiers were holding their mounts behind Sherman's

"Yes, do that, colonel. This damn place has enough rooms to house a regiment. What happened to that journalist, Pohlman?"

"He went back to the city, sir, but he knows about Gilmore."

"He knows too damn much, if you ask me. But I suppose if we can't trust him we can't trust any of them. What about the woman?"

"Well, sir, she gave the sergeant major here a bad time, but I think she can be a lot of help to us."

Spencer and Barlow walked with Sherman to his horse. He took the reins from the trooper, pausing before he mounted.

"How do you have your men deployed, colonel?"

"I have two men inside with the prisoner, sir. There also is one man on the front porch and one on the back porch. There are two men just into the woods on the left, there, and four men in the barn, which is off to the right. The surgeon will be staying to care for Gilmore. Sergeant Major Barlow will be in command when I return to the White House in a few hours."

"Very good. Sergeant Major, if for some reason you can't contact the colonel, don't hesitate to contact me when Gilmore regains consciousness.

Sherman climbed into the saddle. "I received a message today from General Forrest. He discovered that Hollis Connor was recently named the grand wizard of the Georgia Klan. He got the job, according to Forrest, because he is a wild man. Most importantly, Forrest said Connor would be in Atlanta in early October."

"Did he say why, sir—I mean, any indication that Connor knows about the President's visit?"

"No, if we can believe that Forrest would tell us if he knew. I still don't completely trust the man.

Sherman started to leave than paused. "And one more thing, Sergeant Major."

"Yes, sir?"

"Over brandy at some mutually convenient time, I would like for you to explain the technique one uses to drop a two-hundred pound man on his head from horseback."

Spencer and Barlow could hear the general chuckle as he climbed easily into the saddle.

"Gentleman." There was no humor now in Sherman's voice. "The President refuses to reconsider making the trip. I want Connor, colonel—I want him very much. The man is a threat to the President and the nation. Sergeant Major, if you get your hands on him, you will consider it your duty to pound his head to butter."

Spencer and Barlow stood in the yard for several moments after Sherman and his escort had left.

"Sergeant Major, it must be nearly two o'clock. Do you suppose we can find some coffee in that kitchen?"

"I'll be there in a moment, sir. I'd like to check the men first."

Chapter 17

Maremont Hotel
Washington City
October 2, 1870
6:20 p.m.

Hollis Connor hurled the half-filled whiskey bottle with such force that it gouged a hole in the plaster wall of his hotel room.

"God*damn* the incompetent bastard! He must have been caught, and I won't tolerate that kind of carelessness. What kind of half-brained idiots do you hire?"

"Now, Hollis. You really must get control of your temper." Charles Wells said the words more as a plea than a statement. "We can't be certain Gilmore has been caught."

"Then why the hell hasn't he reported in?" Gilmore's question was a shout.

Wells didn't answer. He realized that his only real value to Connor were the contacts he had in England and France, influential contacts he had made during his days as a blockade runner for the Confederacy. Wells' English friends would be helpful when he and Connor had to leave the U.S. with the fortune they expected to make. Even so, Wells felt that he walked a fine line with Hollis, a man whose temper often distorted his judgment.

Connor, his face flushed by the whiskey and his anger, paced the small room. He paused in front of Wells, who was seated in a straight-back chair at a small desk. "If we don't hear from this man of yours by morning, then we'll have to forget about going to see the woman."

"But, Hollis, what hold will we have over Stoval without the woman? Do we have time to find someone else?"

Connor glared at Wells, then resumed his pacing. After a few moments Connor paused, looked back at Wells and smiled, then walked to his bed. He leaned back against the headboard, his hands clasped behind his head. It was clear to Wells that Connor was pleased with whatever thought had entered his head.

"Tell me, Wells. Did you ever sail any of your ships that ran the blockade during the war?"

"Why, no. Of course not." Wells could feel his discomfort growing, his shirt becoming damp under his arms and at the small of his back. "I hired people to do that. I owned the ships and bought and sold the cargoes."

Connor, still smiling, closed his eyes. "I thought as much. You are not a brave and courageous man, my friend. But we both know that. Yet, you are always ready to reap the benefits generated by those with a backbone." Connor swung his feet to the floor, resting his elbows on his knees, staring intently at Wells, the smile gone.

"But the gravy train is over. Very soon you will finally have an opportunity to be brave. I will accompany you to Stoval's home. You will demand to see Stoval on the pretext that you have an urgent message for him. When he enters the foyer, you will calmly, and with great courage, put a bullet into his brain. I want you to kill him the way I killed that nigger."

Wells was stunned. He had to fight the urge to bolt from the room. "You can't be serious, Hollis. I mean...my God, it's one thing to shoot a Negro servant...but the Secretary of the Treasury..." Wells was conscious that his voice was quavering. "Besides, I don't understand why you want to kill him now."

"Because we're running out of time. It appears that we've lost the woman. In fact, we must face the possibility that she may work up the courage to tell what she knows to the authorities, who in turn will warn Stoval. But Stoval will be expecting to be blackmailed, not shot."

"But Hollis, why murder? Why must he be killed? There is already been too much killing. And what about Fisk and Gould? They wanted us to blackmail Stoval with the woman. You know they would never agree to our killing him."

Wells' words were coming in a torrent now. "And I think you are naive to think that they—Gould and Fisk—won't find out that we are responsible for the plot against Grant."

It suddenly was becoming very clear to Wells that Gilmore was mad. For some reason he couldn't explain, Wells was amazed to find that the realization diminished his fear of Connor. Wells wanted out. And he wanted out now.

Connor paused and leaned against the wall opposite Wells. "Yes, Fisk and Gould wanted us to put Stoval in their pocket, and they no doubt would object to our killing him."

Connor's words now were measured, his manner almost polite. "They certainly would object to what we plan for Grant, if only because they are certain that they can make a great deal of money as long as he is President. Grant doesn't understand how the loyalty of those around him can be manipulated by the power of the dollar. But don't you see, Wells, that our objectives are really the same? Fisk and Gould want to control the gold market for two reasons: one, it worked so well the last time and, two, no one would suspect they would try it again. The technique for achieving that objective is where we differ with Gould and Fisk."

"Do you intend to tell them in advance what you're going to do?"

"No. I'm not a fool. I will advise them when the gold market will react. And I'll tell them that the plan to use the woman worked well."

"You realize, Hollis, that you may be putting them in a dangerous position if they take advantage of a market reacting to the deaths of the President of the United States and the Secretary of the Treasury. It will appear that Gould and Fisk knew about it in advance."

"No necessarily. They are too smart not to cover themselves. Besides, there will be so much confusion that no one would have reason to watch them. I've already told Fisk when the market will drop significantly. He and Gould may choose to either dispose of their gold holdings now while the price is up and then buy back when the price bottoms out. Or they may decide to bet on the price dropping. Whatever option they choose, rest assured that very few people in the country would be able to follow their transactions."

Connor pulled his chair opposite Wells and sat leaning forward. "Look, Charles. We're doing essentially what they asked us to do. You're right, they would not agree with our methods. But their rewards—and ours—will be incredibly huge. Think of it, man, there will be complete chaos, the market will disintegrate. With Grant and Stoval gone, the market will be at our mercy.

"And just as important, I will have revenge for the war and Reconstruction. Yes, that will be sweet, indeed."

Wells could smell the whiskey on Connor, who now was animated, his eyes bright and flashing. Wells now had to figure out how he could distance himself from this man and the plot. It still was not too late. But how could he do it safely?

Wells knew that if Connor could read his thoughts at this moment he would instantly kill him. He would have to wait for an opportunity. Connor certainly couldn't be with him every moment. A free moment is all Wells needed. Perhaps if he warned the authorities he would not have to face charges for his involvement to this point. Wells was certain of one thing. He would not kill Stoval.

"Hollis, you are correct, as always." Wells nodded his head vigorously, as if he had suddenly seen the error of his thinking. "Except, of course, about my shooting Stoval. As you said, I am not a brave man. I freely admit that. If I botch the job, the entire plan will be in jeopardy." It was Wells' turn to stand and pace the small room. "What we need is a professional."

Wells stopped his pacing and paused in front of Connor, his arms outstretched as if what he was about to say was the only possible conclusion. "Since I have already disappointed you with the man I hired to watch Rachel's home, I am sure you would prefer to find someone to handle the job. And there is another very important consideration. Stoval should die at about the same time as Grant does, in order to maximize the shock effect. You and I, Hollis, should concentrate on Atlanta and leave someone else here to handle Stoval."

"Well, well, Charles." Connor nodded his head slowly, smiling slightly. "Yes, that makes sense. In two days you and I should be leaving for Atlanta. I think I know just the man to do the job, one who we can be confident will be on the first boat to Europe when Stoval's taken care of. He's here in Washington. Get your coat and we'll go over and see him."

Wells hoped that his relief wasn't apparent to Connor.

October 3, 1870
Millikin Farm
Washington City

"I ain't got nothin' more to say to you, and keep that crazy sonofabitch away from me." Henry Gilmore was sitting up in bed, his head wrapped in bandages that nearly covered one eye. His good eye riveted on Sergeant Major Barlow who was standing at the door with his heavy arms crossed.

Major Malcolm Niblick, U.S. Army surgeon, and Colonel Spencer were standing at the foot of the bed. Rachel Brockton was slightly behind Spencer.

"No, I can not recall ever having seen him before," Rachel said.

"Doctor," Spencer asked, "how would you describe his condition?"

"Well, Colonel," Dr. Niblick said, pausing while he shifted the huge chaw that had permanently distorted his right cheek, "I think he's recovered. But you have to understand that it's hard to be certain with head wounds. He landed on his forehead and his left eye is badly bruised. He's complaining of a ringing in his ears and a headache. But all that should clear up in a couple of days."

Spencer nodded. "Thank you for your help, doctor."

Dr. Niblick had a reputation with high command as a very competent physician. Equally important, he was a man who could keep his mouth shut. He snapped the latches closed on his medical bag and quietly left the room.

"Sergeant, did you make another check of his clothes and saddle bags?" Spencer asked.

"Yes, sir. Nothing."

Spencer also had the report of the men who had searched Gilmore's room in the city. They had returned with some papers, but nothing that would implicate the man in any kind of a plot.

"Once again, Mr. Gilmore," Spencer said as he moved to the side of the bed, "tell us what you were doing late at night in the Georgetown area."

"Dammit, I've told you and I've told you," Gilmore said, flaying his arms in frustration against the mattress. "I'm wantin' to buy a small farm. I'd been out there most of the day just lookin' around to see if that's where I want to buy. I saw you people on the road and, times bein' what they are, I sure as hell wasn't goin' to ride up and say howdy without knowin' who you were."

"What were you afraid of?" Spencer asked. "Even in the dark you should have been able to tell that it was a military unit."

"What was I afraid of?" Gilmore's voice was almost a screech. "What was I *afraid* of, you ask? I didn't want someone to do me like that big dumb bastard standin' over there did. That's what I was afraid of and that's what the hell happened."

"Do you know a man named Hollis Connor?"

"Hell, no, I don't know anybody by the name."

"Colonel Spencer, sir."

Spencer turned to look at Barlow. "Yes, Sergeant Major?"

"If the colonel and Mrs. Brockton would care to leave the room, I'm sure it wouldn't take very long to convince Mr. Gilmore that his language is not appropriate for a lady to hear."

Spencer looked back at Gilmore. Gilmore's good eye shifted from Rachel to Barlow. Spencer was reasonably certain that Barlow wasn't serious, but he wanted Gilmore to think that he was considering the request.

"Now look here, colonel, you know that I don't mean no disrespect to the lady there, I just—"

"I will consider your request, Sergeant Major. But for now, I think we should meet with our other guest.'

"Hey, wait a minute," Gilmore called as the three left the room, "what the hell...what's gonna happen to me? How long you gonna keep me here? Hey! I got my rights! Hey! Someone answer me!"

Barlow stationed a trooper at the door to Gilmore's bedroom, then followed Spencer and Rachel into the living room.

"Well, do we know any more today than we did last night?" General Sherman asked as he rose from his chair when they entered the room.

"No, sir, I'm afraid not. I don't believe his story, but Sergeant Barlow and I are certain that he was hired by Connor to watch Mrs. Brockton's home."

Rachel asked, "General, what if the man is telling the truth? I appreciate that the man may represent a hazard to my family, but to hold him like this just doesn't seem right."

"Whether or not he's telling the truth, Mrs. Brockton," Sherman said, "he ignored a military order to halt, tried to escape, then fired at and wounded a U.S. soldier. To protect his own life, Sergeant Barlow would have been justified in killing Gilmore. Frankly, I can hold him until hell freezes over."

The room was quiet for a moment. Sherman started to light his cigar, then glanced at Rachel and thought better of it. He realized that he'd sounded a little gruff, but he felt moody and irritable, probably because he didn't get enough sleep.

"Mrs. Brockton," Sherman said more pleasantly, "I appreciate your concern for this man. But I am sure that you understand that even if we only suspect Gilmore's involvement, we cannot afford to release him. Too much is at stake."

Rachel moved over to an easy chair. The rustle of the fabric of her dress and petticoats as she sat on the edge of the chair seemed inordinately loud in the huge living room. Rachel looked up to see all three men staring at her. "Yes, general," she said. "I suppose you are correct. It is just that there has been so much violence and hate. And it seems that it will never end."

Rachel's eyes began to fill with tears. Spencer noticed that when Rachel lowered her head, several tears tell onto the bodice of her dress, leaving small dark spots on the tan fabric.

The room was very quiet for a long moment, each man moved by Rachel's fear and frustration. Spencer started to move toward her when he was startled by Barlow's deep voice.

"General Sherman, sir. One of my troopers discovered that the Millikin larder is generously stocked. He's preparing a beef broth and ham sandwiches."

Barlow stepped close to Rachel's chair and stood towering over the woman. "Mrs. Brockton, there is a gazebo in the garden behind the house, and it is surrounded by fall flowers. You may find this hard to believe, ma'am, but I long ago discovered that flowers help me...well, I don't know exactly how to explain it, but they just make me feel better. My dear mother, bless her sweet soul, surrounded our little cottage with them." Barlow extended his hand. "I would be honored if you would permit me to escort you to the gazebo, where we can have lunch served."

Rachel looked up at Barlow, for the first time noticing that, despite his intimidating appearance and demeanor, the man's eyes were dark and warm. She looked at Spencer and Sherman, then at Barlow's huge, beefy outstretched hand. Rachel didn't respond immediately. She reached into her bag for a handkerchief, slowly dabbing at her eyes and nose.

Rachel took a deep breath, tentatively placed her hand on Barlow's, then stood, looking intently for a moment into his eyes. Then she smiled, gripping Barlow's hand more firmly. "You are correct, sir. I do indeed find it difficult to believe that a Union cavalry sergeant major could be moved by the sight and fragrance of something so delicate as a fall flower."

Spencer could not remember seeing Barlow smile so broadly, his huge even teeth contrasting sharply with his dark beard.

"Madam," Barlow said with grave formality as he very deliberately placed Rachel's hand on his left arm and started for the door, "you also will, no doubt, be surprised to learn that when I was a boy, my mother—a tiny, lovely thing she was—feared that the world would treat me cruelly because she said my heart was so tender."

Rachel laughed at the mental image of Barlow cuddled at his mother's breast. She could not imagine him as small, even as a child.

Barlow paused at the door to look back at Sherman and Spencer. "If we may be excused, sirs. I will send someone for you to join Mrs. Brockton and me when lunch is served." Barlow started through the doorway, then paused again. "Ah…as officers and gentlemen, with all due respect, I trust that nothing I've said in this room will be repeated to the men."

Sherman laughed. "Rest easy, Sergeant Major. Your secrets are safe with me, only because none of your men would believe me if I told them."

Later, after lunch, when Sherman and Barlow had gone back into the house, Spencer remained in the gazebo with Rachel. She obviously had come to enjoy the company of the three men, especially Barlow. It was the first time that Spencer had heard her laugh.

"John, your sergeant major is a very interesting man."

"He is indeed, but I have to admit that I've seen a side of him today that I've never seen before."

"Well, it was apparent to me that he was trying very hard to put me at ease, despite the fact that I have given him very little reason to be kind to me. I will always remember his kindness."

Rachel pushed back her chair and she and Spencer stood. It was obvious that neither wanted to go back into the house.

"John, I am…I apologize for any remarks I made that were critical of you or the sergeant major." Rachel walked to the rear of the gazebo where an archway overlooked the heavy woods behind the farm house.

Spencer followed and they stood together for a long moment. He recognized that apologies were very difficult for Rachel.

"I really do understand," she continued, "that you and the others are trying to help me, and I also appreciate that my problems are only a part of a much larger responsibility that you have for the President. I just want you to know that I will cooperate however I can."

Spencer recalled Rachel's flash of fury when she was in his office. Now she seemed warm and considerate. He was surprised that she seemed vulnerable, less confident of herself. Yes, this woman was nothing if not unpredictable.

"Well, you've been through a lot, and I'm certain that I could have been more understanding. And, yes, we are very concerned about the President's safety, but I want to assure you that we also will make every effort to protect you and your family."

"Do you think that you can stop this Hollis Connor?"

"What makes Connor especially dangerous, Rachel, is that he is very determined, despite the fact that parts of his plan apparently have failed. But to answer your question, I just don't know if we can stop him before he makes an attempt on the President's life."

Rachel turned to lean against the railing, facing Spencer. "Why have you remained in the army, John?"

Spencer was surprised by the question. "Why do you ask?"

"Well, you are well educated and you are accustomed to handling great responsibilities. I also have noticed that the people around you, including General Sherman, obviously respect your abilities. Ernst Pohlman has told me quite a bit about you, so I can't help but wonder why you haven't considered the many opportunities available in the business world for someone with your capabilities."

Spencer smiled. Rachel was standing close enough that he could detect the fragrance of her perfume. He felt that he was being enveloped by her large, gray-green eyes. "Yes, I've seriously considered leaving the army. But if I do, I doubt that I would become involved in the business world. Too many of the businessmen I've met seem so driven to make money that they lose sight of what I feel are more important values."

Rachel looked closely at Spencer for a moment to see if she could tell whether he was in any way referring to her. "If you left the army, where would you go...what does interest you?"

"The West, I think. I've seen the mountains of Colorado and Wyoming and, well, I would like to spend some time out there."

"The West? Whatever in the world would you do in an area that is still so...so primitive?"

Spencer laughed, embarrassed about discussing, especially with Rachel, what had been only random thoughts that he'd never really developed into a plan. "I recently had the opportunity to spend some time with General Lee at his college in Lexington. It occurred to me while I was there that...I don't know...I guess I would like to teach at one of the new colleges in the West."

Rachel smiled, her eyes locking with his. "Colonel Spencer, from this moment on, my objective will be to convince you that your future lies here, in Washington—or perhaps New York." She held his eyes with hers. "And I should warn you that—like a good soldier—I rarely fail to reach an objective."

Chapter 18

October 4, 1870
Madison Hotel
New York City

There were eight circular tables in the private dining room. Each table was elegantly set with the fine china, silver and linen that the Madison's elite clientele expected. At one end of the room the chef and head usher spoke in low tones. At the far end of the room, General Sherman and Colonel Spencer sat at one of the tables. Each had been served a glass of the house's finest Portuguese red wine.

"When I can avoid it, colonel, I never like to meet a man on his own ground. But I have been known to accept neutral ground as a compromise."

Sherman and Spencer had carefully planned during the train ride from Washington how they would conduct the interview.

Spencer saw the head usher scurry to the entrance as two men paused at the doorway. The usher bowed with a flourish, then gestured toward Sherman and Spencer as he led the way to their table.

"Remember, we must make them believe that we know more than we do," Sherman whispered. "Let's see just how tough these birds are." Both men rose as their guests approached.

"Mr. Gould, I appreciate that you agreed to take the time to meet with us," Sherman said, shaking Gould's hand. "This is Colonel John Spencer."

Gould's response was barely audible. He hardly glanced at Spencer when he shook his hand, immediately returning his attention to Sherman.

"I must say, general, that your invitation came as a surprise…a pleasant one, I might add. Permit me to introduce Jim Fisk, my business partner."

Spencer was surprised that Gould was so young, perhaps no more than thirty, despite the receding hairline. He was also surprised that the man was so small. Not just short, but fine-boned, almost fragile. Perhaps that's why the man's full beard seemed much too large for his face. Hardly the image he had of the legend of Wall Street. Maybe the man wasn't all that small. Perhaps it was just that his size didn't match his reputation. Spencer was sure of one thing. He'd never seen a man with colder eyes.

As for Fisk, the man the press called Jubilee Jim, Spencer immediately decided that he didn't like him. The man was round, almost lumpy, with eyes that could be described as sinister. Fisk's clothes were expensive and finely tailored, but they didn't give him the edge for which he obviously was hoping.

"Please be seated, gentlemen," Sherman said. "The waiter looks very eager to serve us and in New York that is an exceedingly rare opportunity."

Spencer was not surprised that neither man even smiled.

The usher poured wine for Gould. When he tipped the bottle toward Fisk's glass, Fisk pushed the dark green bottle away, causing the usher to dribble some wine on the white tablecloth. "None of that for me," he said brusquely. "If you know me you know that I drink only brandy. Bring me a bottle of your best."

It was difficult for Spencer to tell whether the usher was more upset over having stained the tablecloth or Fisk's bad manners. The usher backed away from the table, bowing slightly.

"Well, General Sherman," Gould said in his characteristic stage whisper. "To what do we owe the honor of this dinner meeting?"

"We need your help, gentlemen, regarding a matter of national security," Sherman said evenly. "We have reason to believe that you can help us find two men we would like to talk to."

"General," Fisk said, smiling, "we know lots of people. What makes you think we know anyone who would have something to do with national security, whatever that means?"

Sherman didn't answer immediately. He reached out to touch his wine glass, slowly stroking its stem. Only Spencer knew that the general was struggling to control his temper.

"Let me begin to answer that question, Mr. Fisk, by telling you about Colonel Spencer's assignment. He is chief of White House security. His principal responsibility is to ensure the protection and well-being of the President of the United States. The colonel and I are conducting an investigation into a matter that we have reason to believe poses a threat to the President, and perhaps other high officials of the federal government." Sherman paused for a moment. "Let me say at this point, gentlemen, that you should consider every detail of this conversation as highly confidential. In other words, I don't want to read about it in some newspaper."

The usher placed Fisk's bottle of brandy on the table. Fisk carefully poured the dark fluid into a snifter. He held the glass with both hands, rotating it slowly, then smiled.

"General Sherman, you flatter us to think that we can help you. After all, we're just businessmen."

"I am well aware of your reputation, Mr. Fisk, which is why I have asked for this meeting."

Gould told Fisk earlier that he had heard of the general's quick temper. Any kind of confrontation with Sherman, he said, could be dangerous.

"Of course, general," Gould said, "we will help however we can."

Sherman turned slightly toward Spencer. "Colonel?"

Spencer pulled a small notebook from an inside pocket, very deliberately turning a half-dozen pages, then began. "Gentlemen, do either of you know Hollis Connor or Charles Wells?"

Spencer noticed that Fisk's eyes shifted immediately toward Gould.

"Well, yes," Gould said. "We have had business dealings with both of those men. They are what I call fringe people. They have the desire and motivation to make a great deal of money, but they often lack the skill or the intelligence to do so."

"Are you aware, sir, that Connor is the Klan leader in Georgia?"

Spencer thought Gould's surprise seemed genuine.

"I can assure you that if I would have had that information, I would have nothing to do with the man."

"Have you been in contact with them recently," Spencer asked, "say, within the last few weeks?"

"No," Gould answered immediately. "As I indicated, people like that come and go."

"Have either of you ever met or had any business dealings with Mrs. Rachel Brockton, who currently has a home in the Georgetown area?"

"I vaguely recall a meeting with her at a party some time ago," Gould said. "She is a lovely woman who, as I recall, has done very well on Wall Street. But if we have had any business dealings with her, they must have been handled indirectly through one of our associates. You must understand, colonel, that the nature and scope of our business activities involve many people who we never meet."

"Could one of these associates be Roger Brewster who is—or was—president of a major bank in this city? And is there a possibility that you personally, Mr. Gould, gave specific instructions to Mr. Brewster regarding the handling of investments by Mrs. Brockton?"

It now was evident to Spencer that both men were not nearly as self-assured as when they came into the restaurant. He also noticed that Fisk did not even try to answer any of the questions.

"Yes, we know Brewster. He handles many of our transactions. But I am concerned about the way you posed your question, colonel. Are you telling us that Brewster no longer heads his family's bank?"

"The general and I stopped at the bank earlier today, Mr. Gould, and we have had discussions with the police. He is missing, and our concern is that he was the victim of foul play. He is key to our investigation."

Spencer, still holding his notebook, paused for a long moment. "I have one more question. Mr. Gould, do you know a Henry Gilmore?"

"I do not recognize that name." Gould turned to Fisk. "Jim?" Fisk shook his head.

"Colonel," Gould leaned closer to Spencer, conscious of the effect his eyes and low voice had on most people, "certainly you can imagine how Mr. Fisk and I feel about being asked these questions without some clear indication of why you suspect we have some link with these men. As I said earlier, we are happy to cooperate, but I object to being made to feel like a common criminal."

Spencer locked eyes with Gould, willing himself to not even blink.

"Mr. Gould, I am confident that I have intimated nothing that should make you feel like a criminal. But I can tell you this: the Pinkerton people are searching for Connor and Wells. When they are found, they will be charged with murder, among other charges. Pinkerton detectives are investigating—at our request—the disappearance of Mr. Brewster. We have reason to believe that he intended to flee to England, but we also suspect that he might have been murdered before he could leave the country."

Spencer paused for another long moment. "Henry Gilmore, whom I referred to earlier, is in custody and faces charges of shooting and wounding one of my non-commissioned officers."

Sherman spoke next. "All of the names we have mentioned have been linked, in one way or another, with Hollis Connor."

Sherman and Spencer had carefully worked out the wording of what the general would say next. "Mrs. Brockton is at this moment being questioned by military and civilian authorities. We believe that she has information critical to our investigation."

The room was quiet for a long moment.

Sherman had been carefully watching both men, especially Fisk. "I will add, gentlemen, that two men attempted to kill Colonel Spencer while he was personally delivering a highly confidential document for the President. The two attackers were killed. There is evidence that we believe links these two men to Connor and Wells."

"General, who did Connor and Wells kill?"

"Connor is wanted for questioning in the fatal shooting of Mrs. Brockton's servant. There is evidence that the man was badly beaten before Connor shot him. Wells was present. The killing occurred several days ago in Mrs. Brockton's home."

Fisk poured another brandy. All three men noticed that his hand trembled slightly as he tipped the bottle, dribbling some onto the tablecloth.

"Speaking for myself, general," Gould said as he glanced toward Fisk, "I can assure you that I know nothing of these matters."

Fisk straightened in his chair, his eyes locked on Gould. "Well, don't look at me—I don't know a goddamn thing about any of this! In fact, I don't even like being questioned about it!"

Fisk's voice boomed across the room. Spencer noticed that the usher, who at Sherman's request had remained at the far end of the room, snapped his head around at Fisk's outburst. Fisk, conscious that he had angered Gould, sipped noisily from his glass.

"General Sherman," Gould asked, "you still haven't told us what you believe is at the root of all of this. And, more specifically, what do you want from us?"

"We know what the threat is to the national interest, Mr. Gould, and we have taken broad and comprehensive protective measures. I am not at liberty to tell you more than that. What we need from you gentlemen is any help you can give us to apprehend Connor and Wells."

Sherman paused, then said in a tone of voice that was almost menacing, "I want these two men very much, gentlemen, and I will go to any length to get them."

Spencer reached into his pocket for a small leather folder and withdrew two calling cards and handed them across the table. "If Connor or Wells contact you, or you receive any information regarding their whereabouts, please contact me immediately, at any time of the day or night."

Sherman pushed his chair back from the table. "Thank you Mr. Gould, Mr. Fisk, for your time." All four men stood and shook hands. "Again, don't hesitate to contact Colonel Spencer with any information you receive, no matter how insignificant it may appear to be. If for some reason he is not available, his office will contact me. And one other thing—as events develop, we may request a meeting with you again. I want to assure you that this matter has my undivided attention."

When Sherman and Spencer left the room, Fisk and Gould remained seated at the table.

"What the hell do you suppose is going on?" Fisk asked.

"I don't know," Gould said, "and I'm hoping that you really don't, either."

"I swear to God that I don't know anything more about this than you do. I can't imagine what that crazy bastard Hollis Connor is up to."

"Well, two things are certain, as far as I'm concerned. Sherman is one man I don't want to lock horns with. And find Connor and Wells and get them here right away. I want to find out what they've been up to, and then we'll get them out of the country."

Fisk shook his head, as if he were trying to clear the brandy from his brain. "Who the hell do you suppose this Gilmore is? And those two who tried to kill the colonel?"

"I have no idea, but my guess is they were working for Connor."

"Jay, the only thing we've done is to try to arrange for old Stoval to make a fool of himself over the woman. That may raise a few eyebrows, and there may be some pressure on us because of some newspaper stories, but politicians are getting into that kind of trouble every day of the week. Besides, I don't remember that bad newspaper stories ever caused us any real trouble."

"It sounds like there is a lot more to it than that. I want you to get your head out of the sand and take this thing seriously. I'm telling you that Sherman is not to be fooled with. He didn't come up here just to ask for our help."

"Then tell me what the hell he's up to?"

"He's telling us that if we are involved, we had better back off and that we had better put a rein on Connor. I want you to find him Jim. I don't want us to be associated with any of the crazy Klan bastards."

When Fisk reached for the brandy bottle, Gould grabbed his hand. "Listen, Jim. Sherman is smart, and he's the kind of man who doesn't let the rules complicate his life. There is one more thing: it's obvious that this colonel is Sherman's man. That means they are both dangerous to us. And let's not forget what Sherman said about the colonel. As I understood it, he's responsible for the life of the President. Now, what do you suppose all of this has to do with that?"

Gould released Fisk's hand and leaned back in his chair. "Yes,

Sherman is damned smart. He didn't say we're suspects in this thing, but he made it clear that he is watching us. The trouble is I don't know how much he knows. And I don't know what, if anything, the woman told him. And I wonder what has happened to our banking friend."

Gould stood and started to leave the room without looking back at Fisk. "Let's get going," he said. "We have a lot of work to do."

Oct. 4, 1870
Aboard Pioneer II
11:10 p.m.

It was nearly midnight when the three-car military train passed southbound through the outskirts of New York City. Neither Sherman nor Spencer had retired to the sleeper car. An aide had built a fire in the small pot-bellied stove in the day car. He also brewed a pot of coffee, which he'd placed on a low table between the two officers.

Sherman enjoyed traveling by train, as long as he could do so in comfort. Spencer quickly discovered that the general's train was indeed comfortable. The day car was the second car in the train. It was furnished and decorated like a parlor. The two officers sat on facing divans. The warm glow of decorative oil lamps enhanced the richness of the walnut panels. The windows were covered with fringed drapery.

The front car was divided into quarters for the five members of the general's staff. The engine was specially designed by American Standard. More modern versions were available; in fact, the American Standard had dominated railroading until the close of the war. The company had remanufactured the general's version because he had praised its reliability during and after the war. Its top speed had never been determined. The company simply said it would go as fast as the track bed would permit. The train had most recently been outfitted with the new Westinghouse air brake.

It was the third car that Sherman was most proud of. George Pullman had designed the car for Sherman, reportedly at a cost of nearly thirty thousand dollars. The car had four berths and was lavishly decorated with three chandeliers, Brussels carpet, and walnut woodwork. Pullman had named the car the Pioneer II, after the first one that he had designed in 1864. When he presented it to the army after Sherman had become chief of the army, he said the name was appropriate because of the innovations that Sherman had brought to warfare.

Sherman, obviously tired, looked around the car. "Colonel, among the things that I will miss most when I leave the army, this train ranks high."

Spencer had intended to ask the general when they boarded the train in Washington. He knew he had to do it now because there might not be another opportunity to do so in the morning. "Ah...general...I have to use your train."

"Pardon me, colonel?"

"Your train, sir. We'll have to use it for the trip to Atlanta."

"I fully intended to."

"No, sir. I don't mean for us. I suggest we make it available to General Lee, sir, to transport him from Lexington to Atlanta."

"I see," Sherman said. He sipped his coffee, looking at Spencer over the cup's rim. "I will consider your suggestion, Colonel."

Spencer visibly took a deep breath. "Sir, I have already promised General Lee that he could have the train. I did that when I met with him."

"You promised him this particular train? My train? No other military train would have been adequate, in your estimation, for General Lee?"

The expression on Spencer's face was one that seemed to reflect physical pain. "Well, sir, I don't know anything about the other trains. But you told me about this one. Besides, because of his health he will have to be accompanied by a doctor, maybe members of his family, and others. I guess I just felt that he would be more comfortable on this train."

"I see. Well, I must say that was very generous of you, colonel. And yes, I agree with you. Even General Robert E. Lee should find this train very comfortable."

"I, ah, I hope the general isn't too upset with me, but it seemed to be the right thing to do at the time, that it just might help persuade him to make the trip."

"Was he persuaded by the train?"

"I don't know, sir."

Sherman smiled. "Rest easy, colonel. Your decision was a good one. However, you may wonder about your generosity when you—and I—have to take a regular military train to Atlanta. On second thought, that might be the best way to go. The President has asked me not to accompany him. Using this train would obviously make it difficult for me to enter Atlanta unnoticed."

"Yes, sir, I think that's true."

"Well, then, I think I'll retire to the Pullman. We can discuss matters further in the morning.

Spencer stood when Sherman did. The gently swaying car forced him to hold onto the edge of the divan. "Good night, general."

Sherman paused after several steps and turned back to Spencer. "You know, I think we did a good piece of work tonight. The way I see it, we scared hell out of the little round one. I thought he was going to take a bite out of that damn brandy snifter when you mentioned those names. And I think the smart one realizes it's in his interest to help find and stop Connor. I guess what worries me is that he'll do it before we do."

Sherman took a few more steps and paused again. "Colonel, I want Connor. And, by God, we're going to get him."

Spencer remained standing until the general entered the Pullman.

"Will there be anything else, sir?" Spencer, his thoughts on Gould and Fisk, was startled by the aide.

"No thank you, corporal. That will be all."

The aide removed the coffee pot and cups as Spencer sat back onto the divan. It had been a long day, one with a lot of pressure. His head throbbed and he remembered he had not taken his headache powder. The aide turned the oil lamps very low. Spencer sat for a long time, gently massaging his forehead.

The train was on a good section of track. The click of the wheels and the gentle swaying had a lulling effect. But despite his fatigue, Spencer wasn't sleepy. His mind drifted, back to Pedlar Mills—and Jessie McLaws. He wanted very much to see her. Perhaps he could ask her to visit him in Washington. Perhaps she could stay at the Millikan place after Gilmore was moved out. Certainly Jessie and Amanda would be very comfortable at the farm. Yes, he decided, he would ask the general for permission to bring Jessie to the farm. In fact, he would send a message to her first thing in the morning to pack and he would leave to pick her up tomorrow.

Chapter 19

Lynchburg Train Station
Lynchburg, Virginia
October 5, 1870
9:40 p.m.

No one could ever remember a train sitting so long on Lynchburg's main track. The stationmaster, Harvey Combs, said he didn't know much about it except that it was a private train. Combs said he'd received a telegraph message telling him when the train would arrive and that all regularly scheduled traffic would be canceled for the rest of the day.

There were only three passenger cars, the windows covered by drawn drapes. The engine was an immaculately maintained American Standard. Combs said the train was even equipped with the new George Westinghouse air brake. It had arrived just before dark, took on fuel and water, then just sat.

It was obvious that the train was ready to move at a moment's notice because the engine was rhythmically bleeding steam, indicating that the crew was keeping the boiler pressure up. No one got on the train. No one got off. Only the engine crew could be seen.

It all was mysterious enough to keep the interest, even at this late hour, of about thirty people. They stood across the street in front of the stable, talking in low tones.

About twenty more minutes passed before the crowd heard the sound of several horses. In the still night air they could hear flexing springs and steel-rimmed carriage wheels crunching on the gravel road. It wasn't long before two carriages pulled up next to the train. Two men on horseback followed.

At that moment a door on the middle rail car opened and a nicely dressed young man carrying a lantern stepped down and walked to the first carriage. He talked to the driver for a moment, then waved to the open door of the rail car. Two more men got down and approached the rear of the lead carriage where they began to unload baggage from the boot.

The nicely dressed young man opened the carriage door away from the crowd, talking to someone inside.

Bursting with curiosity, someone in the crowd asked, "Can anyone see who's in the carriage?"

"Can't see a damn thing," someone up front said.

"What the hell, I'm goin' up there to see," someone said. "Yeah, let's do it," another said

But the crowd was reluctant to move.

"It's probably some damn rich Yankee. They're comin' down here, you know, to buy up farms we can't afford to own no more."

"That's true. My cousin lost his to a blue belly."

Both riders who had followed the carriages had dismounted and now were standing at the front carriage.

Finally, the crowd saw a figure step down carefully from the front carriage. He looked like an old man. Perhaps he was sickly. The young man with the lantern and one of the riders were helping him. As the young man held the lantern high so the old man could be certain of his footing, someone in the crowd said in voice louder than intended, "It's Lee!"

As one, the crowd slowly moved forward toward the train.

"It is Lee. He's down from Lexington to ride this train."

"You don't suppose he's leaving for good, do you? Look at all that baggage."

The crowd silently moved around the carriages and circled the cone of light around Lee.

The young man with the lantern held it high as the people approached. He was confused, perhaps a little frightened by the silent crowd. He slowly pushed his jacket aside, his hand near the butt of his holstered Colt.

Everyone was startled when the voice boomed from the darkness near the station house. "You folks move back now and let General Lee board the train."

All heads turned toward the voice. No one had seen the man standing there in the darkness near the building. Then the crowd parted as a huge man walked slowly to within a few feet of Lee. In the yellow glow of the lantern the crowd could see that his full black beard was streaked with gray, and that the lower part of his right ear was missing. He was wearing a full-length duster that seemed too small for his massive shoulders. Only those standing closest to him could tell that he held a short, double-barreled shotgun inside the duster close to his right leg, the muzzles pointed toward the ground.

One man in the crowd, wearing the leather apron of a blacksmith, stepped forward into the cone of light.

"General Lee, sir. My name is Jenkins. I rode with Stuart, and I run the stable here. I'm sorry if we've caused any concern to these other people with you, but...but..." The stableman looked uncertainly at the others in the crowd. "Well, general, we're just afraid that you was leaving...I mean leaving for good."

Lee removed his broad-brimmed hat and slowly scanned the crowd. The lantern light played over his silver hair and beard. His eyes appeared soft and tired. At sixty-three, the man looked ancient.

"There is no cause for concern, my friends," Lee said. He smiled warmly as he stepped toward the stableman. "I am just leaving town for a few days to attend a meeting. Mr. Jenkins, it is a pleasure to meet you. I have passed your stable many times, and I must compliment you on the quality of your stock." Lee extended his hand. "Our General Stuart had the same appreciation for fine horses."

The stableman wiped his hands on his apron before clasping Lee's extended hand with both of his. He didn't shake Lee's hand; the stableman just held it for a few seconds.

The crowd didn't want the moment to pass. They wanted to keep Lee with them for as long as possible.

"General Lee, sir," someone called from the back of the crowd, "how's the college doin'?"

"Why, Washington College is doing just fine," Lee said, smiling, searching for the voice in the darkness. "We have a fine group of young men enrolled this year."

"How is the health of your family, sir?" another voice called.

Lee could not respond to a question about the well-being of his family without thinking of Annie, the daughter who died seven years earlier during the height of the fighting. It was a blow from which he never fully recovered. It was only a few months since he had visited her grave in North Carolina. He knew it was their last visit.

"Well, thank you for asking. You may know that my youngest son, Robert, recently was married in Richmond. My son, Rooney, is with me tonight." Lee turned to one of the men who had helped him from the carriage. "Rooney will accompany me on this trip. My daughter, Mildred, stands there by my carriage." All heads turned to see a young woman faintly outlined in the carriage lanterns. "My dear wife, Mary, is in that carriage. Despite the hour, she asked to ride with me as far as this station. They will be returning to Lexington in a few moments." No one could see Lee's wife in the carriage, but all knew that she was an invalid, and some of them knew that she was, and would remain until her death, an unreconstructed rebel.

The big man in the duster stepped closer to Lee. "Excuse me, General Lee. My name is Gideon Barlow. To keep our schedule, we must board the train now, sir."

Lee sensed that the crowd was reluctant to see him leave. Only Virginians could know what it meant to be a Lee in Virginia, and these people knew that for more than a hundred years the Lees had played a leading role in the history of Old Dominion. They had been governors, had served the king, fought in the Revolution, sat in the Continental Congress, represented their country at foreign courts. Two Lees had written their names on the Declaration of Independence, under the flourishing signature of John Hancock. George Washington—whose wife, Martha, was related to Mary Lee—knew the Lees well. He said of them, "I know of no country that can produce a family all distinguished as clever men, as our Lees."

Lee looked at Barlow for a moment, as if he recognized him. "Yes, of course, Mr. Barlow. We will board immediately."

The general looked back at the figure in the coach for a long moment and smiled. He clasped his daughter's hand and kissed her lightly on the cheek.

Then, with his son on his left and his secretary, Clarence Hooper, on the right, he slowly made his way to the train. The crowd moved in cadence with each step Lee took. Each of the onlookers desperately wanted to touch him, but each felt it presumptuous to hold out a hand.

Barlow led the way. He quickly climbed the steps to the middle car, placed his shotgun in a rack, then took a position at the top of the steps.

Lee grasped the handrail, placed his left foot on the first step, then paused, apparently lacking the strength to pull himself up to the second of the three steps. It was only a few moments, but everyone who could see Lee's hesitation wanted to step forward to help. Yet everyone was concerned that offering to help would embarrass the general.

Barlow extended his right hand. "It's easier to mount an unsaddled horse than to climb that first step, general. Take my hand, sir."

Lee looked up, smiled, and accepted Barlow's help. At the top of the stairs, Lee turned to look at the crowd. The people couldn't see his face, just the outline of his figure.

"God bless and keep you, Robert E. Lee." Lee barely heard the words. He couldn't be certain, but it sounded like the stableman's voice. The words were said softly, as if the person were uttering them to himself. But everyone heard.

Lee stood on the platform for a long moment, as if he were searching for words to say. The only sound was the hissing of the boiler. The old man bowed his head, then turned, very slowly, and entered the car.

The train had been gone for several minutes before the crowd, in groups of two or three, began to leave for their homes.

Chapter 20

8:45 p.m.
October 5, 1870
Pedlar Mills, Virginia

"Are you going to be my new daddy?" Amanda was sitting on Spencer's lap near the fireplace.

"Amanda!" Jessie, sitting a chair next to Spencer, was surprised, rather than angered, by the question.

"Well, mommy, you told me long time ago that daddy died in the war." Amanda, her blue-green eyes reflecting her confusion, had turned to look at Jessie. "Now Mr. Spencer wants us to live with him. So does that make him our daddy?"

Spencer gently smoothed the child's blond hair. "Your daddy always will be your daddy. I'm just going to help take care of you. Is that okay?"

Amanda toyed with the cuff of his sleeve. "Were you in the war?"

"Yes I was, sweetheart."

"But you didn't die."

Spencer hugged Amanda closer.

Jessie reached to take the child into her arms. "Come, Amanda, it's time for bed. We're leaving early in the morning so you need to get your sleep."

Later, Jessie and Spencer were seated at the fireplace, sipping coffee.

"So," Spencer said, "*am* I going to be Amanda's new daddy?"

Jessie laughed and rested her head on Spencer's shoulder. "We're going with you, aren't we."

Spencer lifted her chin and kissed her lightly.

"How long will we be staying at this Millikin farm?" she asked.

"Ten days; two weeks at the most."

"Then what happens?"

"That depends," Spencer said softly. "You haven't said you will marry me."

Jessie nodded slowly. "I guess that depends on whether you're going to remain in the army."

"Jessie, the army has been my life for a lot of years. I can't just up and quit. What would I do? How would I support you and Amanda?"

Jessie rose from the chair. She stood by the fireplace, her back to Spencer, lightly tracing the curves of the mantle clock with the fingers of her right hand. "John, the work you do—it's dangerous. Look what happened just across the street when those men tried to kill you." She shook her head quickly. "No. Amanda couldn't deal with the loss of another 'daddy'. And I don't think I could either." She turned to face him. "I know that sounds selfish, but that's what the war and the army has done to us."

Spencer rose and took her into his arms. He held her close. "Let me get through this assignment. Then we'll talk more about it."

6:45 a.m.
October 6, 1870
Aboard Pioneer II

"Sergeant Major, please remind me to thank President Grant for making this train available. I can't ever remember a more comfortable ride. That sleeper car is wonderful."

Barlow, standing behind the divan opposite Lee, had been told not to reveal that the train was Sherman's. Every item—personal or army issue—that might be linked to Sherman had been removed.

"Of, course, general."

"And I do remember you, Sergeant Major. You were my escort when I visited the White House a couple of years ago. As I recall, you were with Colonel Spencer."

"Yes, sir."

"I presume I will be seeing the colonel in Atlanta."

"I'm certain of that, sir. He'll be coming down with the President's party. As you recall the plans, sir, you and the President will be meeting privately tonight in the Kimball House. That meeting will be at six o'clock. The colonel will be present."

"Good. I look forward to seeing Colonel Spencer again…as I do the President, of course."

Barlow noticed that Lee looked pale, his skin sallow in the morning light. The sergeant had intended to return immediately to the forward car as soon as he had brought Lee his coffee. But the general seemed to want to talk, and the rest of the party was still in the Pullman.

"What is the reason, sergeant, that you and your men are dressed in civilian clothes?"

"Sir, Colonel Spencer passed through Lynchburg a few weeks ago on his way to see you. His impression was that the people would be concerned about seeing you board a military train."

"Yes, of course. Yes, that was good thinking." Lee was thoughtful for a moment, then asked, "Sergeant, when Colonel Spencer came to see me, he had been injured. Are you able to tell me more than he did about the incident?"

Barlow hesitated. He hadn't been told not to tell Lee about the attempt on Spencer's life. Yet, he didn't know what risks were involved with telling him.

"All I can tell you, general, is that two men tried to kill him while he was on his way to see you. He killed one of them. The other was killed by person who came to his assistance. The investigation into the incident is continuing."

Lee, concerned, asked, "Has it been confirmed that the attempt on his life was linked to the letter he brought to me from the President?"

"I'm sorry, general, I don't know what more I can say about the matter."

"Of course, Sergeant Major, I apologize for asking. It is just that...well, this whole matter involving the reunion is apparently much more involved than I imagined."

Lee turned in his seat to look out of the window at the heavily wooded countryside.

"Where are we now, sergeant?"

"We passed through Charlotte about twenty minutes ago. We're not making very good time now—although we'll arrive on schedule—because the track from Lynchburg to Charlotte is all pre-war and not in the best of shape. We felt that you would get a better night's sleep if we kept the speed down. Then we were delayed for a while getting through Charlotte. The track from here to Atlanta is all new."

"That was very considerate of you people. What time will we arrive?"

"We are estimating arrival at about one-thirty this afternoon, general."

"Will we be passing through any more towns?"

"Yes, sir. In about ninety minutes or so we'll go through Spartanburg. A little more than two hours after that we may see Athens, Georgia, off to our left."

Lee knew why the track east of Atlanta was new. Sherman had destroyed most of it on the march to sea, after the man had turned much of Atlanta to ashes. Lee felt that he would never understand war on such terms."

"Would the general like to have breakfast now or would you prefer to wait for the other members of your party?"

"I think I will wait. Thank you, Sergeant Major. I am not very hungry this morning."

"Then excuse me, sir. I'll check on the men forward."

Kimball House
Atlanta, Georgia
October 6, 1870
9 a.m.

Joe Johnston—formerly a full general in the CSA—had always taken great pride in the comment made by a gunnery master sergeant in one of his units. The highly respected sergeant was the older brother of an artillery colonel who had relayed the comments to Johnston. The sergeant had told his brother, "Ole' Joe Johnston's got a head as cool as General Lee's. I'll float my stick with him anytime." In fact, there were many in the South who considered Johnson a more effective commander than Robert E. Lee.

The gray-bearded and balding Johnston didn't feel especially cool-headed today, and he hadn't for some time. He was in a small room he used as a temporary office in the Kimball House on Pryor Street. In less than twenty-four hours the officer corps of the Army of Northern Virginia, and a number of special guests, would hold its first reunion in the main floor ballroom. Of course, it wasn't a full reunion. The war was still too fresh for that. Nor would there be a lot of hoopla—no street signs or parades or speeches extolling the virtues of the late southern cause. This would be merely a dignified gathering of nearly two hundred veterans, all of them former senior officers. The reunion would begin with a banquet. There would be more speeches the following day about such things as how the economic recovery of the South might be expedited or how organizations might be formed to assist veterans. Then, with one more dinner the following evening, the group would quietly disband.

Johnston's troops had been among the last of the Confederates to surrender, weeks after Lee gave up. Sherman received Johnston's surrender of all Confederate troops to the Rio Grande. A great deal of mutual respect developed between Johnston and Sherman, both during and after the war.

The reunion had been Johnston's idea, and he'd worked on it for almost a year. The prospect of having many of the South's top officers together again was truly exciting. He knew there would be criticism from some quarters, and there had been. Johnston was especially worried how the Ku Klux Klan might react to President Grant's appearance before the group. He knew the Klan had the power and influence to cause him real trouble.

In the last few days, however, he had really begun to wish that he'd never come up with the idea. First, there was the confidential message from General Lee's aide, who said the general probably would attend, but that he didn't want that fact known until he actually walked into the room.

Then there was the message, delivered by a courier from Washington City, from the chief of Grant's security. Incredibly, the message said that Grant would attend and that he and Lee would address the gathering, standing together. That message also told Johnston to keep the President's visit confidential, and further implied that he would be held accountable if word leaked out.

Both messages stipulated that Johnston was not to make arrangements for quarters for either Lee or Grant. The military would handle the President's accommodations, the message from the White House said.

Lee said he would arrive on the afternoon of the sixth on a private train. He would spend that night on the train and would depart Atlanta immediately after the banquet.

Security for both men would be handled by the President's chief of security, a Colonel John Spencer. Spencer's message also said that an Associated Press correspondent would cover the reunion.

Joe Johnston shook his head. What had begun as the very agreeable prospect of meeting again with old friends and comrades was rapidly degenerating into a political circus. Johnston held Lee's message in one hand and Grant's message in the other. He looked from one to the other, shook his head again, and very deliberately began to tear them into very small pieces.

Georgian Hotel
Atlanta, Georgia
October 6, 1870
12:30 p.m.

It was just about one hundred yards, straight-line distance, from Joe Johnston's third floor office to the second floor hotel room across Pryor Street. In fact, if Johnston would have walked to his office window and looked at the building across the street, he might have seen a man looking at the Kimball House from the second story window of the old hotel.

Hollis Connor was watching the main entrance, but he was doing so very carefully, reluctant even to pull the tattered shear curtains back for a better view.

Jason Markham was sprawled on the double bed in the corner. Charles Wells, seated in a straight-back chair against the far wall near the door, couldn't understand how Markham could be so casual, so relaxed.

Markham was a hired gun. He had a good ranch in Texas, and he and Connor jointly owned countless acres of prime rangeland. Wells knew that in a few years cattle would be a very good business. Wells also knew that the relationship between Connor and Markham involved more than just business. Wells had seen Markham cleaning his Sharps rifle earlier in the day. The way the man handled the weapon, Wells knew that he was a practiced killer.

Both Markham and Wells had heard Connor go over the plans several times, and they could tell that he was about to do so again.

"It appears that you will have a minimum of fifteen seconds," Connor said without looking at Markham, "presuming that Grant moves directly from his carriage to the front door. You will have more time if he stops to talk to someone."

Connor moved to the chair at a small table and poured a drink. He held the bottle toward Wells, who shook his head.

"I've looked over the banquet room. There are ceiling-to-floor draperies to the right of the dais. But behind the drapes is a door leading to a hallway that has an exit to the alley. It's a very wide door, apparently so that equipment can be unloaded from freight wagons."

Connor gestured with his glass toward Markham. "If you fire and miss, Jason, then it's all over. We'll have to get out. Whether or not you shoot, I want you to follow through with your plans to get out of the country for a few months. Wells has arranged for you to get your money from one of his friends in London. If you don't get a shot, then it's up to my friend here and me."

Wells got up and walked to the table to pour himself a drink.

"Charles, at the appropriate time, you and I will enter the main ballroom when Grant stands to speak. We will move deliberately toward the front of the room. We will both fire on my order. Our escape will be across the dais and through the curtains that lead to the hallway. About fifty feet down that hall is another door that leads into an alley, where two horses will be waiting for us."

Wells swallowed the two fingers of whiskey in one gulp. "Don't you think they'll have guards in that hallway?"

Connor gestured toward Markham. "Jason will take care of anyone in that hallway.

When we're certain that Grant is dead, you and I, Charles, will go immediately to the train station. We already have tickets for the nine o'clock train to Washington. No one will suspect that we would be so casual about making our escape. We should be in New York within two days, which should be just in time to take advantage of some market conditions working in our favor."

Connor leaned back in his chair, obviously pleased. "Gentlemen, it's a fool-proof plan."

CHAPTER 21

Foster House
Atlanta, Georgia
October 6, 1870
2 p.m.

President Grant's train arrived in Atlanta at 4 a.m. Although his military training gave him an appreciation for the need to take security precautions, he felt smothered by what he considered unnecessarily restrictive measures to ensure his safety. He was more chagrined than angry at having to skulk into Atlanta in the dead of night.

Spencer had arranged to have Grant stay at the Foster House, owned by a northern businessman who recently opened a clothing store and a restaurant in Atlanta. The city's rapidly expanding economy was attracting a great deal of northern money, which even some southern radicals had to agree was good for the city.

The Foster House had been the home of an industrialist, William Carter Dodds, who until the end of the war had owned the Georgia and Atlantic Railroad. Dodds had also been a successful planter, at one point owning more than 800 slaves. Even when his slaves were gone and he could see the firestorm consuming Atlanta, Dodds still hoped he could salvage some part of his small empire. But then his superintendent told him what Sherman's troops were doing to his railroad. The track was being ripped up and placed over bonfires fueled with rail ties. Then the soldiers bent the glowing center of each rail around the nearest tree. The result, the superintendent said, was what the troops were calling "Sherman's bow ties."

Dodds' wife said that, after receiving the message, he had calmly gone upstairs to the master bedroom. It was obvious that when Dodds had pulled the trigger on the gold-inlaid dueling pistol, the barrel had been in his mouth.

"Can you believe it?" Grant said to Ernst Pohlman, who sat across from him in the parlor. "Spencer won't even let me sit on the front porch."

Pohlman chuckled. Grant had paced through the house like a caged cat for nearly an hour before slumping into the stuffed chair to light a fresh cigar.

"Well, Mr. President. We both know that he takes very seriously his responsibilities for your safety. Besides," Pohlman said lightly, trying to improve the President's dark mood, "if Spencer didn't, you can imagine how quickly General Sherman would have him transferred to some lonely outpost in Indian country."

"Oh, I know that, Ernst. But don't you see what this looks like? The President of the United States must remain cooped up, surrounded by six guards, while the general who lost the war is free to roam the countryside." Grant's anger was building again. "It's a statement about conditions in this country that I don't like a damn bit. No, sir. Not one damn bit."

"I understand, Mr. President., but you must see that this is a special circumstance. Spencer believes that this man, Hollis Connor, may be planning an attempt on your life, an attempt that appears to be motivated more by avarice than politics."

Grant, who had been waving his cigar like a conductor's baton to accentuate his words, bit down hard on the Havana and shifted it to the corner of his mouth.

"I know, I know," he sighed, leaning back into the chair. Nothing was said for several moments. Then Grant smiled. "It's just that I was never rich enough as a boy to have a nanny, and I'm having some trouble getting accustomed to it." He laughed at the thought of it. Then he leaned toward Pohlman, pointing at him with the glowing cigar. "But don't you dare tell Spencer I said that." They both laughed.

Pryor Street
Atlanta, Georgia
October 6
4:15 p.m.

Passersby couldn't help but admire the handsome couple walking casually arm-in-arm toward the Kimball House. The couple smiled warmly at people. The woman, in a lavender dress that obviously was created in Europe, was stunningly beautiful. One woman angrily yanked her husband's sleeve when he turned to stare.

"How long must we continue with this?" Rachel Brockton asked through clenched teeth as she smiled and nodded to another couple.

"As long as it takes," Spencer said. When they had begun their walk, it was evident that Rachel was very nervous.

"There, across the street." Rachel said the words breathlessly.

"Which one?"

"The man going in the opposite direction, the one in the tan suit with a walking stick."

They both watched the man. When he came close enough for Rachel to see his face better, she shook her head. "No, I'm sorry. From a distance he looked like Connor." She shook her head again and stopped walking. "John, I'm worried now that I won't be able to recognize him. I've played that horrible scene in my mind so many times now that his face is a blur. It's strange. When he killed Nelson, everything seemed to happen in slow motion. I can remember every detail, except for the faces. I'm not even sure now that I would recognize Nelson if he were here today."

Spencer reached with his left hand to touch her hand on his left arm. "You will know him when you see him, Rachel. Don't worry."

When the couple resumed walking, so did Captain James Griffin. He also wore a civilian suit, the jacket of which had been nicely tailored to cover the revolver he carried in a unique shoulder holster of his own design. Griffin, who served on Sherman's staff in St. Louis, had been assigned to assist Spencer because the captain had three qualities that Sherman admired. The man was highly intelligent, totally unflappable under pressure and was without a doubt the finest pistol shot the general had ever met.

Griffin's assignment was to protect Rachel at any cost. He was ordered to keep her in his field of vision at all times, unless relieved of that responsibility by Spencer or Sherman.

As Rachel and Spencer approached the Pryor Street entrance of the Kimball House, Spencer was not surprised to see that many people had already begun to arrive. Most of the early arrivals were motivated by their eagerness to meet old comrades-in-arms; others by the desire to ensure a choice table.

"We'll stand near the entrance for a few minutes to see if you recognize anyone," Spencer said. "Then I'll take you up to your room so that you relax for a half-hour or so. It's going to be a long evening."

Spencer reached for her hand. "Remember, now, if you spot either Connor or Wells, I want you to quietly and carefully point them out to me, then step back to Griffin. He'll get you out of here. If for some reason you are separated from either Griffin or me, get back to the Foster House—any hack will know how to get there. Wait there for one of us."

"John, I have to admit that I am very frightened."

"Well, my dear, I have to admit that I am too."

They glanced at each other, then they began to laugh.

"You surprise me, colonel."

"Why is that?"

"I had no idea that Union cavalrymen could laugh, let alone have a sense of humor. Would you mind taking me to my room for a few minutes so I can freshen up?"

Spencer told Griffin to remain in the lobby, but to come up and get him if anyone matching Connor's description arrived.

The Kimball House had been open only a few weeks. Built by Atlanta's energetic entrepreneur, Hannibal I. Kimball—who at the moment was facing a scandal over the misuse of state funds—the six-story hotel with its gas chandeliers and steam-powered elevators cost more than $600,000 to build and was described as the finest hotel south of New York.

Even though Rachel would spend the night at the Foster House with the rest of Grant's party, Sherman had suggested that a room in the Kimball be reserved as a convenience for Rachel during the long evening. It was a corner room on the fifth floor. Outside the room was a small sitting area that was ideal for either Spencer or Griffin to wait for her and to guard the room.

Rachel and Spencer were alone in the elevator as it nosily began to move. It stopped for a moment just short of the forth floor, then jerked into motion again. Rachel clutched Spencer's arm. "Have these things ever been known to fall?"

"This is the first one I've every ridden." Spencer reached forward to open the door at the fifth floor. She reached for his hand as they slowly walked down the corridor toward her room. Spencer had her wait in the corridor while he checked to make sure the room was unoccupied. When he held the key out to her, she didn't respond immediately. Then she reached out and closed her hand over his. "Please, I would like you to come in."

When Spencer closed the door behind them, they stood awkwardly, avoiding each other's eyes. Slowly, tentatively, her arms encircled him. They held each other for a long moment. Spencer knew that Rachel was a very spirited woman, but he was discovering that she also was compassionate, sensitive, and more vulnerable than he ever would have suspected.

Rachel looked deeply into Spencer's eyes. Then she circled his neck with her arms, kissing him passionately.

When Rachel sensed that Spencer wasn't responding, she took a step back. Her face flushed with embarrassment. "I'm sorry, John. That was presumptuous of me."

"No," Spencer said quickly. "Don't think that. It's just that I—"

"There is someone else?"

Spencer nodded. "She should be waiting for me when we get back to Washington."

There was a long moment of silence that was broken by a knock at the door. Rachel stepped quickly to a mirror to examine her hair and makeup. She could see that her face still was flushed.

Spencer moved to the door. "Who's there?" he asked, his right hand near his revolver.

"It's Griffin, colonel. May I speak with you for a moment?"

Spencer hesitated, then opened the door only a few inches so that Griffin could not see Rachel.

"Colonel, there have been quite a few new arrivals." Spencer couldn't tell whether he or Griffin was more embarrassed by the interruption. "I'm, ah…well, I'm concerned, sir, that I won't be able to recognize Connor and Wells if they are among them."

"I understand, captain. Mrs. Brockton will need a few minutes more, then we will join you in the ballroom."

"Of course, sir. Pardon the interruption."

When Spencer closed the door, he noticed that Rachel was smiling, seemingly perfectly composed. "If the opportunity presents itself," she said. "I hope you will tell me about your lady."

Aboard Pioneer II
Atlanta, Georgia
October 6
5:10 p.m.

Rooney Lee was concerned. He tapped lightly on the door to the dressing room in the Pullman car. "Father, are you well?" There was no response.

Clarence Hooper was standing slightly behind Rooney. "Knock again, Rooney," Hooper said. "If he doesn't answer, we'll force the door."

The door opened so suddenly that Rooney and Clarence felt embarrassed, as if they had been caught peeking through the key hole.

General Lee was standing in his trousers and undershirt. He seemed confused. Rooney noticed that his father's left arm trembled as he held the door open.

"Please...don't be concerned," Lee said, his voice very soft. "I just felt a little dizzy for a moment. I will be dressed in a minute and join you in the day car."

"General, why don't we reconsider going tonight?"

"Clarence is right, father. I just don't think you are feeling well enough to go."

Lee's mind drifted back to the year of Gettysburg, when he first suffered severe chest pains. He had to be moved from his tent cot to a private home where he spent several days recovering. He knew it was heart disease. After the loss and pain of Gettysburg that summer, neither the Confederacy nor Lee ever recovered. Now the pain in his chest and left arm was worse than ever.

"Please, I will be fine," Lee's right hand fluttered as he waved them away. "We must go tonight. Give me a few more minutes."

"Then at least have Doctor Bannock come in to see you," Rooney asked. The doctor at that moment was in the forward car treating one of the engine crewmen who had burned his hand.

"Yes, if that will ease your concern, you may send for the doctor."

"I'll get him, general," Hooper said. "Please wait here." Hooper hurried away.

Lee put his hand on his son's shoulder. "Rooney, I will be fine, really. It is just the same old problem and, like always, it will pass. Why don't you wait for me in the day car?"

Rooney hesitated, then reluctantly nodded agreement.

Hooper joined Rooney after escorting the doctor into the Pullman car.

"We've got to stop him from going, Rooney. I've never seen him so weak."

"I know, but how do we stop him?"

At that moment Barlow came in from the forward car. "Is the general about ready to leave?"

Neither man responded for a moment. Then Rooney said, "Sergeant Major, I must ask you to relay a message to the President. My father is ill, and he should not attend the reunion tonight. Doctor Bannock is examining him now."

Barlow looked from one man to the other. "Gentlemen, I understand

and appreciate your concern for the general. And I say this with all due respect, but before I agree to deliver such a message, I will have to talk to the general myself."

Hooper barely managed to control his mercurial temper. "Do I understand, sergeant, that you are suggesting that we are not telling you the truth?"

"Not at all, sir," Barlow replied calmly. "But a number of people have made a great effort to bring about this meeting. The President will be there, despite the very real prospect that someone will try to kill him. I'm sorry, but I must discuss this with General Lee personally."

Hooper shook his head, taking several steps toward Barlow. "Look, sergeant, I appreciate the risk that the President is taking, but he has something to gain from doing so. The risk the general would take is more complicated than that posed by an assassin's bullet. Not only is his health precarious, but his appearing with Grant could destroy him."

"I am sorry, Mr. Hooper," Barlow said, "but I don't know enough about the politics of the situation to argue those points with you. But it seems to me that General Lee and the President have both agreed to accept whatever risks there are because they believe that what they're trying to do is more important than their political futures, or even their lives."

Barlow took his suit jacket from a small closet near the door. "My orders, gentlemen, are to escort the general to the Kimball House, and to have him there at six o'clock for a private meeting with the President. Only General Lee can tell me that he is not going to attend that meeting."

"Sergeant Major." The three men turned to see Lee standing in the doorway to the Pullman. Doctor Bannock could be seen behind him. "You must forgive my son and Mr. Hooper. Their motives are pure. It is their judgment that is clouded." Lee smiled as he slowly walked to the divan. When he was seated, he looked at his son and Hooper, then locked eyes with Barlow.

"Rest assured, Sergeant Major, that you will complete your assigned mission tonight. Now, please refresh my memory regarding the arrangements."

Rooney interrupted before Barlow could answer. "Doctor, what do you have to report?"

Dr. Virgil Bannock was nearly sixty. Even though he had served the Confederacy throughout the war as a surgeon, he had never met Lee until the general became president of Washington College. The doctor had been present at the surrender and had remained near Appomattox to treat the wounded long after the fighting had ended. Rather than return to his native Richmond, where his wife had died shortly before the war, he moved the relatively short distance from Appomattox to Lexington and began to build a practice. He met the general a year later during a reception at the college. The two men had developed a close friendship.

"Yes, Virgil," Lee said, "please put this matter to rest."

Bannock, still standing near the door, walked closer to the group and placed his medical bag on the floor next to the divan. "I'm sorry, general, but I really can't do that." Bannock cleared his throat nervously before he continued.

"There is no doubt that it is your heart again, general," Bannock said, looking directly at Lee. "But we don't know precisely what the problem is."

Bannock looked at the others. "As I am sure you know, this illness first occurred in late March of sixty three, no doubt brought about by the stress of command. We are certain that the general's heart was damaged at that time. I have discussed the matter with those doctors who initially treated the general, as well as other experts in the field. I regret to say that we are not able to accurately diagnose the problem."

Hooper asked, "The point is, doctor, what is your recommendation regarding the reunion? Is it safe for the general to go?"

Dr. Bannock slowly shook his head. "Gentlemen, if I had my way, the general would not be involved in any activity or responsibility that involves hard work or tension." Bannock turned to Lee. "And the general knows that I include in that category the administration of a college."

Bannock paused for a long moment, as if struggling to find the right words. "Certainly, tonight's activities will be stressful, of that there can be no doubt. I would prefer, general, that we go back home and just sit under one of those trees on your campus."

Frustrated and confused by what the doctor had said, Hooper

exploded. "Damn it to hell, doctor! Should he go to this damnable meeting tonight—yes or no?"

Lee, surprised by Hooper's language, held up his hand. "Clarence, please. We must remain calm." Lee looked up at this friend, who was standing to his right. "So that there is no misunderstanding, you all should be aware that Doctor Bannock advised against my making this trip and against my going to the meeting tonight. And he did so clearly and forcefully. I, in turn, made it clear that the decision of whether or not I attend involves much more than medical considerations."

Lee rose from the divan and looked carefully at each of the men in the car. Then he turned to Hooper.

"Clarence, you have done a good job of preparing statements of our position on issues vital to the South." Lee's voice was strong now. "I will present those statements to President Grant when I meet with him tonight. Further, I will attempt to extract an agreement from the President which makes clear that our support of his position on reunification will require his support for our position on issues that we believe are vital. Now, we must not be deluded into thinking that the President will support our position without question. Negotiation will be inevitable."

Lee paused, recalling the conversation he had with Spencer some weeks before, when the young colonel said in almost so many words that Lee might have used his prestige to help unite the country. What pained Lee was Spencer's suggestion that Lee might be so consumed with the past that he was forfeiting his responsibilities to the future. What of the young men he was helping to prepare for the future? Did that not meet his obligation? Apparently Spencer felt that he should have been more visible to the South, as well as to the North; that he should have spoken out on the promise and the reality of Reconstruction. Perhaps he could have done more. Lee had a fleeting image of the lonely figure in the tattered Confederate greatcoat, struggling to stand at attention, a basket of spoiled apples at his feet. Mostly, he remembered the man's lifeless eyes.

"So, the matter is closed," Lee said with finality. "We must not let this opportunity pass. Now, sergeant major, please continue with your briefing."

Barlow, who had been fascinated by Lee's words, hesitated for a moment while he collected his thoughts.

"Yes, sir. A carriage is waiting alongside the train. It will carry you, your son, Mr. Hooper and the doctor. One of my men and I will follow on horseback. We are scheduled to arrive at Kimball House—about twenty minutes away—at six o'clock. We will use the side entrance and meet the President in a private room on the second floor."

Rooney asked, "Will all of us be able to attend the private meeting?"

"My orders, Mr. Lee, are that the general is welcome to bring anyone to that meeting."

Barlow looked around the car to see if there were other questions, then he continued. "At seven o'clock, general, you and the President will be escorted to a small waiting room off the banquet room. You will meet with General Johnston to review how the introductions will be made. You will speak to the group first, at about eight o'clock. Considering that no one in the audience will know in advance of your presence, you obviously can expect a lot of, shall we say, excitement when you walk into the room. It will probably be several minutes before you have the opportunity to speak."

Barlow was now visualizing the written plan in his mind's eye, reciting the words from memory. "Your comments, of course, will be of your own choosing. The President asked if you would agree to provide him in advance with a copy of your prepared remarks."

Lee nodded.

"The President also leaves to your good judgment, sir, the words you choose to inform the audience of his presence and his desire to speak to them."

Barlow paused while he recalled the security measures. "Now, if there is a threat to the President, Colonel Spencer has the responsibility to escort him from the building. I also will immediately escort you and your party back to this train. Whether or not there is an incident, this train will leave for Lynchburg at ten o'clock tonight."

Lee nodded and looked around at the others. "Thank you, Sergeant Barlow. Your details of the agenda coincide, as I recall, precisely with those I received in the message from Colonel Spencer." Lee looked at his pocket watch, then got to his feet, wincing as he straightened. "Gentlemen, we already are behind schedule. I suggest we leave immediately. Rooney, help me with my coat, please."

Barlow hurried forward to alert his men. He reminded the engine crew to keep steam up so they could move at a moment's notice. He took the short-barreled shotgun from the rack and handed it to the carriage driver, a corporal in his early twenties. "Son, keep this scattergun under your seat." Barlow placed his hand on the young man's shoulder. "Remember, I don't want you to get down from that rig for any reason. If nature calls, use your boot. I want you to park at the side entrance and don't move for a damn soul except for me. Understand?"

"I understand, Sergeant Major."

Barlow now had to resolve a dilemma he'd struggled with since this assignment began. The LeMat was much too large to hide under his jacket. In fact, Sherman had suggested that he carry a much more concealable Colt single action in .36 caliber. But Barlow felt too comfortable with the old LeMat to give it up.

He took the revolver from under his berth, pulled up his trouser leg and shoved the barrel into his boot. Then he took a strip of soft leather and tied the revolver across the cylinder to his leg. Barlow had already practiced retrieving the gun. He found that he could slip the knot on the thong and draw the gun in less than three seconds. He knew that would be too much time in some situations, but he felt that having the LeMat's firepower would be worth the risk.

When Barlow jumped down to the gravel alongside the track, he noticed that Sergeant Davis was mounted and was holding Barlow's horse by the bridle. Davis and the other troopers were assigned to Barlow from the Atlanta military district. Rooney and Hooper were assisting the general into the carriage.

When he was mounted, Barlow discovered that what he had not considered is that on horseback, his trousers were stretched taut around his trunk-like legs, and he could clearly see the outline of the LeMat. He decided not to worry about it when he realized that he wasn't worried about anyone who would question him about it.

The carriage and the two riders moved slowly along the red clay road that paralleled the rail line, a spur that had served a now abandoned factory. There was no other traffic on the road so Barlow began to review once more how the events of the evening were scheduled to proceed.

The party had been on the road for no more than five minutes when Barlow noticed a commotion in the carriage. Then he heard Hooper's high-pitched voice: "Stop! Stop the carriage! Stop, damn you!"

Barlow spurred his horse the few yards to the carriage and jumped down. When he opened the door, he saw General Lee with his head back against the cushion. His eyes were open, but they were flat, unseeing. The general's mouth had gone slack

Dr. Bannock, who had been sitting across from Lee, was unsuccessfully trying to get closer to him. "You two," Bannock said to Rooney and Hooper, "get out so I can have more room."

Barlow touched Rooney's arm. "What happened?" Rooney didn't take his eyes from his father. "I don't know," he said in a flat voice. "I asked him a question. He started to answer, but stopped in mid-sentence. It doesn't appear that he can talk or hear us."

Barlow stepped closer to the carriage. "Excuse me, doctor, shall we take the general to a hospital?"

Bannock didn't respond. He was closely examining Lee's eyes, then felt his pulse. After nearly a minute Bannock turned to Barlow and started to say something when Lee moved his arm. Bannock immediately leaned forward and began to lightly massage the side of Lee's neck. Rooney climbed into the coach on the other side and took his father's hand. "Father, it's me, Rooney. Can you hear me?"

Lee stirred, groaning softly deep in his throat. With his head still against the cushion, he turned to the right, toward Barlow and Hooper. Then he turned to his left, toward his son. Rooney could feel, ever so lightly, his father attempt to squeeze his hand.

Slowly, with great effort, Lee raised his head and forced himself to sit straight. He looked at the anxious faces around him. "I am...sorry, gentlemen...if I have caused you concern." The old man's voice was so soft that Barlow and Hooper didn't hear all of the words. "I am better now...we can continue."

Dr. Bannock slowly shook his head. "Robert, my friend, we are going home."

The doctor reached into his medical bag and retrieved a small pad of paper. He quickly wrote something on it, then gave it to Barlow. "Sergeant, that's the name of a very prominent surgeon. I know him only by reputation. Fearing the worst when I was invited on this expedition, I researched his credentials and sent him a message informing him that I might require his services on this day. I told him nothing else. Send someone to fetch him and bring him to the train."

Barlow took the paper and handed it to Sergeant Davis. "You heard him. Ride hard and bring the doc to the train quick as you can. Move!"

"Sergeant," Bannock called, "let's get the general back to the train immediately."

Lee shook his head. "No, doctor, we are going to the reunion."

"General. You can't possibly do that."

"Yes, I must. But I won't stay long."

"Father, you need to be in bed."

"Son, I gave my word. I must go."

Dr. Bannock sighed heavily. "Robert, you as stubborn as a..." Shaking his head, the doctor reached into his black bag and withdrew a small bottle of a yellowish liquid. "If you must go, I want you to take a sip of this."

Lee clearly was better now. He smiled and tapped the doctor on his knee. "How do I know that won't put me to sleep?"

"Frankly, General, I wish I'd thought of that. Here, take it."

Lee took the medication, then ordered the carriage to proceed.

Chapter 22

A.C. Wylie Building
Atlanta, Georgia
October 6
6:50 p.m.

Hollis Connor peered briefly over the ledge of the fourth-story window. The sun was very low and the street was in shadow. Dozens of carriages were randomly parked on Pryor Street.

Connor was surprised that he wasn't angry. He realized that he probably hadn't believed that he would be lucky enough for the whole matter to be dealt with by a rifle bullet. He knew what had to be done now.

He moved from the window to stand near Markham, who was crouched behind a low, heavy table that he had arranged as a shooting bench. The barrel of the Sharps lay braced on a small sandbag supported by a short stack of business ledgers he had found in the office. The muzzle pointed at the Kimball House portico.

"Well, Jason, it looks like we won't get him from here."

"Yep," Markham replied without moving his eyes from the entrance below. "If he's there, he got in through some other door."

Connor started to say something, then looked around at Wells. "Why don't you watch the back stairs, Charles. We don't want to be surprised by anyone."

Connor waited until Wells was gone before speaking quietly to Markham. "I'm going to need your help inside—I need you to back me up." Connor pulled a small silver flask from an inside pocket. He took a sip, then leaned closer to Markham as he handed him the flask. "I've been thinking long and hard about this, Jason. As long as we're going to kill Grant, we might as well kill Lee."

Markham slowly tipped the flask and took a long swallow. He looked at Connor for a long moment. "Why?"

"Don't you see it? With both of them dead, there will be chaos, in the North and South. The markets will—"

"I don't care about any of that," Markham said with a wave of his hand. "What I'm thinking is that if we kill them both it'll be harder to get away clean."

"Just the opposite, my old friend. When Wells shoots Grant and I kill Lee, you will be in the hallway to make certain it's clear. I'll push Wells through the curtain back onto the stage."

Connor laughed. "Standing there with a smoking gun in his hand should make him the prime target. They'll probably shoot him down. If they don't, I will. But no matter what happens, there should be enough confusion for us to get away. I'll need you, Jason, to keep the back door clear and to help me stop anyone who comes through the drapes after us."

Markham nodded understanding. "Okay, but you got to pay me double."

Conner didn't hesitate. "Deal. We've got more than a half hour before Grant is supposed to talk," Connor said. "We might as well relax right here."

More than two minutes had passed before Wells recognized the opportunity that Connor had handed him. There was no reason why he couldn't just rush down the stairs and get away. But to run required courage, and his fear of Connor was so strong that he didn't know if he could do it.

Despite his desperation, Wells smiled at the irony of it. He was afraid to run away to save his life because he might be killed trying it.

Wells walked very quietly back toward the corner room where he'd left

Connor and Markham. He listened at the door for a long moment. He could just barely hear murmuring voices. He turned and started for the stairs. Once had had made the decision, he had to fight the almost irresistible urge to flee through the hall and go pounding down the steps to freedom. As he forced himself to walk slowly down the stairs, he couldn't shake the image of a bullet crashing into his back, the lead ball's energy flinging his lifeless body down the stairs. Only when he reached the bottom of the stairs did he risk looking up. That's when he knew he was free.

Wells also knew he had been a fool to get mixed up with Connor. The man was insane. Connor would either be killed or captured tonight. Either way, Wells knew he eventually would be implicated. He began to run through the alley behind the building. He would cross Pryor Street far enough south so that he couldn't be seen from the window. He would go into the Kimball House and tell them. After all, he thought, he hadn't done anything seriously wrong. He certainly hadn't killed anyone. Perhaps they'd let him go back to England.

Kimball House
Atlanta, Georgia
October 6
7:05 p.m.

President Grant was seated at the far end of the large table that dominated the room. He was staring at the end of his cigar as he slowly rolled its glowing tip in the large, cut-glass ashtray.

Sherman stood a few feet to the President's right. Joe Johnston, obviously uncomfortable, stood at the far end of the table. Spencer was at the door. Ernst Pohlman had left several minutes earlier to assess the crowd in the dining room. He was particularly interested in seeing whether former generals James Longstreet and George Pickett would show up.

When Sherman led the group into the room several minutes earlier, they had witnessed a spectacular display of Grant's temper. Grant instantly recognized Sherman, despite the fact that Sherman had shaved his beard and wore civilian clothes.

"Cump! You pig-headed...!" Grant was livid. "You are risking everything. I told you that if you—"

"Sam, hold on," Sherman said calmly, his hand up. "No one has recognized me and I'll leave this room before Lee arrives. I'll wait outside the building to make sure there isn't any trouble."

There was a knock at the door and Barlow entered the room. He turned to Spencer. "Colonel, General Lee will be here in about ten minutes. But there is a problem, sir: he's sick. The way the doctor talked, it's his heart."

"How sick is he?" Spencer asked. "Will he be able to stand and speak?"

"Sounded to me, sir, that he'd do it or die trying," Barlow said.

"Well, gentlemen." Everyone turned to look at Grant. "That's the mark of our General Lee. I believe we're ready to—"

Someone began to frantically knock on the door. When Spencer opened it a young usher, obviously flustered, almost stumbled into the room. Grant turned his back, but he needn't have bothered. The boy was too rattled to notice him.

"Mr. Johnston," the young man said excitedly, "a man by the name of Mr. Griffin sent me up here to tell you something he said was extremely important." The young man seemed to have trouble catching his breath.

Sherman leaned close to Grant. "Griffin is a captain on my staff."

"Go easy, son," Johnston told the young man, "and tell me what this man Griffin said."

"He said...he said...that I should tell you that he is holding a man who is very dangerous, and that you would know who to tell about it."

"Was there any kind of fuss when Griffin caught this man?" Johnston asked.

"Well, yes, sir, but not much. Mr. Griffin pulled a gun on the man, and then marched him into room number six off the dining room. I don't suppose many people saw that. But I was serving drinks and I saw it. That's why Mr. Griffin picked me to tell you."

Spencer touched the boy's arm. "Son, did Mr. Griffin say what the man's name is?"

"I almost forgot about that. He said his name is Wells, sir."

Spencer turned to Sherman, "General, I recommend that you remain here with the President until Barlow and I can find out what's happening down there." Spencer knew that Sherman was armed.

"How can I help, Colonel?" Joe Johnston asked.

"It would be very helpful, sir, if you would guard the hallway," Spencer said. "If you keep this young man with you, he can serve as your messenger if the need arises."

Spencer then motioned to Barlow and they quickly ran down the hall.

Room six was where Grant and Lee would have waited before speaking to the veterans. It was furnished as a small sitting room about ten by fifteen feet.

Wells was sitting in the far corner when Spencer and Barlow entered the room. He appeared to be badly shaken. Griffin and Rachel were standing near the door.

Griffin handed Spencer a Navy Colt revolver. "He was carrying that. He says he won't talk unless we can give him some guarantees."

Spencer walked closer to Wells. He could tell that the man was frightened, his eyes darting to each person. "My name is John Spencer, Mr. Wells. I don't know what guarantees you want or expect, but we don't have time to discuss them. I want the answer to just one question. Where is Hollis Connor?"

"You must understand, Mr. Spencer," Wells began hesitantly, "that I regret ever becoming involved in this mess. All I want is some assurance that I can leave the country and go home to England."

Spencer started to say something when Barlow reached around him. "Excuse me, colonel, but with your permission I'll handle this."

Barlow grabbed Wells by the lapels of his jacket and lifted him out of the chair. Barlow then turned and slammed Wells against the wall, the man's head thumping heavily against the plaster. Wells, his boots dangling a good six inches above the floor, was pinned to the wall by Barlow.

"Now, Mr. Wells," Barlow said ominously through clenched teeth. "Do you really want me to ask the question again?"

Wells tried to talk, but he was dazed by the blow to his head, and the pressure against his chest from Barlow's clenched fists made it difficult to breath.

"Sergeant Major," Spencer said. "I think he's ready to tell us. Let him down."

Barlow permitted Wells' feet to touch the floor. Still holding him by the lapels, Barlow steered Wells toward the chair and dropped him into it.

Gasping for air, Wells nodded his head. "Yes...Yes, he's across the street...the Wylie Building." Wells paused to take huge, shuddering breaths, then continued. "He plans to come here through the alley entrance. He will stand behind the curtain...he will shoot Grant when he stands to speak."

"Is there anyone else with him?" Spencer asked.

"Yes. A man named Jason Markham. He's a Texan. He has a Sharps rifle set up on the fourth floor. He was supposed to shoot Grant when he got out of his carriage at the Pryor Street entrance."

"No one else?"

Wells shook his head.

Barlow asked. "Which entrance in that building did you use? I know you didn't go through the front door."

"The side entrance, next to the Republic Block Building. They will come out that way."

Spencer turned to Griffin. "Take Mrs. Brockton up to the room where the President is waiting to meet General Lee. Joe Johnston is in the hallway outside the room." Spencer picked up the Colt lying on the table. "I doubt that Johnston is armed. Give him this. And Captain, as soon as Mrs. Brockton is safe, I want you to come over to the Wylie Building as quickly as you can. Guard that side entrance. If they get by us, it'll be up to you."

"Colonel," Griffin said evenly, "with respect, sir. I suggest your place is at the President's side. Barlow and I should go to the Wylie Building. If we can't stop Connor, only you will be left to protect the President."

"I fully appreciate my responsibilities, captain, but the sergeant major and I have worked together for several years. You will remain in this building and he and I will handle Connor."

Barlow opened the door to the hallway. "Colonel, can I speak to you a moment—privately?"

They stepped out into the hall. "Sir, I think the captain is right. It would be better if you stayed with the President and General Lee. The captain seems like a good man, and we can handle the likes of Connor."

Spencer didn't respond and turned back into the room. He looked at Griffin for a long moment. He felt trapped by Griffin's comment and what Barlow had said. Yet, he wanted Barlow to be at his side when they dealt with Connor. Perhaps that was why he was so curt with his instructions for Griffin.

"I want the situation handled in that building," Spencer said to the Griffin. "Is that clear?"

"I understand, colonel."

"If we can, I want to quietly arrest those people and get them out of town without anyone here knowing about it. If there's shooting inside the building, the noise from the orchestra and all of these people hopefully will cover it. And take that young usher with you. Station him outside the building. Send him to me if there's a problem."

"John." Rachel's voice was barely audible. "This man, Connor, is very dangerous."

Barlow reached down and pulled up his trouser leg. He slipped the knot on the leather thong and drew the huge LeMat from his boot. Holding the revolver with the barrel pointing at the ceiling, he smiled and said. "Ma'am, there's no need to worry."

Griffin touched Rachel's elbow. "You should move into the ballroom, Mrs. Brockton." She hesitated a moment, her eyes on Spencer as she left the room.

Spencer turned back to Wells. "You will have to go with the captain and the sergeant major. You know the building, and you know where they're waiting."

Wells shook his head vigorously. "No. Absolutely not. Connor will kill me the instant he sees me."

Barlow took two steps toward Wells. He gestured with his thumb toward the door. "Move!"

When Wells started to walk to the door, Barlow grabbed him. With his left hand gripping the back of Wells' neck, Barlow placed the barrel of the LeMat under the man's chin, pressing it against his throat. "If you try to run, or if you don't instantly follow any order you get from the colonel or me, I'll make you eat the barrel of this thing. Do you understand me?"

Barlow released Wells and then tucked the LeMat inside his jacket, holding the weapon against his body with his left arm.

"Colonel," Barlow smiled, "Mr. Wells and I are ready."

CHAPTER 23

A.C. Wylie Building
October 6
7:20 p.m.

Griffin couldn't argue the point. Barlow was right. The sergeant major wanted to lead the way because of the LeMat's firepower. It was clear they would have to keep Wells between them, so Griffin would be last up the stairs. He didn't like it. If he had to shoot, he was worried about Wells getting in the way. Besides, Barlow made too big a target, and if the sergeant major were hit, Griffin didn't welcome the prospect of explaining to Spencer how and why it had happened.

Griffin worried about the possibility that Connor had already left the building and was in the Kimball House stalking the President. If Connor happened to see Sherman, Griffin had no doubt that Sherman also would be a target. If Connor did get past them, it would be up to Spencer to stop him.

Griffin, Barlow, Wells and the young usher had crossed Pryor Street far enough to the south to be certain they weren't seen. Once across the street they ran down the alley behind the Wylie building. Griffin felt that they had as much information about the layout of the fourth floor as Wells could give them. But he knew he'd find that out in a few minutes.

They paused at the side entrance for nearly a half-minute to steady their breathing. It was nearly dark. Only the upper stories of the Kimball House across the street were lightly bathed in the orange glow of the setting sun. Griffin knew there would be heavy shadow and pockets of darkness inside the building.

It was time. Griffin touched the young man's shoulder. "What is your name, son?"

"Peter Linder, sir."

Griffin guessed the young man couldn't be more than sixteen. He pointed across the street to the Kimball Building. "Peter, I want you to stand over there. If you see anyone other than the sergeant or me come through this door, I want you to run to Colonel Spencer and tell him. Is that clear?" Peter Linder, his eyes wide, nodded briskly.

Griffith waited a moment until the young usher crossed the street. Then he nodded to Barlow, who carefully opened the door. As Barlow moved up the stairs, Griffin was surprised that such a large man made hardly a sound. At each landing they paused to listen.

Leaning close to the window to see his watch, Connor decided it was time to leave. Markham's single-shot Sharps rifle was still loaded. He had packed the extra ammunition into a leather bag that he slung over his shoulder. In the failing light, Connor checked the cylinder of his revolver, making sure there was a cap over each chamber.

Connor led the way across the darkening floor to the stair well. It was at that moment that he remembered Wells. Panic and anger churned his stomach. What a fool he'd been to leave Wells alone. He'd always suspected the coward would run at the first opportunity. Where would Wells go? Probably on the first train back to New York, Connor thought.

What worried Connor more now was that, down deep, he knew his confidence was slipping. Why did he ever bring Wells into it? He always knew the man would lose his backbone when it came to the killing. Too many elements of his plan had failed because too many people had failed him. For a moment he considered forgetting the whole thing. He and Jason would get on the train and head for Texas. But what would Jason think? And what about all that money? No, he had to go through with it.

He didn't want his best friend, his only real friend, to think that he was a coward like Wells.

When they got to the stairs, Connor looked around to make sure that Wells was indeed gone. They quickly started down the stairs.

Chapter 24

A.C. Wylie Building
October 6
7:24 p.m.

The landing between the third and fourth floors was the worst possible place for it to happen. Barlow had just reached the landing when Connor and Markham were halfway down the stairs from the floor above.

Both groups froze. In the dim light, Barlow could see the first man clearly. The second man was little more than a shadow. He couldn't tell if either man was holding a weapon.

Barlow's voice boomed and echoed in the stairwell. "You men—stand where you are. Don't move." With the LeMat leveled, Barlow slowly moved toward them.

It's possible that no one would have died if Connor hadn't recognized Wells's upturned face. "You bastard; you *miserable* bastard!"

Connor fired and the muzzle flash in the shadowed stairwell was a huge, jagged tongue of flame. In the momentary burst of light, the bullet caught Wells just below his chin, tore through his windpipe, and severed his spinal column. Wells crumpled instantly, the back of his head bouncing grotesquely as his body slid head-first down several steps.

Barlow had the LeMat set to fire the shotgun barrel. At such short range the grapeshot would take out both men.

An instant before he could pull the trigger another shot was fired. It was a thunderous, deafening roar that for an instant turned the darkened stairwell into day. A great cloud of white smoke billowed down the stairway.

Markham's .50 caliber rifle bullet smashed into the left side of Barlow's chest, shattering two ribs where it entered. A large rib fragment was protruding from the gaping exit wound just below his shoulder blade.

Barlow thought it strange that he felt no pain. In fact, his mind was clear. He knew he'd waited too long to fire. But he still had time. He still held the LeMat. All he had to do was raise it a few degrees and fire. But for some reason the damn thing had suddenly become so heavy. As Barlow strained to raise the LeMat, he could hear the air rushing from his shattered left lung.

Connor fired two quick shots. One bullet struck Barlow near the groin; the second ball hit just above his belt buckle. Barlow slowly slid into a sitting position, leaving a wide swath of blood on the wall behind him.

At the instant Markham fired, Griffin was several steps below the landing, his way blocked by Wells' falling corpse. In the momentary spasm of muzzle flash, Griffin saw Barlow convulse when the rifle bullet slammed into his chest. It was a fragmentary, ethereal image shrouded in gun smoke.

Stepping backward up the stairs to find Markham, Griffin snapped off two shots with his Colt, a split-second after Connor fired at Barlow. Griffin's first bullet ricocheted off the banister. The second round hit Connor in the upper left shoulder. Griffin's eyes were searching for the second shooter when he heard Barlow's LeMat fire. It was the shotgun barrel. Griffin heard a scream. Markham's Sharps rifle tumbled over the railing and clattered down the stairwell.

Griffin and Connor, separated now by less than a dozen feet, swung their weapons toward each other at the same instant.

The usher, Peter Linder heard the gunfire, and a minute or so later he saw Griffin stagger through the side door, his right arm covered in blood. "Boy," Griffin called. "Tell Colonel Spencer that I killed the man with the rifle and wounded Connor, but he got away through another exit." Griffin held his handkerchief over his wound to staunch the bleeding. "And boy, tell the colonel that his sergeant major is dead."

John Spencer was standing outside the second floor room occupied by the President when Joe Johnston appeared at the far end of the hall. Behind him was Robert E. Lee, followed by his secretary, Clarence Hooper. Sherman and Rachel had left several minutes earlier to join the reunion crowd. Spencer opened the door and told the President, "He's here, general."

Lee entered the room first. He and Grant stood at opposite ends of the long, rectangular table. For a long moment neither man said a word. Then the President stepped toward Lee, smiling and holding out his hand. "General, I'm very pleased to see you."

"Mr. President, it is good to see you again."

They held their handshake for a moment, each looking into the other's eyes. Recalling Barlow's report, Grant could clearly see that Lee was ill.

"Why don't we be seated, general. Can I get anything for you?"

"Only some water, please." Grant nodded to Joe Johnston, who left the room and asked an usher to bring in a watcher pitcher and glasses. Johnson asked the usher to remain outside the door to prevent anyone from entering the room.

Lee motioned toward his aide. "This is Clarence Hooper, Mr. President, who serves as a key assistant at the college and who served as a major on my staff during the war. With your permission, I would like Clarence to attend this meeting."

Grant nodded, then motioned for Spencer to sit to his right. "General, I know that you are acquainted with Colonel Spencer."

For the first time since he entered the room, Lee smiled. With some difficulty, Lee stood and reached across the table to shake Spencer's hand. "You look considerably better than you did the last time we met, colonel."

Spencer chuckled. "It's good to see you again, general."

Clarence Hooper remained seated and merely nodded.

Joe Johnston, standing by the door, was about to leave when Grant motioned for him to join them. Johnston took a seat at the far end of the table, near the door.

Grant cleared his throat. "General Lee, let me begin by expressing my sincere appreciation for not only attending this affair, but also for your agreement to invite me as your guest. I believe that this evening you and I can make a positive impact on the future of our nation."

Lee did not respond.

Grant glanced at Johnston at the far end of the table, then at Spencer. "General Lee, when and how had you planned to introduce me?"

"Before we discuss that, Mr. President, I have something I would like you to review." Lee made a hand motion toward Hooper, who opened a leather briefcase and withdrew several sheets of paper. Lee placed the papers on the table in front of him, then rested his clasped hands over them. "I would like you to consider these five issues, which are the result of a study conducted by a team of our advanced students—which, by the way, included three students from the North. With your endorsement of our position on these issues, I am confident that Reconstruction will become more fact than hope."

Lee slowly slid the papers toward Grant. The President read each page, then folded them and started to put them into an inside jacket pocket.

"No, Mr. President, I would like to get your commitment tonight, before we leave this room."

"Are you asking me to make a decision tonight on these issues?"

"Yes, sir."

"General, these are complex issues with which I alone cannot deal. Congress and other governmental bodies must be involved."

Lee placed his elbows on the table and leaned toward Grant. "I am sorry, sir, but I must insist. Certainly as President you have such authority." Lee sat back in his chair and crossed his arms over his chest.

Grant, his growing frustration reflected in the tone of his voice, said, "General, the only commitment—in fact, I will make it a promise—I can make is that these matters will be seriously considered. As soon as any decision is made, I will have Colonel Spencer report to you personally on any progress being made."

Grant put the papers into his pocket. "I'm sorry, sir, but at this point that is all I can promise."

The room was quiet for a long moment.

Johnston heard a commotion in the hall and quietly left the room. A moment later he returned. "Mr. President, I just spoke with the usher who accompanied Mr. Griffin and Sergeant Major Barlow to the Wylie building directly across the street. The assassin, Connor, who has threatened your life, escaped from the building, although he may be wounded. His accomplice was killed, and Mr. Griffin is wounded." Johnson looked at Spencer. "I'm sorry to say, colonel, that it appears Sergeant Major Barlow was fatally wounded."

Both Grant and Lee looked at Spencer. Grant shook his head slowly. Lee lowered his head, his clasped hands resting on the table.

Spencer quickly rose from his chair, started for the door, then stopped and turned to face Grant. "Sir, it's clear now that you cannot go into that room. We have to assume that Connor is in there waiting for you."

Clarence Hooper rapped the table with his knuckles. "General Lee, for the first time I agree with the colonel. We should return to the train immediately. Standing next to the President will also put your life at risk if this madman is out there."

Lee looked at Hooper and made a calming gesture with his left hand, then turned toward Grant. "What is your decision, Mr. President?"

Grant wondered how many men had shed blood because he wanted to speak to these people. Was he just being stubborn? Would it really make any difference? What could he say to John Spencer to ease the young man's pain over the loss of his sergeant major? The two obviously had a very special relationship going back to the war. Would Spencer be able to function with Barlow gone? Grant considered that if Spencer—who he depended on for security—was seriously affected by his sergeant's death, would standing in front of the crowd be a foolish risk for himself? Grant doubted that Lee would be an intentional target. But he could be the victim of a stray bullet. What would Cump say? He knew what Cump would say.

Grant locked eyes with Lee. "Well, general, I would like to hear your opinion of what we should do."

"I would say, Mr. President," Lee said softly, "that you and I have faced decisions considerably more difficult than this one. We both have traveled a difficult road—in more ways than one—to be here tonight."

Grant nodded slowly. "I repeat, general, that these issues"—he tapped his jacket pocket—"will be seriously considered." He took out his pocket watch. "General Johnston, it is almost time for you to introduce General Lee to your guests."

Johnston stood. "Yes, sir. I'll speak to them for a moment, then introduce General Lee. I suggest you wait at the end of this hallway where a doorway leads into the ballroom. You'll be able to hear the general introduce you."

Clarence Hooper, obviously angry, snatched up his briefcase and walked into the hall. Johnston followed, and they waited for Lee. When they were gone, Grant and Spencer stood alone in the room.

"John, I don't know what I can say about the loss of Sergeant Major Barlow," Grant said, resting his hand on Spencer's shoulder.

"I guess I always believed that Gideon Barlow was indestructible. When we're done here, sir, I'd like to get him out of that building. I'd like to take him home with us."

"Of course. Where will you be in the ballroom?"

"With your permission, I'd like to ask General Sherman to help me keep an eye out for Connor. I can't cover that crowd myself, and without Barlow…"

Grant hesitated a long moment. "I don't like having General Sherman in the audience, but I suppose we don't have much choice. But if those old soldiers see through his disguise, we may have a lot more to worry about than your Mr. Connor."

"Thank you, sir. I'll go brief General Sherman." Spencer hesitated a moment. "Sir, if there is any problem in that room—and I'm not talking just about Connor—I will escort you into this hallway. Barlow told a trooper to have your carriage ready to go on a moment's notice. General Sherman will meet us at the carriage."

Grant patted Spencer's shoulder. "I suppose we'd better get this over with."

CHAPTER 25

Grand Ballroom
Kimball Building
October 6
7:30 p.m.

At one end of the ballroom, Joe Johnston stood on a low dais that was the focus of the twenty round tables at which were seated the nearly two hundred guests. To one side of the dais were dark green velvet curtains. The curtains were slightly parted in front of a door, on the other side of which stood Robert E. Lee. The door was ajar so Lee would hear Johnston's introduction. Grant stood with Lee in the hallway, and they heard Johnston begin.

"Gentlemen," shall we do this again next year?" Johnston was surprised and pleased by the enthusiastic applause and cheers. "Shall our next gathering be in Richmond?" The crowd clearly agreed. Johnston paused and looked around the room. "Gentlemen, as we close this year's gathering, I wish to express my pleasure for the opportunity to meet with so many former comrades-in-arms.

"Before we adjourn, I would like to introduce a special guest—a man for whom we all have the utmost regard, a man who also would like to express his pleasure to be in the company of the men gathered in this room, a man who needs no formal introduction." Johnston turned toward the curtains and called, "Will you join us now, sir."

Sherman, Rachel Brockton, and Ernst Pohlman were standing in front of the door that led to the kitchen at the rear of the ballroom. During the course of the evening, Rachel had searched for Connor among the guests. Although she could not clearly see the faces of every single man, she could judge by the physical size and hair color of the faces she couldn't see that Connor was not in the room.

Sherman and Spencer had met a few minutes earlier. Sherman said Rachel had not spotted Conner in the room, and they should plan for Connor to burst into the ballroom, either from the rear door or from behind the curtains near the dais. Spencer said he would stand with the President and remain in the hallway behind the curtains.

In the long moment before the curtains parted, a nervous energy swept the crowd. One man was heard—only by the men at his table—to mutter, "It's *Lee*! It's *got* to be Lee!"

When Robert E. Lee stepped onto the dais, a low roar began that quickly rose to a crescendo of applause and cheering that echoed from the chandeliered ceiling and tapestried walls. All the men were standing and several had climbed onto their tables to cheer and applaud, while a rhythmic chant began to dominate the room. "*Lee! Lee! Lee!*"

During the war Lee had many times been cheered by his troops. Now he was uncomfortable with the reaction. He raised his hands in an unsuccessful attempt to quiet the crowd. Joe Johnston was standing next to him, applauding and smiling broadly.

For almost five minutes it continued unabated—the applause, the cheers, and the chants by the former senior officers of the Army of Northern Virginia. Then, gradually, the sounds began to ebb.

Wearing a light gray suit and dark tie, his hair and beard shimmering in the multitude of gas lights, Lee waited patiently. The room became very quiet. There was not even the sound of silverware on china. The silence, in fact, was an almost painful contrast to the din that had preceded it.

Lee's eyes moved slowly across the room, in an apparent attempt to look into the eyes of every man present.

"Thank you, gentlemen. Thank you very much." Lee's voice was so soft everyone strained to hear him. He smiled. "Rest assured that I do not plan to bore you with a long and windy speech." Polite laughter drifted across the room.

"Let me say first of all that serving with you men, and leading the Army of Northern Virginia, will always be the highlight of my life."

The crowd erupted into another long cheer.

"I don't know how history will treat what we tried to accomplish. But I am confident that history, whoever writes it, cannot ignore the valor and dedication of every man in this room."

Lee paused as his eyes scanned the room, as if he were trying to memorize the faces. He smiled. "I promise that if I am able, I will be with you next year."

His words were greeted with cheers and applause.

When the room was quiet, Lee's smile faded. "The fact that there may be criticism in some quarters regarding next year's reunion in our capital is at the root of what I would like to briefly discuss this evening.

"Despite the fact that five years have passed since the war's end, there still are factions in this nation who believe the South has not been sufficiently punished for what they call our insurrection. Consequently, there are areas of the South that today are suffering more than they did during the war.

"To that end, I have been asked by the nation's president to lend whatever support I can to ensure the success of Reconstruction."

A low murmur spread across the room.

"And I have agreed to do so."

A man at one of the nearest tables stood. "With respect, General Lee, why would you agree to cooperate with Grant?"

"Let there be no doubt that I firmly believe we now are one nation."

Lee looked around the room. "Based on research conducted by Washington College, we have identified a number of issues that we believe are critical to the well being of the South. I have presented those issues to the President, and I have received his assurance that our issues will receive every consideration."

"How can we believe him, sir?"

"We can believe him because it has been my personal—as well as my professional—experience that President Grant is indeed a man of his word. But I don't expect you all to take just my word for that."

Lee paused and looked back to the curtains.

"Gentlemen, the President has asked for the opportunity to speak to you so that you can make that judgment yourself." The men exchanged looks of disbelief.

"I will ask him to join us in a moment, but first I am compelled to say that although I do not fully endorse his Administration, his desire to put the bitterness behind us and to make every effort to unite the nation has my complete support.

"President Grant, will you please join us."

John Spencer stood in the doorway but did not step through the curtain with the President. Spencer wanted to stand near the President on the dais, but Grant ordered him to remain in the hallway. The door that led from the hallway to the alley was about fifty feet to his right. He had no way of locking the door, so he frequently glanced down the hall.

Chapter 26

The Kitchen
Kimball Building
October 6
7:45 p.m.

Washing the pots, pans, and the dinnerware used to feed two hundred people required a kitchen staff of seventeen. The crowded room was made uncomfortably warm by the heat generated by the activity and by the clouds of steam from the water tanks where the dinnerware was being washed. There also were a number of waiters in the kitchen who were helping to store leftover food. The food scraps, empty food containers and other trash were dumped into a wooden barrel near the door. When the barrel was filled, it was dragged a few feet through the propped-open door into the alley. An empty barrel there was pulled back into the kitchen.

One of the waiters stepped out into the alley for a moment to enjoy a breath of cool evening air. When the butt of Hollis Conner's pistol struck the back of the waiter's head, the man collapsed instantly. Conner pulled the man behind the line of barrels, then removed the waiter's red vest.

The bullet fired by Captain James Griffin in the stairwell across the street had struck Connor high in the left shoulder. Conner had applied a compress to stop the bleeding, but his left shoulder had become so stiff and painful that he had difficulty putting on the vest. He slipped the Navy Colt revolver into the left side of his belt. He was confident he would be able to draw it instantly with his right hand. The vest would hide the weapon, as well as the blood-stained shirt.

Connor peered into the kitchen. On a table near the door was a stack of small circular trays used to carry drinks. On the top tray was a knife with a nine-inch blade. On wall shelves near the table were dozens of metal decanters.

Conner had walked through the Kimball building the day before the veterans arrived. He knew of the door behind the curtains that led to a hallway, which in turn led to another door that opened into the alley.

Wells was dead, as was Connor's old friend, Jason Markham. If Grant was going to die, Conner now realized he alone would have to make it happen. Connor planned to enter the ballroom and shoot the President point-blank, then escape through the curtains and into the hallway. Since he had decided to also kill Lee, Connor was confident that the veterans would be too shocked at act. Perhaps, Connor thought, doing it alone would be safer.

The reunion guests clearly were stunned when Grant walked across the dais to stand at Lee's side. The veterans did not know how, or whether, to greet former Union General and now President Ulysses Simpson Grant. The men seemed as confused by Grant's appearance at their reunion as they were by the fact that he was standing next to Lee. The silence was awkward, and Grant seemed uncertain of how to begin.

Lee turned toward Grant, smiled, and began to very deliberately applaud. After several moments most of the veterans joined in applauding, but it could hardly be considered enthusiastic.

When Grant held up his hands, the applause died quickly.

"Thank you, General Lee."

"And I wish to extend my sincere thanks to you, the distinguished senior officers of the Army of Northern Virginia." Grant hesitated as he scanned the room. He smiled. "I suppose that as long as I live, I will have the nightmares created by the men in this room."

Polite laughter rippled through the audience.

"I asked General Lee if I could be with you this evening to make the point that a former Union officer could join a reunion of former Confederate officers—and not be instantly scalped."

Most of the men smiled and more than a few laughed.

"However, gentlemen, I fully appreciate the fact that the evening is still young."

This time the laughter was full and genuine. Grant turned more serious.

"Those of us in this room have lived through the most wrenching experience in our nation's history. More than a half-million men gave their lives, and many more—including, I am confident, an appreciable number in this room—will until the end of their days carry the physical and mental scars created by that conflict."

Grant's voice now was low as he emphasized his words. "The real tragedy, gentlemen, is that the casualties in that war—every single one of them—was an American.

"I realize that for many of us the scars remain deep and troubling. I am not suggesting that we can put the war behind us. That, at least for our generation, is probably impossible. But, somehow, we all must find a way to put behind us the issues that fueled the conflict—we must put them behind us if this nation will ever achieve its potential."

Grant turned toward Lee. "General Lee agreed to stand here with me—shoulder to shoulder—to demonstrate that if he and I can stand together, then the rest of the nation certainly must be able to do so."

General Lee nodded agreement and he and the President shook hands.

The veterans stood and applauded.

At that moment, Hollis Connor moved quickly through the door from the kitchen. He was carrying a tray on which sat two water-filled decanters. He turned his face away as he stepped past Sherman and Rachel, moving toward the front tables nearest the dais.

Rachel gasped, clutched Sherman's arm, and pointed. "My god, I think that's him—that waiter!"

The standing veterans quickly obscured Sherman's view of the man.

"Stay here," Sherman ordered. He drew his pistol, held it close to his leg, the barrel pointed toward the floor, and moved among the veterans.

When the crowd stood to applaud, Spencer moved through the curtain to stand at the back of the dais where he could more clearly see the crowd. Deep in his gut Spencer knew something was about to happen. He knew the President would be angry if he walked out to stand near him. "Listen to your gut," he told himself. "That's how Gideon would handle it." Gideon. Spencer felt a momentary spasm of regret over the loss of his friend. But he had to put Barlow out of his mind—for now.

Because the dais was about two feet higher than the ballroom floor, Spencer was able to see movement near the middle of the room. He could see a waiter holding a tray moving through the crowd. There was something about the waiter. What was it about the man? He was not looking at the veterans; his eyes were locked on the President. It must be Connor!

As Spencer moved toward Grant and Lee, he realized he could not shoot unless Connor came very close to the dais. If Spencer's fire killed or even seriously wounded one of the former senior officers, he knew there would be serious consequences.

The waiter placed the tray on one of the front tables and reached with his right arm to draw a revolver. It *was* Connor!

There was only one thing Spencer could think of to do. He would have to stand in front of Grant and take Connor's bullet. Perhaps he still might be able to kill Connor. Perhaps the veterans would overpower Connor.

As he moved closer to the President, Spencer saw that Lee and Grant were standing very close to one another. "My god," he thought, "what if Connor hits Lee as well? What if I protect Grant and Lee is hit?"

Spencer moved quickly now. As he began to run, a thought flashed that he should not draw his weapon. If one of the veterans was armed, he might draw it and fire if he thought Spencer was a threat to Lee. "I'll have to charge Connor and hope I can reach him before he fires." When Spencer reached the edge of the dais he dove, arms extended to grab Connor.

Connor drew his pistol and fired two quick rounds. The first bullet hit Spencer's right hand, severing his forefinger and thumb and exited from his forearm near the elbow. The second round struck Spencer in his right waist and passed through his body. That bullet grazed the President's right arm near his shoulder.

Spencer's body slammed into Connor, knocking the pistol from his hand. Both men careened into several veterans.

Connor almost immediately jumped to his feet and reached behind the small of his back to draw the knife from his belt. He made several slashing motions to force the veterans back, then he turned toward Grant and Lee. Spencer rose to a sitting position and tried to grab Connor's leg, but he couldn't hold on.

With the knife held low, Connor started for the dais, less than twenty feet away. Many of those in the ballroom would recall later that President Grant stepped in front of General Lee.

General Sherman, his pistol drawn, ran through the crowd, roughly shoving the veterans aside. He could see Connor now. Sherman sent two guests sprawling as he pushed forward and leaned across a table to place the barrel of his pistol near the left side of Connor's skull. When he pulled the trigger, Connor dropped instantly.

Chapter 27

Kimball Building
October 6
8:35 p.m.

Concerned that there could be another assassin in the crowd, Sherman quickly led Grant and Lee through the curtains and into the alley. Sherman asked one of the veterans to help Spencer, whose hand was wrapped in a towel. Two more carried Connor's body.

As a precaution, General Sherman sent an aide late that afternoon to the Union Station just down the street from the Kimball Building. He had written a message to be telegraphed to the military barracks less than a mile north of Atlanta. He ordered the senior officer, a Colonel Martin Stoner, to send a squad of six troopers and two surgeons with two ambulances as fast as possible. The troops and the ambulances were to wait in the alley next to the Wylie Building across the street from the ballroom. The troopers were in the alley when Grant and the others came across the street. The surgeons had already treated Captain James Griffin. His arm was in a sling. The President's left arm wound required only a small bandage.

The lieutenant and his men came to attention when they saw Grant and Lee. Sherman told the officer, "Assign two men to stop anyone who tries to enter this alley." The young officer, who clearly didn't recognize Sherman without his beard, looked at Grant."

"Do it now, son," Grant ordered.

Grant looked back across the street and saw that Lee was being helped by his aide into a carriage parked in the alley behind the Kimball Building. Grant turned to Sherman. "I want to talk to Lee before he leaves."

Sherman sent a trooper across the street to the carriage. A moment later the soldier returned. "Sir, General Lee's aide said the general is not feeling well and they are returning to their train."

Grant said quietly to Sherman, "Cump, I want to see him before the train leaves."

Captain Griffin stepped forward. "Sir, I can ride to the train." Sherman hesitated, looking at the young officer's bandages, then nodded. "Take General Johnston with you and tell them we will be there within the half hour." Sherman then told the men carrying Connor to put the body in one of the ambulances and told Spencer to get into the other one.

"Sir," Spencer said, "I want to see Barlow."

"Nothing can be done for him, John," Sherman said. "Get into the ambulance so the doctor can treat those wounds and we'll bring the sergeant major down."

Spencer turned and started for the door into the Wiley Building. Sherman reached to stop him when Grant put his hand on the general's shoulder. "Let him go."

There was a commotion in the street. Sherman saw that the soldiers had stopped Rachel Brockton and the journalist, Ernst Pohlman. "Let them pass, lieutenant," Sherman ordered.

When Rachel reached Sherman, she asked, "Where is John?"

Sherman nodded toward the building. "He went in to check on Sergeant Major Barlow. He was killed by Connor."

"Oh, no." Rachel turned away a moment. But what about John? I saw him shot. It looked like he was seriously wounded."

Grant stepped forward. "Mrs. Brockton, we're going into the building to get the colonel, but I agreed to let him see his sergeant. Wait here with Mr. Pohlman, and we'll bring him down in a few minutes."

Chapter 28

Wylie Building
October 6
8:55 p.m.

Grant and Sherman entered the side entrance to the Wiley Building. Sherman led the way up the stairs. When they started up toward the third landing, they could see a body sprawled on the stairs, its head pointed toward the landing below, a narrow stream of blood flowing down several steps. As they moved near the body, Sherman recognized Wells. He paused to draw his weapon, looking up toward the third floor landing, and motioned for Grant to remain where he was.

When his eyes were level with the landing between the third and fourth floors, Sherman thought he could see Barlow sitting with his back to the wall and Spencer kneeling next to him.

Sherman stepped closer, but it was too dark to see clearly. He climbed the stairs to the fourth floor landing where he found another body. He searched the fourth floor office area until he found a lamp on one of the desks.

When he returned to the third floor landing, Sherman held the lamp high. Now he could see that Sergeant Major Barlow's eyes were glassy, lifeless. The floor was slick with blood. He saw the wide swath of blood on the wall behind Barlow. The sergeant's body was drenched in blood. The old LeMat revolver lay in his lap.

Spencer's hand was on Barlow's shoulder. "Old friend," Spencer said softly, "I should have been with you." Sherman saw Spencer's head drop.

"Come on up, Sam," Sherman called.

When Grant stepped up to the landing, Sherman could see his friend bite down hard on his cigar. They saw that the towel had come off Spencer's wounded hand. The thumb and forefinger on Spencer's right hand were missing and his forearm was bleeding heavily. The fabric of his jacket sleeve was slit almost to his elbow.

Sherman held the lamp high so Grant could see the landing above. "There's another body up there, Sam. Wells told us that Connor and a Jason Markham were the only ones in the building. He said Markham was the shooter. I saw the rifle lying at the foot of the stairs."

Grant didn't respond for a moment, shifting his cigar from one side of his mouth to the other. Grant looked into Barlow's unseeing eyes. Spencer was semi consciousness as Grant stepped close to him and kneeled down. Resting his right hand on Spencer's shoulder, Grant reached out with his left and gently closed Barlow's eyelids.

Spencer looked at Sergeant Major Barlow's face for a long moment. Then, very slowly, Spencer's head came forward against Grant's chest. The President, as he held Spencer close to him, could feel the young officer's body go limp.

Alarmed, Grant looked up at Sherman. Sherman kneeled down to check Spencer. He was quiet for a moment. "I think he's okay, but he's lost a lot of blood."

Grant turned up the lamp. He and Sherman carefully pulled Spencer into a prone position. Spencer was conscious again, but he clearly was in shock.

"Cump, let's get his jacket and shirt off so we can see if he's got any other holes in him. We'd better cut it off so we don't move him anymore than we have to."

Sherman opened his jackknife and began cutting at the jacket. "Sam, did you know that during the Wilderness fighting Barlow there went behind the lines to find Spencer? He'd been wounded pretty bad, I guess. I heard that Barlow carried him like a baby for nearly two hours, dodging Reb skirmishers the whole time."

"Yes, I knew," Grant said as he held the jacket for Sherman's knife. "There was something special between them. My guess is that this boy would sooner be the one sitting against that wall, and that we'd be working like this on his sergeant major."

With his jacket and shirt removed, they could see that Spencer had been hit low in the side. The bullet that severed his fingers had also torn the flesh on the inside of his right arm.

"Looks like the bullet in his side went in and out," Sherman said. It doesn't look very serious, but you can never be certain."

They used Spencer's shirt to staunch the bleeding, then Sherman stood to remove his own jacket and wrapped it around Spencer.

Spencer was lapsing in and out of consciousness.

Sherman looked closely at Spencer. He could see that his breathing was shallow. His eyes were closed.

"Boy's lost a lot of blood," he said again. "Let's get one of the doctors up here."

Sherman called down the stairwell for a doctor.

Grant looked around the landing, then up toward the floor above. "Hell of a place to fight," he said. "It's obvious that they ran into each other on these stairs."

"I'd guess that the one on the landing above and Wells were the first ones to go down, since they're the farthest away. That means that Barlow must have been hit early because he clearly was hit with a rifle bullet."

"Looks like he was hit with at least two pistol bullets as well," Grant said.

Sherman nodded. "I checked Barlow's LeMat. He'd only fired the bottom barrel, and that's what Markham was hit with. But Markham was also hit with two of Griffin's bullets, see there, low in his belly and the thigh. Markham would have died, but not for a while. I'd say Barlow killed Markham."

Both men were silent for a long moment. "It's my guess," Sherman said softly, "that Barlow fired the last shot up here. That's hard to believe, considering how badly he'd been hit."

Grant nodded.

Sherman lighted a cigar. Again both men were quiet for a long moment, each with his own thoughts of the fighting and death they'd seen.

"Cump, the man you shot in the meeting room, was he Klan?"

"Yes. He was their leader in Georgia."

"Why?" Grant asked softly. "Why would he want to try?"

"Hell, you know the answer, Sam. "For one thing, you just recently pushed the legislation through congress to ensure voting rights for the Negroes. Bedford Forrest told me it one of a long list of grievances that motivate the Klan."

"What about the British?"

"Nothing to worry about. It was just a case of low-level bureaucrat trying to make his mark. I've reported him to his government."

"We owe General Forrest something for helping us."

"You pay him, Sam. I never have much to do with any general whose ass I couldn't kick in the field.

Again, both men were quiet for a long moment.

"Sam, early on you asked me to do what I could for Spencer. You said he was a good man, and he's done a damn fine job for you. What would you do, Sam, if I sent you a recommendation that we give Spencer his first star and that he comes to work for me?"

"I'd send your recommendation to the Senate with my full endorsement." Grant hesitated, then asked, "But what about his wounds? Can he remain in the army?"

"As long as I'm running things, that won't be a problem. And I expect to be around a long while."

Grant looked at Barlow. "What can we do with the sergeant major?"

"He's going home with us, Sam."

"Good," Grant said. He knelt down to feel Spencer's forehead. "I don't think the army's newest brigadier general would have it any other way."

Grant pulled the coat higher around Spencer's head. "Cump, I also want you to do something for Griffin. That young man did a good job here tonight."

Sherman's voice was almost a whisper. "Sam, over the years, it's been our curse and good fortunate to serve with men like Spencer, Barlow and

Griffin. The problem is that it seems the good ones are always the first to fall."

Grant stood and looked into Sherman's eyes. "Cump, there's something I want you to do as soon as Spencer is cared for. Make the arrangements as soon as possible for me to see Lee."

Sherman didn't respond for a long moment. In the dim yellow light of the lamp, he could see that his friend's weak eye seemed to have drooped lower than ever.

"If that's what you want, Sam," Sherman said softly, "I'll go down now and arrange for a carriage."

Sherman had gone down two steps when he paused and looked back at Grant. "Sam, what you wanted to accomplish here...you tried...you did your best. No man could have done more."

Chapter 29

Pioneer II
October 6
Atlanta, Georgia
9:45 p.m.

The carriage had been sitting some distance from the train. The glow from the engine's firebox indicated the train was ready to leave. Lights could be seen in the day car and the Pullman, even though the drapes were drawn.

Sherman could vaguely see General Johnston walking quickly back to the carriage.

"Well?" Sherman asked when Johnston opened the carriage door.

"General, I don't think that train is going anywhere. The engineer said that Sergeant Major Barlow ordered him not to move that train until he personally told him to."

Sherman turned to Grant. "If you're ready, Sam, we'll drive up there. I'll talk to the engineer."

"Yes, I'm ready."

The carriage pulled up alongside the day car.

"Joe, would you please knock on the door?" Sherman asked. "Tell whoever answers that the President would like to spend a few minutes with General Lee. You will go into the car with the President. One more thing—the President would like to meet privately with the general."

The coach door opened almost instantly when Johnston knocked. Sherman could see a young man in shirt sleeves talking to Johnston. A moment later, Johnston climbed up into the car.

Less than five minutes later he returned to the carriage.

"I saw three people in the car: General Lee's son, Rooney; Clarence Hooper, his secretary; and a Doctor Bannock. Dr. Bannock said that the general is conscious but he's worried about Lee's heart. He's in the Pullman car in his bed. I think this Hooper is an ass—excuse me, Mr. President—but the general's son and the doctor said they thought General Lee would be honored to spend a few moments with the President. The only thing is, sir, they'd like the doctor to be present."

Sherman looked inquiringly at Grant.

"That's fine," Grant said. The President stepped down from the carriage. He paused to draw deeply on his cigar, then tossed it aside and climbed into the car.

It took a moment for Grant's eyes to adjust to the bright light in the day car. Rooney was the first to extend his hand. "Mr. President, I am Rooney Lee."

"It's a pleasure to meet you, Mr. Lee. I want you to know that I share your concern about your father's condition." Grant locked eyes with Rooney while he shook his hand. "Mr. Lee, I also want you to know that I sincerely regret whatever effect the strain of this trip might have had on your father's health."

"Thank you, sir. My father wanted very much to be with you tonight. In fact, he wanted to attend the reunion even after he suffered his attack earlier this evening. He believed in what you wanted to accomplish."

Grant nodded slowly, gripping Rooney's hand once more. Then he moved to the next young man, who had to be Hooper.

"You must be Clarence Hooper. It is a pleasure to meet you."

Hooper's handshake was weak, half-hearted. Grant remembered Johnston's comment.

"Mr. President. I'm Doctor Bannock."

"Yes, doctor. Thank you for permitting me to see the general. What is his condition?"

"He is very weak, Mr. President. It's been a recurring problem with his heart. Frankly, I'm very concerned. His condition has never been this bad."

"Doctor, I am sure he is in good hands, but is there any help I can get for you?"

"Thank you, sir, "Bannock replied. "One of your men found a surgeon I knew of in Atlanta. He's a very good man who specializes in this kind of condition. He examined the general shortly before you arrived. He said there was nothing he could do and recommended that we take the general home." Bannock paused for a moment. "I'm afraid, Mr. President, it doesn't look good."

Grant nodded, glancing toward Rooney.

"I gather that you gentlemen have no objection to my seeing General Lee for a moment?"

Dr. Bannock gestured with his left arm. "This way, Mr. President. He's in the Pullman car."

The car was dimly lighted, except for a lamp on a small table next to Lee's bed. The general's head was elevated by two pillows. Someone had thoughtfully placed a chair next to the bed.

When Grant stepped to the side the bed he saw that Lee's eyes were closed. Grant was struck by how much Lee had aged. Lee's hair and beard were white as snow. His skin seemed almost transparent.

Dr. Bannock touched Lee's shoulder. "General...General Lee. The President is here to see you."

Lee's eyes opened. He blinked several times, as if he were trying to focus his eyes. Then he nodded. "Mr. President," he said, his voice weak and phlegmy, "I apologize for not standing, sir, but the good Dr. Bannock has confined me to this berth."

Grant smiled. "General Lee, no apology is required." Grant saw Bannock step back outside the cone of light.

"Mr. President, it is important for you to know that I wanted this evening to be a success." Lee paused to catch his breath. "Who was the assassin?"

"That is being investigated now, but I am confident that you were not the target."

"What Colonel Spencer did was...was very brave," Lee said. "He is a special young man. Was he badly wounded?"

"His wounds are being attended to. We expect a full recovery."

"Thank God. I also noticed, Mr. President, that you stepped in front of me when the assassin charged the stage."

Grant made a small gesture with his hand, as if to dismiss what he had done. "I'm told that you will be leaving for Lexington in a few minutes, where I hope you can get some rest and recover your health."

Lee nodded. "God willing, I will get better. There is still much to do."

It was quiet for a long, awkward moment. Grant considered whether he should leave.

Then Lee broke the silence. "Mr. President, you should also know that I had intended to bargain with you tonight. I expected something in return for standing with you in front of the men."

"I am aware of that, General. I am confident that together we can work on the issues you have identified and reach solutions that will please you."

Lee shook his head. "No…no, not for me. For the people of the South. They have suffered for too long."

Grant didn't respond. He felt that whatever Lee had in mind sounded too involved for him to discuss in his present condition.

"You and I can plan to discuss all that at some later date, general."

Lee's raised hand fluttered. "No, there may never be another time. The paper that Hooper and I prepared. We should discuss one or two of those issues now."

Grant didn't respond.

Lee was obviously exhausted, and he closed his eyes for a moment, then said, "It was your Colonel Spencer. He told me…" Lee paused again.

"Spencer? I don't understand, general."

"He told me…not in so many words…but he said that I might have done more…"

Grant noticed the fine beads of perspiration on Lee's forehead.

"…He said I was more concerned about preserving the past than helping to build the future."

"General, I am sure that Colonel Spencer didn't mean—"

Lee waved his hand. "Please, permit me to finish, Mr. President. I felt that I was helping the South by providing for the education of our young men...but perhaps...perhaps that was the safe way to do it...perhaps I could have done more to help unite the country..."

Grant saw that Lee was frustrated because his weakened condition prevented him from making his points more forcefully.

"Your Colonel Spencer may have been correct. He didn't say it directly..." Lee paused to breathe deeply. "...but he thinks I should have worked as aggressively for a political solution as I did for a military one."

Lee locked eyes with Grant. "Mr. President, you and I...we must share in the blame for what has occurred...and is occurring today. In some ways," Lee continued, "the South has suffered more during Reconstruction than it did during the darkest days of the war."

Grant felt a momentary surge of anger. Or was it hurt? Perhaps it was envy. From his days as a young officer in the Mexican war, Grant had admired Lee. Lee was the perfect soldier, the perfect Christian, the family with prestige and power. Lee's troops cheered and adored him. Even today much of the North thought more highly of Lee than it did of the President and the general who had led the North to victory.

Deep in his heart, what Grant had always wanted most from this man was his respect.

Grant heard Lee speaking, but the words weren't registering. Grant and Lee were not enemies, as they once were. Nor would they ever even approach a friendship. Grant knew and accepted that. But he now realized that Lee would go to his grave finding fault with him as a general, and now as a President.

"...Mr. President, if it is God's will that I recover, then you should know that I will take a public stance...on issues that...I think are vital."

It was apparent that Lee had grown very weak. Grant felt the presence of Dr. Bannock.

"General Lee," Grant said as he rose from the chair, "we—you and I—are accustomed to being on the opposing sides of issues. But what is most important, general, is that you recover. When that time comes, and I am confident that it will soon, I will come to Lexington and we can discuss your issues—if that is agreeable to you, sir."

"Yes...yes...perhaps you can talk to the students."

Lee extended his hand. Grant smiled and took Lee's hand, surprised that the grip was so firm. Their eyes met for a long moment.

As Grant turned to leave, Lee asked. "Mr. President, please convey my compliments to Colonel Spencer and Sergeant Major Barlow. Will I have an opportunity to see them before we leave?"

Grant hesitated a moment. "I'm sorry. That won't be possible, but I will relay your compliments. Have a safe journey, General Lee."

Grant and Sherman remained in the carriage for long minutes after the train pulled off the spur onto the main line. Neither man said a word. Joe Johnston was patiently waiting in the darkness several feet from the carriage.

Grant retrieved a cigar from an inside pocket. To Sherman, the ritual for preparing the cigar seemed inordinately long. He fished a match from his jacket pocket, scratched the flame to life with his thumbnail, and held it out. Grant leaned forward and drew on the cigar as he slowly rotated it over the flame. In the soft light of the match, Sherman was struck by how his friend had aged.

"Sam, I told you that it wasn't a good idea to see him." Sherman wondered whether he should continue. "Look, you two are like flint and stone—whenever you come together you make sparks. You are a damn good man, Sam Grant—as long as you are Sam Grant. You can't be anyone else and you shouldn't try. You are depending too much on people you shouldn't trust."

Sherman's words were coming in a torrent. He was watching for a reaction from Grant, who was drawing steadily on the fresh cigar. Sherman could tell the moment that Grant climbed into the carriage that the meeting hadn't gone well.

"Damn it, Sam, politics is like an old army mule. You can't always depend on it to go where it's needed or when it's needed. Sometimes you've got to kick it in the ass. You're in another war, Sam. Fight it like you did before. When no one else could do the job you went out and did it."

Sherman's voice was rising. Joe Johnston and the driver could clearly hear his words. "Sam, pick the goddam politicians the way you picked your commanders. Most of those people who are around you now—you need to kick their asses out of their offices. You can tell me to shut up, Sam, but I—"

"All *right*! I just *did*!"

After a long, awkward moment, Grant sighed. "Cump, no one else can get me worked up the way you do."

"Hell, Mr. President," Sherman said lightly. "That's my job. The problem is that since I moved my headquarters away from those Washington political vipers—present company excepted, of course—I have the army running so efficiently that I've got nothing else better to do than to keep your blood pumping."

Grant was over his anger. "Well, at least try to look busy, old friend, from even as far away as St. Louis. Otherwise, I just may order you to tour every fort in the far west to see how well prepared they are to deal with hostiles."

Sherman could tell that his friend's mood now was melancholy, and he seemed exhausted. "Well," Sherman said with mock indignation, "if you're going to pull rank on me, we might as get the hell out of here."

Sherman opened the carriage door and motioned for Joe Johnston to get in. When he was seated opposite Sherman, he reached into his pocket. "General, I almost forgot to give this to you."

Johnston handed Sherman a small revolver, a Colt Patterson.

Sherman held the weapon up to the carriage lantern.

"Where did you find this?"

"Spencer was carrying it. The doctor gave it to me. But notice, sir, that it has your name engraved on it."

Sherman could see that the top half of the revolver's right grip had been blown away and that the cylinder was damaged by the bullet that struck Spencer's waist. None of the chambers had been fired.

Sherman showed the gun to Grant. "I gave it to John Spencer when he came to me with your letter for Lee. I told him to save it for his first-born son, that it might have some value some day."

Sherman slipped the revolver into his jacket pocket. "I don't think Spencer would want his son to have this damn thing. He clearly intended to save you—and probably Lee—by putting himself between the two of you and that killer's bullets."

Chapter 30

October 11, 1870
Washington College
Lexington, Virginia

Mary Lee held her husband's moist hand. He was feverish and had been muttering incoherently for hours. The doctors told her the end was near. She insisted that she be wheeled into the room. Silently, hour after hour, she held his hand.

The muttering now was almost constant. Suddenly, in a clear battlefield voice, Lee said, "Tell Hill he must come up!" Perhaps he was thinking of the fighting at Sharpsburg where the late arrival of General A.P. Hill saved the day.

All through the night Mary Lee prayed, as she had prayed for her husband through two wars. There were only vague movements now, and occasional muttering.

When the sun rose, the students of Washington College were straggling to the chapel. They knew the general was waging his final campaign.

At half past nine there was a small restless movement, a soft muttering, then the final words in a clear voice, "Strike the tent."

Chapter 31

4:30 p.m.
December 21, 1870

Spencer had left the White House less than an hour earlier. The horse's hooves were muffled by the more than three inches of snow that covered the road. The air was calm, permitting the huge snowflakes to flutter and drift as they fell. The branches of the pine trees along the road were sagging under the weight of the wet snow.

John Spencer was chilled by the flakes that fell between his collar and neck. He tugged his hat down lower on his head and pulled up his collar. He and the mare seemed almost covered with snow.

The cold air made his right hand throb. Strange, but the pain never reminded him of Connor. It was Barlow's final moments of life that filled Spencer with mixed feelings of guilt, sorrow and pride. He always would be haunted by Barlow's horrific wounds, suffered when the heavy rifle bullet smashed the air from his lungs. How could Barlow have raised the LeMat to fire the shot that killed Markham?

Then the attack by Connor. The electrifying pain when his hand was hit. Then his legs buckled when the bullet struck his side. Fortunately, his pistol had deflected the full force of the bullet, but fragments and hit him in the waist.

It was a decision Spencer knew he must live with. He should have been with Barlow in the Wylie building. Perhaps he could have saved his friend. Griffin was a reasonably competent man, but he wasn't as experienced. Yes, he'd made the wrong decision.

As he replayed again and again in his mind his decisions and the events, however, he began to develop a more objective assessment. Griffin himself had reminded Spencer that his primary responsibility was for the President's safety. Yes, his gut told him that he should have been with Barlow, but he began to realize that logically, he made the only choice possible—the right choice. And was it his gut or logic that guided his actions when he confronted Connor? Perhaps it was both: Logic told him he couldn't fire at Connor because of the risks to the veterans, and it may have been his gut that guided him to sprint across the stage and dive onto Connor. Sherman had complimented Spencer's decisions—a rarity for the general.

Perhaps, after all these years, he finally would be free of that recurring nightmare in the Wilderness.

Spencer wanted to check his watch, but he was reluctant to open his coat to dig it out of his pocket. He decided to urge the mare into an easy trot for a while. He was eager to see Jessie and Amanda. Perhaps, he thought, his right hand would be warmer if he put it into the pocket of his heavy wool jacket.

There wasn't another soul on the road, but Spencer didn't expect there would be in this weather. The mare was a smooth trotter and he was making good time.

Spencer regretted the disappointment in Sherman's eyes, but he couldn't deny the compliment that Sherman's regret implied. It was after he was transferred to a hospital in Washington. Sherman came to see him. The general gave him a small, velvet-covered box. It contained a single silver star.

Sherman said the star had been his. In a few days, he said, the President would submit Spencer's name to the Senate with the recommendation he be promoted to the rank of brigadier general in the regular army.

Yes, Sherman was disappointed. But Spencer didn't try to explain his decision.

When he was discharged from the hospital, Spencer received a message from Sherman asking him to come to the White House. The final meeting with Grant and Sherman took only a few minutes. It seemed as if no one knew what to say.

Finally, the President gave Spencer a heavy leather-bound case. A small, engraved silver plate was attached to the top of the case.

The case was lined in rich crimson velvet, with edge piping in cavalry yellow, all perfectly fitted to hold a well-used .44 caliber LeMat. Another engraved silver plate was attached to the lining.

Spencer reached back with his good hand to check that the case was in his saddlebag. The snow wasn't falling as heavily now. In fact, there were shafts of sunlight through scattering clouds to the east. Spencer slowed the mare to a walk. A light breeze came up and Spencer could feel the cold more intensely.

Rachel visited Spencer twice when he was in the hospital. She talked of opportunities in Richmond, perhaps even Atlanta, which was growing so rapidly. It was during her second visit that she met Jessie. Although the women chatted amiably, Rachel could not help but notice the warmth and depth of the relationship between Spencer and Jessie. It was Rachel's final visit.

While Spencer recuperated, he told Jessie that he wanted to leave the East, that there were enough crippled veterans in Washington.

He talked of the young men he'd seen at Lee's Washington College. Spencer told Jessie that perhaps Lee's decision to avoid the politics of Reconstruction may have been the correct one. Perhaps Lee, better than anyone, knew that the wounds for the generation that had lived through the war would always fester and seep. Perhaps no one, not even a Lee, could have eased so much pain.

Lee wanted to plant the seed for the nation's new growth with the young people, the students who came to him because of his prestige, his dignity and his name and all that it had come to mean. Spencer told Jessie that he deeply regretted even suggesting to Lee that he had not fulfilled his obligation to the future.

Spencer told Jessie that perhaps he, too, might teach—but not here, not in the East. He asked her if she and Amanda would go with him to one of the far western states, away from the hate and bitterness.

Except for some very high and thin clouds, the sky now was a deep blue. The Virginia countryside was dazzling, and he was anxious to see Jessie and Amanda. At a crossroads, Spencer had to squint to read the sign. It read: Milliken Farm.

Afterword

Ernst Pohlman

On October 8, 1870, President Grant invited Pohlman to the White House. When Pohlman arrived, he found that Grant also had invited Joseph Medill and the other editors who had met some weeks before in Chicago.

Grant urged the editors not to report any of the events that occurred in Atlanta. He explained that Lee was near death and would be unable to defend himself from the criticism of powerful southern groups that would have opposed such a meeting. Lee's image and reputation in the South might be damaged, Grant said. After heated discussion, Pohlman was instrumental in convincing the other editors to comply with Grant's request.

In the weeks that followed, Pohlman and Rachel Brockton were often seen together at Washington Restaurants and cultural events.

On December 3, 1870, a small story appeared in the Washington papers noting that the AP's chief editor would cover the Franco-Prussian war. He planned to be in Europe for at least four months.

On the battlefield, observers noted that Pohlman covered the fighting as he had during the American Civil War, moving quickly on horseback from one hot spot to the next, often more aware of events than the generals.

Pohlman's dispatches to America were read with great interest by

Grant and Sherman. As Lincoln had before them, they looked forward to discussing with Pohlman the tactics, strategies and the personalities of the generals.

Early one morning, two weeks before he was scheduled to leave for America, Ernst Pohlman was knocked from his horse by shrapnel. Because he had been in the thick of the fighting, neither side could reach him as he lay between the lines. Two Prussian infantrymen crawled to Pohlman in the late afternoon. They found that he had bled to death.

Rachel Brockton

In late January, 1871, Rachel Brockton's father died in his sleep. Two months later she moved her son and Mattie back to Richmond. In 1874, Rachel became the director of a Richmond bank. Her specialty was the management of investment portfolios for principal clients.

The press speculated that Rachel Brockton was probably one of the wealthiest women in the nation. She was noted for civic and cultural contributions. Her son became a history professor at a New York university.

Rachel never remarried.

John Spencer

John Spencer and Jessie McLaws were married on Dec. 24, 1870 in Washington City. General of the Army William T. Sherman and President Ulysses S. Grant attended the ceremony. Three months later John and Jessie moved to Denver, where he received a university appointment as a professor of history.

Spencer never again had any personal contact with either Grant or Sherman. But within two weeks after John and Jessie Spencer gave birth to a son, they received a letter from St. Louis. The letter advised Spencer that his son, at the proper age and upon meeting certain minimum requirements, was guaranteed acceptance to the U.S. Military Academy at West Point. The letter was signed by William T. Sherman.

Historical Note

General William Tecumseh Sherman

Sherman's name was placed on the army's retirement list on Feb. 8, 1884. He moved to New York, where he enjoyed life to the fullest. He was regularly seen at the opera, theater and important parties.

When Ulysses S. Grant was lowered into his tomb in New York's Riverside Park overlooking the Hudson, Sherman sobbed like a child.

Sherman would be ranked among the nation's most eminent military leaders.

Perhaps Sherman's greatest disappointment in life occurred when his son became a priest. He loved his son deeply, and he felt that the church had lured him away. He became embittered and ill. When he was delirious and near death, he called his son's name. Sherman died on Feb. 14, 1891.

Ulysses Simpson Grant

A distinguished British historian commenting on Grant's abilities as a military strategist and tactician said, "We must go back to the campaigns of Napoleon to find equally brilliant results..." His strategy to take Vicksburg in 1861 is considered by some to be among the most brilliant in military history. Lincoln said after the capture of Vicksburg, "Grant is my man and I am his the rest of the War."

Although Grant did not profit from corruption among members of his administration, he failed to take action even after their guilt was established. In his selection of subordinates, he favored military colleagues over those with political experience. At the end of his second term, Grant wrote to Congress that his "...failures have been errors of judgment, not of intent." Several historians in recent years have taken a more positive view of Grant's Presidency.

Grant and his family were destitute in 1884 after he was swindled out of his life savings. At the time, Presidents did not receive pensions and he had forfeited his military pension when he became President. At about this time, he was diagnosed with throat cancer.

Penniless and terminally ill, Mark Twain offered Grant a generous contract for the publication of his memoirs. Grant completed the book a few days before his death in 1885 at age 63. The memoirs sold over 300,000 copies, earning the Grant family over $450,000. Twain promoted the book as "the most remarkable work of its kind since the *Commentaries of Julius Caesar*," and such writers as Matthew Arnold and Gertrude Stein regard Grant's memoirs as among the finest ever written.

Nathan Bedford Forest

A former millionaire slave trader and plantation owner, Forrest was a brilliant cavalry leader whose tactics still are studied in war colleges. When Robert E. Lee was asked to name the greatest soldier who served on either side, he is quoted as saying, "A man I never met, sir. His name is Forrest."

Forrest's racist views moderated in his later years. Addressing an African-American organization, he was quoted as saying, "We are born on the same soil, breathe the same air, live on the same land, and why should we not be brothers and sisters?"

Forrest spent his fortune equipping his troops during the war and supported Confederate charities after the conflict. Critical of Reconstruction until his death in 1876 at age 56, he said Reconstruction had taken the South out of his countrymen's hands.

Footnote

On September 21, 2006, the curator of military artifacts at the U.S. Military Academy at West Point received a package marked to his attention. The accompanying letter explained that the contents of the package were among the effects of the great-grandfather of the undersigned.

The writer said he presumed the article had some historical significance. If the article had any significance for the family, the writer said, its meaning had long since been lost. The letter was signed by a graduate of the academy—John Spencer IV, lieutenant general, U.S. Army. The return address was the Pentagon, Washington, D.C.

When the curator opened the package he found a finely tooled leather case. On the cover of the case was an engraved silver plate tarnished with age, which read:

Col. John Spencer
In Honor of a Soldier Who Did His Duty
My Sincere Respect and Appreciation
U.S. Grant 1870

Inside the case the curator was pleased to find a .44 caliber, 10-shot LeMat, of the type favored by some Civil War Confederate officers. The curator felt that the weapon would be a fine addition to the academy's collection. There was another silver plate—attached to the case's rich crimson velvet lining edged with cavalry yellow piping. The simplicity and brevity of the engraving made it even more intriguing than the cover plate.

It was inscribed:

Sergeant Major Gideon Barlow—U.S. Army